ROGUE LIO

SIMON BARNES is an
journalist (*The Times, Spectator*) and author
of *Horsesweat and Tears*, as well as several
books on wildlife and conservation. *Rogue
Lion Safaris* is his first novel. He lives in
Hertfordshire.

Simon Barnes

ROGUE LION SAFARIS

HarperCollins*Publishers*

HarperCollins*Publishers*
77–85 Fulham Palace Road,
Hammersmith, London w6 8jb

This paperback edition 1998
1 3 5 7 9 8 6 4 2

First published in Great Britain by
HarperCollins*Publishers* 1997

Copyright © Simon Barnes 1997

The Author asserts the moral right to
be identified as the author of this work

ISBN 0 00 649849 3

Set in Sabon

Printed and bound in Great Britain by
Caledonian International Book Manufacturing Ltd, Glasgow

For Bob, Jess and Manny with grateful thanks;
for CLW with eternal gratitude.

It is customary on these occasions to make some kind of disclaimer: I would like to begin by doing the opposite. The geography and ecology of Mchindeni National Park is based on a real park Somewhere In Africa; every observation of wildlife and every interaction between wildlife and people come from my own notebooks. The single exception is based meticulously on a personally communicated eye-witness report. However, the politics and the administration of the park are entirely fictional, as are all the human characters to be found there. I would also like to acknowledge the most frequently used reference material: *The Serengeti Lion: A Study of Predator-Prey Relations* by George B. Schaller, *Portraits in the Wild* by Cynthia Moss, *Roberts' Birds of Southern Africa* by Gordon Lindsay Maclean and the bird-sound recordings of Baron Robert Stjernstedt.

I

South

I

George Sorensen, ectomorphic, myopic, leotropic, pointed to the crown of an umbrella thorn, where three vultures sat waiting.

'Lion?' he asked, but with George, questions were often really statements. Lion: for sure: and I knew George would want to move in. Dread and delight, familiar fellows, gripped me again.

George pointed a courteous finger skyward, and said to Helen: 'Striped kingfisher. A duet. Remember what we said about pair-bonding? Hear them? All right, we'll move in, shall we?'

I heard at his word the razor-stropping duettists, male and female, at their hundred-times-a-day ritual of conquest and sex, and looked to the umbrella thorn. Three white-backed vultures: in a second thorn tree a little beyond, two more vultures, these white-headed. It was likely, then, that something lay dead beneath: and likely that lion had killed it. The vultures had not descended to the cadaver because the lion were still there. Very likely. Say, two to one on.

Well, naturally, lion had killed, and naturally, George wanted to move in. Between us and the thorn trees lay a small-ish expanse of grass, parched and painted pale tawny by drought: lion-coloured.

George was seldom aware of people when lion were present, so, as was my habit, I checked the company, a short job, for we had but one client with us. Helen was a rather stately Englishwoman the far side of sixty, with tea-party manners. Vague, frail-looking and ladylike, she had done far better than I had expected when I (arriving rather more than forty minutes late, unfortunately) had met her at the airport five days ago.

3

She had walked not swiftly but tirelessly, and she had taken great delight in the wilderness we had shown her. A client who falls in love with the bush warms a safari guide's heart. With perfect politeness, she had denied any feeling of disappointment in our failure to find lion for her. Now, on the morning of her departure, we seemed no more than a couple of hundred yards from invisible and uncountable lion. And on foot, of course. But Helen didn't look like a panicker.

'Why not?' I said. 'Phineas?'

Phineas, long and lean, with impossibly graceful fingers, was holding his rifle by the extreme end of the barrel and resting the weapon's point of balance on his shoulder. This was not a suitable position for immediate action, but then I had never seen Phineas use his rifle as anything other than a leaning post and undergrowth-basher. He turned to me and offered a kind of facial shrug, a brief thrusting out of his lower lip. He stooped, picked up a handful of dust and let it trickle through his elegant fingers. A little cloud hung in the air and drifted towards us. Phineas nodded.

In the far distance, I heard the triple scream of fish eagle. Phineas motioned us to follow with a small movement of his head. We were at it again. Why not?

Well, as a matter of fact, *The Safari Guide Training Manual* provided a long list of reasons why not. The book was adamant on the point: with lion, there is no such thing as a safe distance on foot. Its author concluded reluctantly that feeding lion could be approached within two hundred yards, but then only if the wind was blowing from them to you, and the country was open and undergrowth-free, and every lion could be counted and accounted for.

The *Manual* had been produced by the Ministry of National Parks and Tourism, and it was a masterpiece of terror. Its persistent but never stated theme was the dread of the bad publicity that would follow the devouring of tourists by lion, or the impaling of tourists by elephant, or the bisection of tourists by hippopotamus, or the flattening of tourists by buffalo, or the vivisection of tourists by hyena.

None of us followed the *Guide*'s instructions to the letter, even though infraction of its code could mean the withdrawal of the Safari Guide licence. A certain amount of rule-bending was *de rigueur* for those who wished to be Cool in the Bush. We all liked to swap tales of our daring when we met up, at the airport or at the Mukango Bar. But no one thought George was Cool in the Bush. Most people thought he was a suicidal maniac. But then George had no aspirations towards coolness. He did not see lion as a virility test. He just liked them. He couldn't get enough of them, couldn't know enough. And he could never get close enough. He wasn't in the least brave: but he was recklessly, perhaps, I sometimes thought, terminally, curious. Some people had tried to tell me that George was addicted to danger, but I knew better than that. I had worked with him long enough to see what the Cool-in-the-Bush brigade missed. George could not possibly be addicted to danger, because he was never aware of whether he was in a dangerous situation or not. It was an alien concept to him. No, it was not danger he was addicted to. It was lion.

So, for that matter, was I. George had shown me the way, so perhaps I was addicted to George too. Or perhaps just to the bush.

George once described the correct method of approaching lion as 'cosmic courtesy'. Accordingly, we did not walk straight towards the umbrella thorn, and we did not walk away from it. We struck a line of about forty-five degrees. The path took us by a large brake of bush: once clear of it, they were revealed. Lion. A sand-coloured knot, 150 yards away, around an equivocal black shape. Ahead of me, I heard Helen give a brief gasp. As for me, I felt a warm clutch at the belly: the Darlin' Girl Syndrome, I sometimes called this sensation, naming it for a horse that had once filled me with the same mixture of fear and delight.

And George walked on, neither creeping nor hurrying. Neither fear nor love was discernible: only his eternal curiosity. I watched the lion with the usual rapt anxiety. They were aware of us, but intent on their meal: all save one. She raised

5

her yellow eyes from the carcass before her and with them followed our progress. And we walked on. And on. At length, we halted by a small bush, one that did not conceal us at all. It was another aspect of cosmic courtesy. We were not so bold as to approach openly, nor so timorous as to lurk behind cover. We were neither good nor bad, neither prey nor predator.

A walk through drought-dried grass fills your ears with the noise of your own passage. In the sudden silence of stopping, the sounds of the lions' banquet came towards us. They were devouring a buffalo, a colossal and absorbing task. In the clarity of the morning, I could hear the slicing of the carnassial shear.

'Buffalo,' said George, to Helen and also to a small tape recorder, plucked from the bulging pocket of his khaki shirt. 'Male.'

'Definite male,' I said, an ancient joke.

'Clearly old, and presumably one of the group of five old males seen near the Tondo confluence yesterday. Remember to check the area this afternoon, try and find the same group, see if it has been reduced to four.'

'Do you think these are the lion we heard last night during supper?' Helen asked.

George shifted his specs to the extreme end of his nose, giving himself an air of prim stupidity. There was a new cigarette burn in his shirt, I noticed, just above the left pocket. There were moments when, even to me, George looked like a dangerous lunatic, one quite incapable of comprehending his own interests. It was hard to remember that he was a businessman: hard for him too, I suspected. 'Well, yes, certainly, or at any rate probably, because it was rather a good chorus last night, wasn't it? Not a full pride chorus of course, but I counted half a dozen individuals, I think, and we are now in the core area of their territory, around the Tondo confluence, this being the Tondo Pride, of course, territory insofar as lion *have* a territory, which they do, of course, but rule one of lion is that you must never make rules about lion, because lion certainly won't stick to them.'

George paused for a moment, perhaps contemplating the inevitability of leonine lawlessness. 'Where was I? Oh yes, well, they probably didn't kill last night, there's rather a lot of buff left, and they are all tucking in, no one lying around digesting and waiting for second helpings. I suspect they killed at first light, and it is a little unusual that the vultures should be here so early. Check the thermometer when I get back to camp, maybe it's warmer than it's been so far this season, thermals available for the vultures earlier than previously.' This last to the tape recorder. 'But I could get a better idea if I moved around a little, and saw how much of the buffalo is left –' George took a step forward, and Phineas stretched out a long arm and placed a hand mildly and briefly on George's shoulder. It looked like nothing more than a gesture of affection. 'Oh, Phineas, really, I was only going to – oh! Auntie Joyce!'

I heard Phineas's voice, soft and delighted. 'Ohhh. She is *crazy*, that one.' For one of the lionesses, no doubt sensing a momentary lack of cosmic courtesy in George's attempted advance, had, in a sudden instant of action, rolled to her feet. To receive the stare of an irritated lion is rather like being struck in the chest by a death ray. Enormous, unreadable yellow eyes, tiny dots of pupils in the ferocious morning light. One lion after another followed her lead, not standing, but raising a head from the carcass to stare at us: four cosmically discourteous intruders.

It was a near-certain fact that if we turned and ran at this moment of tension, the lion would pursue us. In the bush, nothing inspires pursuit so much as flight. But Phineas remained still, leaning on his gun, smiling very faintly to himself. He liked his animals fierce. George too was still, muttering quietly to his machine, recording details of position around the kill. I was also still, from long habit. Relish of the scene fed on its distant but distinct peril. I felt a slow smile crawl up my face: I wanted no other life than this. What if it should end? But I thrust the thought aside. And then, abruptly, Auntie Joyce sat down on her haunches, front paws together, like a domestic cat. She continued to watch: she was no longer considering immediate action. Stand-off.

Auntie Joyce, George said, was the oldest lioness in the pride 'and probably the pride's leader, insofar as lion have a leader, which they don't of course'. She was easily the most crotchety. Lion on a kill are disposed to be peaceful and preoccupied, but Auntie Joyce didn't go by the rules any more than did George. At the moment of stand-off, I moved half a pace sideways: I wanted to see how Helen was taking all this. No sign of panic. Quite the reverse. I wondered then how many people – how many men – had seen that expression on her face. Eyes wide, mouth slack, quite motionless. She was enraptured: ravished by the eyes of Auntie Joyce. Terror and beauty, or terrible beauty, had undone her. And all the while the lion but forty yards away.

We stood for a further fifteen minutes in flesh-ripping silence, while Auntie Joyce stared unwinking. At last, and slowly, she lowered her body to the ground and lay on her chest, her eyes never leaving us. We remained still. And then, almost reluctantly, she lowered her head and began once again to feed. Silently I released a long sigh. George did not. He had not for an instant ceased to alternate long stares at the lion and muttered comments to his tape recorder. I sometimes wondered what people would conclude if our party were ever devoured by lion, leaving nothing behind but bones, Phineas's unready, inedible weapon and George's tape recorder, like the little black box of an aeroplane disaster. Our finders would have every detail of the positions the lions took up relative to each other, how long each fed, where each one rested, who rested alone and who sought company. George could recognise every individual in the pride from scars and nicks, from size and age, from the individual freckling of whisker spots. So could I, for that matter, though rather less certainly. George loved information: he was a scientist long before he became a safari guide, and he believed devoutly that God dwelled in the details. I was never wholly convinced that George transcribed all those tape-recorded notes. Certainly, the tapes themselves were endlessly re-used and re-recorded, stratum upon stratum of leonine detail: a Grand Canyon with endless layers of lion. George's mind was rather like that.

Phineas caught my eye and made a little gesture: let's move in still closer. I grinned back at him. The previous night, we had had a silly conversation about who was the more terrified by George's way with lion. 'That time we had to climb the tree, Dan, we were stuck up the tree for half a day.' 'Phineas, you don't want the story of the definite male again, do you? That was worse than anything you've told me about.'

But George was now counting vultures; he had seen two lappet-faced vultures on the far side of the umbrella thorn, and was asking his tape recorder why no hooded vultures had shown up. I looked at him, made a head gesture: we withdraw? 'Oh, well, all right, I suppose so. Helen, are you all right? Do you want to move in a little closer and take a photograph? Oh no, you don't have a camera, do you? Happy? Don't want a closer look? Very well then. All right. Phineas?'

'Lead us out, Dan,' Phineas said quietly.

I did so: forty-five degrees, cosmic courtesy, Phineas between us and the lion, rifle uselessly across his shoulders. Auntie Joyce watched every step of our crackling retreat.

About five minutes later, Helen had shifted from enraptured silence to compulsive talking. 'Why did you call that lioness Auntie Joyce?' she asked.

'Perhaps you'd better answer that one, George,' I said. I couldn't bring myself to speak of the human Joyce: a female of infinitely worse temper, our sworn enemy in all her dealings.

'Oh, well, really, just a joke, really; we called her after the lady who met you at Chipembere, off the plane from England, the lady who looks after our interests in Chip. Silly joke.'

Helen let it pass. Delight had filled her: and it filled me too, in the delight of showing. 'The most beautiful thing I have ever seen in my life, how can I ever thank you? So wonderful, so marvellous, and all the time I felt so *safe* with you and Phineas and everyone.' Helen, in neatly pressed khaki slacks, a shirt

9

buttoned at the wrists for fear of the sun, and a straw hat suitable for the sport of bowls, was in a frenzy of leonine love.

'Safe?' I said, smiling at her pleasure. 'I never do.'

'Oh, you're just teasing.'

'I am not. George has taken me closer to lion than any sane person would consider safe.'

'Definite male,' George said, rummaging around obscenely in the pockets of his shorts until he came up with a box of matches. He lit the cigarette he had just, with great concentration, rolled; a small shower of burning shards fell to earth. 'Collared barbet,' he said smokefully, vaguely brushing at the front of his shirt. He expected no reply to this observation.

The country was open as we returned to Lion Camp, and the discipline of the walk broke down. We moved in a line abreast, instead of the *Manual*'s strictly ordered single file. 'But surely the lion are fairly safe here,' Helen said. 'I remember when we went for a drink at Mukango Lodge, one of the guests was telling me how docile the lions in this park were.'

'Pretty docile,' I said. 'They only killed three people in the wet season this year.'

'*Really?*'

'Oh yes,' George said. 'One schoolboy, poor little sod, one jealous lover, and one old pisscart – oh, I do beg your pardon, Helen.'

Helen waved the apology aside. 'Jealous lover?'

'Chap from one of the villages,' I said. 'Apparently he thought his girl was dallying with another man. He wanted to catch the pair of them at it, and so he stayed up all night to spy on her. Lion took him while he was sneaking about.'

'Found bits of him all over the village next morning,' George continued callously. 'Lion buggered off before dawn, I'd say, and the village dogs had a tuck-in before the village woke up. Terrible to-do. Lion prints all over the shop.'

'Was it the same lion every time?'

'They thought so. There was a lot of talk about the Rogue Lion at the time. Lot of jokes at the start of the season.'

'It was the same,' Phineas said. 'I was with the party of

scouts that went to track him. The warden, Mr Mvuu, he said to shoot him before he eat a tourist. But this lion, he is a very clever fellow. One day he kill the schoolboy, next day gone. We tracked him, but always he is ahead. As if he knows we are tracking him. North, always north. We travelled north until we lost him. We tracked him into the North Park, long long way, very beautiful trip, we make camp in a very special place, many many lion there. And that is where we lost him. Too many lion tracks, and he got lost amongst them.'

'It was a male then?' Helen asked.

'Oh yes. Big tracks, big fellow.'

Helen laughed suddenly. 'Is that why it says Rogue Lion Safaris on your Land Cruiser?'

'Oh dear. Does it still show?' George asked, dropping his cigarette butt to the ground and leaving it to smoulder.

'Of course it bloody shows,' I said, automatically treading out the cigarette.

'But I painted over it,' George said peevishly.

This demonstrated very clearly George's selective vision of reality, no doubt an essential adaptation for his survival. 'Your paint job makes it more obvious, not less.'

'Oh dear. Do you think another layer will do the trick?'

'We'll have to do something before Joyce comes out again.'

'Oh God. We're in enough trouble as it is.'

'But why are you called Rogue Lion Safaris?' Helen asked.

'We are called Lion Safaris,' George said, rather primly.

'The people at Mukango Lodge called you Rogue Lion Safaris. So did that nice boy who looked after me while I was waiting for you to turn up at the airport.'

'Bloody Lloyd the Stringer,' I said, or rather muttered beneath my breath.

'I really can't apologise enough for being so late that day,' George said. He didn't explain that we had found a leopard on the way, and had watched it for half an hour while it stalked fruitlessly about in the unconcealing daylight, after what had plainly been an empty night of hunting. 'But, no, I think people like Lloyd think that, well . . . the point is that our operation is –'

'Not so dull as the others,' I suggested. 'Rather more concerned with the bush than with anything else. I bet it was van der Aardvark who wrote on our vehicle, or his eejit assistant, your friend Lloyd. Even money it was them. Better, I'll take six to four.'

We dropped into the Tondo, a dry riverbed, floored with sand, a wet-season river that flowed, when it flowed, into the mighty Mchindeni River itself. We made our crossing about a hundred yards upstream from this confluence. Ahead, a couple of hundred yards further, we could see the tiny scatter of huts that made up Lion Camp. From any sort of distance, it always appeared absurdly vulnerable and small: no mighty stockade against the perils of the bush, rather, a small hiding place lurking beneath the ebony trees. The few huts, each walled with bamboo matting and wearing a small hat of thatch, looked, from the banks of the Tondo, like abandoned laundry baskets. To one side, no more obtrusive and as deeply stained with the colours of the bush as the huts, the vehicle. Bush-weathered, it seemed as if the camp and the vehicle had all sprung from the floor of South Mchindeni National Park.

Then, coming to meet us at an unprecedented run, was Joseph Ngwei, trainee safari guide. 'George!' he shouted. 'George, why aren't you at the airport?'

'Airport?'

'Well, I *am* catching a plane today,' said Helen mildly. 'Isn't it this morning?'

'Oh dear,' said George, quite unperturbed. 'I wonder what time it leaves?'

'I heard van der Aardvark's vehicle leave more than an hour ago,' Joseph said, voice filled with urgency. This was a reference to the camp across the river from us, invisible but intermittently audible. 'That can only mean he is going to the airport himself. So the plane must be leaving at ten.'

It was now close to nine, and the journey normally took a couple of hours. 'Oh dear,' said George cheerfully. 'Well, we'll probably make it. Possibly anyway. Have to miss breakfast, though, awfully sorry. I suppose we'd better be off pretty soon, really. Have you packed, Helen? I suppose you'd better pack.'

There were times when even George's most devoted supporters wanted to pick him up and shake him. 'I already put Helen's kit on the vehicle,' Joseph said. 'Excuse me for taking the liberty, Helen. And Sunday has made some egg and bacon sandwiches for breakfast, they're on the front seat. So just go, George, yes?'

George gave no sign of appreciating this initiative. 'All right then. We'd better be off.'

'I'll just check my hut,' Helen said.

'Have we got anyone to collect?' George said vaguely. 'Have you got the bookings book, Joseph?'

'No one to collect, George, we're empty.'

'Are you sure? I'm certain we had a booking.'

'We did. There was that big Wilderness Express party, but they're not coming, are they?'

'Oh God. I'd forgotten that. What on earth possessed Joyce to get rid of them? I wish you hadn't reminded me. Oh dear. Oh dear. Oh well. Better go, I suppose. Helen? Anybody else coming? Joseph, Dan?'

'I'm coming,' I said. 'I might see someone I know.'

'He means he might get the chance to lust at Mrs van der Aardvark,' Joseph explained to Helen.

'Slander,' I said. 'Not my type at all, that one. You coming, Joseph?'

'I'll stay,' Joseph said. 'I have some work to do.'

'Writing to Gianna,' I explained to Helen, counter-teasing. 'Dear Gianna, I send my love from the shower cubicle . . .'

'Sex mad, my staff,' said George. 'Are you ready, Helen?'

When Helen had taken her place at the front of the vehicle, I climbed on behind. It was the standard vehicle of the Mchindeni Valley, a Toyota Land Cruiser with an open truck bed and a pair of benches fixed in the back, one bench higher than the other: a mobile platform for game viewing. But somehow, it didn't look like standard transport. It was older than most of the vehicles run by the other camps. The doors of the cab had been removed, against conventional wisdom. Naturally, there was no windscreen. The vehicle looked as if it had done several seasons too many, mainly because it had. It had hit too many trees, had heaved itself through too many thorn bushes, had climbed the walls of too many dry riverbeds. Every square inch of its surface bore testimony to a million passages through all but impenetrable bush.

The company logo had been applied near each of the forward wheel arches: a Metro-Goldwyn-Mayer lion surmounted by the words 'Lion Safaris'. The word 'rogue' had been crudely painted beside this on each side in thick black varnish by an unknown hand. George had painted over this still more crudely in borrowed white emulsion. All in all, it was not a vehicle that inspired confidence in a non-bush-hardened client.

'Well,' said George. 'Either we catch the plane or we don't.' He let in the clutch with his customary violence; my hand flew in a long-established reflex to my hat, once a racing trilby but now, like the vehicle, showing signs of hard use in the bush.

George's driving was impatient at the best of times. On the road, the roads being merely graded tracks, he was a perfectly dreadful bush driver. Off the road (off-road driving naturally forbidden by the *Manual*), he was reckoned to be even worse. In point of fact, he was superb in this area, but the ride was never less than alarming. Most bush drivers tended to cruise gently, giving the animals the best possible chance of being unamazed. George preferred to roar about the bush, crash-halting when a nice animal came into sight, catapulting the clients out of their seat, desperately clutching cameras and binoculars while exclaiming with delight. This morning, George had a licence to hurry, and he hurried. Bush roads are not designed for speed ('never exceed 20 kph,' said the *Manual*) and the drive was rather like doing the Cresta Run on a tin tray. I stood, preferring to take the bumps through my legs rather than my back, removing my hat and standing on the brim to keep it safe. Impala flew from our roaring progress, puku scuttled away like huge fox-coloured rabbits. A party of zebra watched us amazed from the middle of the road, forcing George to lift his foot for a second. 'Stupid bloody animals, don't know what you see in the bloody brainless things, Dan . . .'

I pointed to one as we swept past and shouted over the engine's noise: 'Stallion!'

'Definitely!' George shouted back. 'Bateleur, see, Helen?' He crammed his foot to the floor again, still staring skywards at the eccentric tailless eagle of the Mchindeni Valley.

Helen craned her head back as we sped away, catching a fleeting glimpse of the gliding bird, and catching my eye as she did so. 'Do you know what I say?' she asked me, in a thoroughly unladylike yell.

I bent down. 'What?'

'Bugger the bloody plane!' It was the first time I had heard her use an improper word. Both the word, and the sentiments were, I think, new to her. 'Yes, bugger the plane. That was the most wonderful morning of my life.'

'I believe you have fallen in love with Auntie Joyce,' I said.

She turned to me again, and didn't speak. Instead, an absolutely colossal grin. Then she asked: 'Will we make it?'

We hit a bump, and I, in my unbalanced crouch, briefly flew, rescuing my hat with an adroit dab of the foot on touching down again. 'Even money,' I said. 'Better, I'll take six to four.'

2

I had never intended to be a safari guide. I was always going to be a racehorse trainer, like my father. I had grown up with racehorses. For twenty years, or since I could walk, I had been, or at least had seen myself as his right-hand man. I had been assistant trainer, mucker-outer, yard-sweeper, groom and work-rider. My father was a widower – I could hardly remember my mother – and he had never remarried. Horses were his life. He was English, but 'by an Irish sire out of an English dam', as he always put it. English enough in normal circumstances, he would become progressively more Irish with strong emotion or strong drink. Neither state was unusual; his stage Irishisms were deliberately self-mocking, deliberately endearing: 'Sweet Jaysis, the focken dry season's upon us,' every time a bottle was finished, which was often.

He ran a string of a couple of dozen beasts, a mixed band of jumpers and flat horses. There was never a horse of any great distinction, but he, we, had a winner here and a winner there, 'and God send nothing worse'. He loved horses, gambling, drink and chasing women, the women making a distant, hard-panting fourth. A big, bonhomous, bibulous man, he was greatly and widely loved, if seldom very profoundly. People tended to feel protective of him; I did myself. He was the most easy-going man in the world: generous and comfortable with clients, employees, women, horses. Perhaps that was why his horses never won quite as often as they might have done: he was a man without ruthlessness. But boundlessly optimistic: and as long as the horses won sometimes he was content.

Legends accumulated around him: he was that sort of man. They centred on his eccentricity and his extraordinary ability with horses. The best of these was the Derby winner he found wandering about on a motorway late at night, having dumped its rider and taken off that morning: how my father, having persuaded the frightened animal to trust him, led it home across country, arriving in the horse's yard at two in the morning in full evening dress, leading a million pounds' worth of horse in one hand, an open bottle of champagne in the other, a smouldering cigar in his mouth. In fact, it was not a Derby winner, nor a motorway, and the champagne and cigar were later embellishments. But the story was true, the racehorse was indeed a good one (Falco Spirit, went on to win the Cambridgeshire) and my father was certainly wearing a dinner suit. I know, I was there. I had picked him up after a dinner with one of his owners in Newmarket, and was driving him home. I remember seeing the horse and stopping: and then my father's calm, matter-of-fact gentleness: 'All right, me fella, what do you say to a few mints, now?' Inevitably, he had a packet of Polos in his pocket: you could always tell my father's movements around the yard by following the minty breath of his horses. Everyone in racing loved the story: well, everyone in racing loved my father. But they never sent him their best horses.

I spent most of my youth being told what a wonderful man he was: he was a genius with horses, a genius with money. How did he manage to run a small business so successfully, and with such style? What was his secret? I didn't know then, but his secret was that he wasn't and didn't. It was something I should have known: and perhaps remedied. But I didn't.

I finally learned the truth of my father's business a few days after he died of a heart attack at the races. I took a little comfort in the inevitable witticism that ran through racing at the time: he had dropped dead from the sheer shock of seeing one of his own horses win. This was meant affectionately, on the whole, and I took comfort where I could find it. For I was struck down with grief, which is a kind of madness: a refusal to believe that it was not possible to turn the clock back just a few days: to, say, take over the bookwork, run the business, save the day, romp home a winner. Had I done the bookwork, would he be alive now? I could not bear such a thought, but I kept on thinking it all the same.

To my eternal regret, I was not with him at the races that day. I had been in the middle of my finals at university. I was completing a degree in zoology. My childhood, not lonely but somewhat isolated, had been divided between horses and nature. I had been a bird-watcher, a flower-presser, and a maker of soon dead pets from wild rabbits, hedgehogs and baby birds. I had jars full of beetles and I had watched many moths emerge raggedly from hoarded chrysalises. The first great love of my life was a stoat I had as a pet for a glorious few months, until it escaped. I was an only child in a stableyard set a fair distance from the village: horses, birds and wild beasts peopled my childhood: these, and my affectionate, chaotic father.

I read, of course, incessantly. My early heroes were Mowgli and Dr Dolittle; later heroes were the great interpreters of animal behaviour: Jane Goodall on chimpanzees, Cynthia Moss on elephants, George Schaller on pandas and gorillas, George Sorensen and Peter Norrie on lion. My copy of their book, *Lions of the Plains*, was nightly perused in wonder, till it became a mass of dog-ears and pencillings. I had a few friends from neighbouring yards; my second great love after the stoat was the daughter of a trainer, a kind and lovely girl of much horsiness: very much my type. Perhaps I would have married her, had I not wanted to go to university.

My father had not exactly approved of my ambition to go to university, but he tolerated it well enough. Tolerating things was his strong point. 'Horses have got four legs, and if you can count to four, you've got enough focken zoology for me,' he had said, but only because he felt it was expected of him. Besides, I was never a student in the traditional sense of the term, having hundreds of affairs, exploring the far reaches of the universe, plotting global revolution. There was a girl in my second year, but she went off to study epiphytes in the Amazonian rain forest. She was, in a different way, very much my type. Things might have turned out otherwise, but probably not. I was still very much involved with racing and horses. I just did my course work and left for the yard. I would arrive at my provincial university at around noon on Mondays, still smelling of horses after riding out two lots. I would stay in residence until Friday lunch time, and get back to the yard in time for evening stables. I knew very few people outside my tutorial group. University was not a formative experience, it was a sideshow. My real life was bound up with horses: with my father's horses, our horses. I had never considered the possibility of life without him, or them. And so, at his death, I found myself in free fall, plummeting under the gravity of grief.

My first coherent thought about the future, after I had been summoned from the exams by bad news, was that I would simply take over the running of the yard rather sooner than I had expected. Surely, I thought, it was just a matter of picking up the bookwork; I knew the horse side of things backwards. Without ever thinking the matter out at all clearly, I had envisaged taking an increasingly dominant role at the yard, my father gracefully assuming a back seat. It would be a painless transition, a gradual shift in the emphasis of a partnership that had already worked well for twenty years and more. But like lappet-faced vultures, troubles came down to roost.

I had never bothered much with the business side of stable management. Nor, I soon learned, had my father. There were debts: debts to inspire horror and despair. The yard was so heavily mortgaged it was effectively valueless. Repossession was inevitable. The six horses he – we – I – actually owned had not in fact been paid for. They had to go back. We owed the feed merchant, the farrier, the vet, we owed Weatherbys, we owed several jockeys. We even owed for a couple of horses that we no longer possessed. The wine merchant had not been paid either. This was not a mess, this was disaster. My entire legacy was debt. Solicitors wrote to me in scores, their offices telephoned me hourly. My father's, our, my solicitor would not let me touch a penny of the estate, such as it was. Practically everyone in racing had a prior claim on it. Including the solicitor himself, as it happened.

Clearing up was, inevitably, a grim business. The owners took their horses away one by one, all with kind words and regrets, none more so than Cynthia, the tearful owner of Darlin' Girl, who had been a faithful owner and, off and on, a faithful mistress to my intermittently faithful father. The lads were paid off: some grousing, some in tears. I organised a funeral, distractedly: my father had been a sentimental, non-practising Catholic, barring annual drunken forays to midnight mass. The undertaker kept ringing me up to ask unanswerable questions, like how should my father be prepared? What were his favourite hymns? I remembered his drunken improvised hymn of victory one afternoon about a year before, accompanied by a mad jig round the yard with two Tesco bags brimming with tenners. It went something like 'We've stuffed the focken bookie and he's lost his focken balls', but perhaps that wouldn't do. Any bloody hymn. 'The Lord Is My Shepherd' is very popular at these occasions, sir. What? Oh yes, the one about the quiet waters by? Yes, sir. Excellent, jolly good. Though neither water nor quiet had ever played a big part in his life. And what should he wear, sir? Plain wooden overcoat, cheapest in the shop. Very good, sir. And what shall I do with his effects? His what? Burn the bloody things. I'm afraid I can't do that, sir. Will you take delivery of them? All right, all right.

And so I had to sign for this miserable bundle of junk. A large rumpled suit in Prince of Wales check, mud round the turn-ups and a red wine stain over the breast pocket. Brown brogues that needed mending. In the suit pockets keys, Polos. A wallet containing the usual odds and ends. A pair of unusually good race-glasses. A brown racing trilby. My legacy. The rest of the estate was being fought over by my father's creditors and their solicitors: carrion feeders, hyenas and lappet-faced vultures.

I picked up the wallet: a familiar enough object, enormous, but seldom full, save after the occasional thundering coup against the bookmakers, when wallet, pockets and sometimes carrier bags would overflow with tenners. The wallet contained little of note. I took out the credit cards, and dutifully snipped them in half. There were two twenty-pound notes; these I pocketed, wondering if this was a crime and deciding that it almost certainly was. And there was also an inordinately thick wodge of betting tickets, fat as a pack of cards. I smiled with troubled affection: it was rare for my father to be in possession of entire betting tickets. They were generally ripped asunder and scattered to the four winds as the horses thundered past the post.

And then my heart performed a crash-halt. After a long moment, it restarted: galloping a finish, tumultuous rhythm. In the last race my father had bet on, his horse had won.

A week later I was richer by several thousand pounds. I did not tell any of the solicitors. My father had bet cunningly and well, placing a great deal of money with a wide selection of bookmakers. He had bet at odds from thirty-three to one down to fives. This was, I had no doubt, intended as a desperate coup to save the yard from extinction. Alas, victory had not been enough: the yard and he were gone. But I collected the money on his behalf. All the bookies paid up. There was no legal obligation for them to do so, but they did, some with good humour, some with resignation. One or two were reluctant, but I browbeat them with threats of the dreadful publicity that would follow any meanness. Popular Trainer's Son Left Destitute by Heartless Bookie. Popularity: that was the trump card. Everyone had liked my father; many would be furious if he was cheated, as it were, beyond the grave. One of the Great Characters of Racing, said the obituaries, and the bookies, sensitive flowers when it comes to bad publicity, decided it was better to cough. And they coughed and they coughed. For the last time in that house, pockets and carrier bags overflowed with my father's tenners.

In the final analysis, then, my legacy was this: one pair of binoculars from Leitz of Germany; one racing trilby from Bates of Jermyn Street; and vast wads of tenners. Make a life from that. All right, I will. The madness of grief is much like the madness of love, and so madly I rose to the challenge offered by this legacy. I had no close relatives, no close friends, nowhere to go. I had to vacate the house within six weeks. The logical course was to find a job as assistant trainer somewhere; and it wouldn't have been hard. But I couldn't face the idea. I was used to our yard, our system, our horses: my horses. I worked with my father, the idea of working *for* someone was impossible to contemplate. Just about everything was impossible to contemplate. And so, distracted by grief and overcome with bewilderment, I coldly and deliberately permitted myself a season of insanity. It was intended to be no more than that: a season of madness to be followed by a return to my sort of life, my type of people.

After the funeral, massively attended, and the boozy party paid for by my father's last wager, I returned to the university. A mixture of compassion and respectable work over three years had secured me a respectable degree. They had no objection to my doing an MSc, once I had told them I could pay my own way. It would be research-based. Subjects for this were discussed, methods suggested, many useful contacts were provided. I spent money on telexes and telephones. Within a fortnight it was all fixed. I was going to turn myself for a season into one of the heroes of my childhood.

I flew on a single ticket to Cape Town, and there I bought a beaten-up but still effective Land-Rover. It was a Series One, a model much treasured by Land-Rover enthusiasts. The metal shelf can be used for opening beer bottles; the headlights are placed close together, giving the vehicle a slightly cross-eyed look. Subsequent models had the headlights conventionally placed: 'No good,' George was to say later. 'Can't hit trees.' I drove north into Zimbabwe, and there I took up residence in a centre for field research in one of the national parks. I stayed there for just under a year, living in a bunk in a sort of long house for field scientists. I did not abandon horses, not exactly: in fact, for the first time, the two halves of my childhood were in unity. I produced a fat thesis on the subject of friendship in zebras. I did not dare to call it 'friendship', of course: in ethology, which is the study of animal behaviour, anthropomorphism is considered the sin of witchcraft. My paper was entitled *A Record of the Interactions and Associations between Non-related Animals in Three Breeding Groups of* Equus Burchelli *Plains Zebra*.

I collected enormous quantities of information: how long unrelated females stayed in each other's company, and what they did together. I noted a thousand nuances of horsy behaviour, and, deep in Africa, I felt profoundly at home. For each gesture, each shared behaviour, was something I had witnessed at home, when my father and I had turned the mares out into the big field 'for a buck and a kick and a pick of focken grass'. I made hundreds of graphs and pie charts and bar charts. It was all rather like making up an owner's bill. Don't give them a focken great big figure and let them boggle at it: give them lots of small amounts instead. God dwells in the details.

I was given enormous help by Dr Jessica Salmon, who was doing a colossal piece of research for one of the international wildlife organisations. She had done her doctorate at my university, hence the contact, and she was now researching every imaginable aspect of zebra ecology. Her project, lavishly funded, had involved the blood-typing of a large number of animals; thanks to her, the non-kinship of my chosen zebras was an established fact. Her groundwork gave my research its validity. She was planning a popular book to follow her research: 'I want to do for zebras what George Sorensen and Peter Norrie did for lion all those years ago,' she said. I was delighted that she used some of my own observations in her final, massively authoritative work, all properly, generously acknowledged, and a grand piece of work it turned out to be as well. But that is by the way.

My own paper was finished after a year or so, and so was my money. I got the work typed up in Harare, and posted it – two copies under separate cover, naturally – back to England. I had always thought that I would then post myself, but I did no such thing. I resolved to try my luck, to try 'one more year' in Africa.

I met someone who had worked in tourism, in South Mchindeni National Park, further north. He had worked as a safari guide for Philip Pocock. I was suitably impressed: Pocock was something of an African Legend, a former white hunter who had turned rabid conservationist and grand old man. I was given a letter of introduction and recommended to give it a try. Still uncertain of why, I drove on.

I reached the Mchindeni Valley a couple of weeks before the dry season, also known as the tourist season, or sometimes just as The Season, officially began. The camp operators were setting up for six months of beasts and tourists. I found my way to Mukango Lodge: this was the first tourist operation that had been established in the Valley. Pocock still ran it. I sought him out, and dealt him my letter of introduction. This seemed to go all right. He gave me a beer, talked about zebras and the research centre. He was not hiring staff himself, but I had timed this visit well: it turned out that he was holding a party that night for all the tourist operators in the Valley, a traditional pre-season ritual. I was invited to the do, and offered a bed for a few nights, until I had found a job. Philip Pocock was a crusty and difficult man, but always very kind to me.

The gathering that evening was large, and somewhat overwhelming. I knocked back several beers as a defensive measure, erected my academic status as a wall. I had expected the gathering to be all male, but there was a fair number of women as well. Most camps, I learned, employed a European woman as caterer; after a year on a research centre, each one seemed a dazzling nymph. Most of the people were white, but there was a small number of Africans among them. One of these, who worked as a safari guide with Philip, discoursed learnedly with me on zebras. I met a short but terribly wide man with a penetrating Afrikaner accent, who talked solid business at me. 'The logistics of running a business on a six-month operation are frightening, man. You've got to be good to survive out here, man.' I met an intense English birding type called Lloyd,

24

who confused me mightily with his talk about red-billed and Cape and Hottentot teal. He told me more than once that he had seen a palmnut vulture that day. 'A crippler,' he said. 'An absolute bloody crippler.' I was familiar enough with birding slang to follow him. He introduced me to his camp's caterer, whose beauty caused me to freeze instantly, like an alarmed impala. However, she treated me with impenetrable English snootiness, and when she heard I was looking for a job, she looked me up and down, and laughed. I decided that I hated her. Her freckled, sun-bleached appearance had rendered me more or less incapable of speech, but more attractive still was the thought of throwing her into the Mchindeni River to take her chances among the hippo. Not my type at all: she looked like the sort of owner who every week announced she would take her bloody horse elsewhere. Focken take him. He'll not win nothing without a rocket up his arse.

I moved on, finding myself in conversation with a clownish individual in baggy shorts: shorts, I couldn't help noticing, that had a kind of open-work crochet pattern around the crotch, a pattern created, presumably, by tumbling shards of cigarette. He looked like the party bore, and my first thought was to wonder how to escape. He was lanky without being in the least bit tall; he had a haircut of grey stubble that appeared self-administered, or rather, self-inflicted. I was struck by the almost cosmic filthiness of his clothes. He seemed utterly out of place in this pleasant, civilised gathering. He asked, in an unexpectedly mellow tone, what I had been doing.

I told him, in a rather superior fashion, about friendship in zebras, for I was a field scientist, no mere safari guide. 'How terribly interesting, I've always wondered about doing another study, perhaps of a herbivore, though I'd never thought about zebras, confusing things, after my stuff with, well, those lion, you know.' For this, of course, was George Sorensen, *the* George Sorensen, African legend, co-author of *Lions of the Plains*. I was instantly ashamed, instantly impressed. I noticed that his glasses had been fixed across the bridge with Elastoplast. (In fact, I was to notice that George changed this bridge far more often than any other of his garments, Elastoplast replaced by Sellotape, replaced by masking tape.)

I also had the weird impression that the cigarette he was smoking was made from newspaper. This turned out to be the case. 'The *Guardian Weekly*,' he explained. 'Airmail edition. Best for cigarettes. May I roll you one?' I accepted. The tobacco, thick, coarse and crackly, delivered a powerful and pungent smoke. We discussed the usual problems of field work, and he asked with great attention about my zebras. The key to ethology is the recognising of individuals: no, I had not used coloured ear-tags, or anything of the kind. 'Well, I have read that every zebra has a distinct stripe pattern, of course,' George said. 'But then I have also read that every snowflake is unique. It has always seemed an impossible business to me.'

'It's just a matter of getting your eye in,' I said. 'Same with all animals. A racehorse trainer can recognise every horse in his string. Zebras are easy – easier than lion, I would have thought.'

'I've always found zebras exasperating. I can't even tell males from females half the time, not without a long hard look.'

'Well, I will take a bet that I can tell the dominant stallion from any breeding herd of zebra within, say, five seconds of seeing the herd, and I'd be right seven times out of ten. I'd bet better than even money. These cigarettes are good.'

'Aren't they? I get the tobacco in the village just down the road from here. How can you pick out the stallion so fast? Without peering at the undercarriage for half an hour?'

'Body language. And the position he takes up relative to the herd. And especially the way the herd responds to him. Once you've got the hang of it, it's amazingly straightforward.'

'How terribly terribly interesting,' George said, without a shred of irony. 'Do you think you could show me? Perhaps we could take a drive tomorrow? I assume you're staying here. I could pick you up after breakfast.'

'Why not?' I wonder now how many hundred times I have asked this same non-question of George. Why not, indeed.

3

I suppose it does sound rather melodramatic, but all the same I don't suppose I ever *will* forget the sight or vision that greeted us as George, Helen and I turned into Mchindeni Airport. George, eschewing the tarred road, had taken an intriguing and bouncing short cut across open country – 'I think a spot of bundu-bashing is in order' – crunching and pitching through the scrub. Negligently wiping out a small bush, he jumped the vehicle heroically back onto the road, pounding up to the front of the airport building, eyes skyward as he remarked, 'Wire-tailed swallows' above the engine's roar, and made, passengers listing crazily forward, his trademark crash-halt.

There, watching every yard of our arrival, was the sight or vision, and it affected my pulse rate as dramatically as the morning's lion. This was Mrs van der Aardvark, no less, or to be formal, Caroline Sandford, caterer and deputy manager of Impala Lodge, mistress to Leon Schuyler, who, behind his extremely wide back, was nicknamed van der Aardvark. He was the owner and manager of Impala Lodge, the grandiosely named camp that lay across the river from our own.

She was dressed in khaki shorts and a singlet in umbrella-thorn green and gave an impression of arachnoid limbs. Her straggle of leucistic hair was worn in a style that looked self-administered or self-inflicted, perhaps with wire-cutters. Arms, shoulders, neck, face, legs: all copiously freckled: endless constellations, galaxies and nebulae of freckles, freckles that caused me to wonder, but not for the first time, with the curiosity that is at the base of the erotic impulse, exactly how far, and in what form, those freckles extended.

She was laughing as we pulled up, absolutely roaring with

laughter. She was also apparently talking, which was not unusual, but inaudibly. George switched off the engine, and it was as if her personal volume had been switched on. 'It's like the clown's car arriving at the circus, I keep expecting it to explode and all four wheels to fall off. Really, George, where did you learn to drive?' She turned to me as I stood on the back replacing my hat, and she smiled, something that always had on me the approximate effect of swallowing a large Jack Daniels in one go, ice cubes and all. 'And you with your trilby and George with his broken specs and, really, Leon and I are labouring night and day to drag this park up-market, and here come the pair of you standing for everything we try not to do.' She was beautiful and I adored her, but I didn't like anything she said or did.

I jumped neatly to the ground and observed, 'There is a difference between money and class, but not everyone knows that. Has the bloody plane gone yet?'

She smiled patronisingly: Impala Lodge would never get into such a mess about planes, oh dear me, no. 'It's only just landed,' she said. 'They're running about an hour late.'

'There you are, you see,' George said smugly, as if he had personally arranged all this.

'I'll get Helen checked in.'

'What a shame,' Helen said. 'I was beginning to like the idea of being marooned.'

'Marooned with this pair of lunatics?' Caroline asked her. Truly an insufferable woman. But she seemed completely unaware of either of the two effects she had on me: hopeless desire and helpless anger.

'I wouldn't wish to stay anywhere else in the world, given a choice,' said Helen, suddenly and rather magnificently reverting to her tea-party manners. 'Let alone in Mchindeni Park.'

I pointed a finger at Caroline's freckled nose. 'Class,' I said. 'You see, there are some clients you can't poach from us, and that's the classy ones.' Then I seized Helen's baggage from the back, and George and I escorted Helen herself into the airport building, a long, low hall thronged with tourists and safari guides from all over the Valley.

The meeting of planes was also a meeting of the clans. The dozen or so camps in the Valley were widely separated, relative solitude being rather the point of visiting a wilderness. Everyone knew everyone else at the other camps, but we tended only to meet when collecting or despatching clients. An airport run was always an opportunity to talk shop, swap gossip, lust at caterers and so on.

We steered Helen through various groups of already-checked-in tourists clutching boarding passes and phony items of African fetish, and a couple of hunter types looking sneeringly superior. At the head of the queue, actually checking in, we found Leon Schuyler: van der Aardvark himself. 'Ullo, George, killed any clients this week?' He accepted his boarding pass, yielding the check-in to Helen, and turned to us: a chunky, much moustached man, extravagantly epauletted and wearing at his belt a knife that reached almost to his knees. As his nickname suggested, or shouted, he was of Afrikaner extraction, but he had been born in Chipembere, the capital city. He had lived in Africa all his life, educated at school and university in South Africa, returning to the land of his birth to set himself up in the safari business. He was, in a distinctly African way, a great problem-solver: a man of practicalities. He was also said to be very good indeed in the bush and was much respected in the Mchindeni Valley. 'Leon will know how to do that,' people said, and he generally did.

'Oh, not many,' said George. 'None to speak of, really.'

'Is it?' said Leon, one of the great Afrikaner question tags.

After a brief pause, George remembered his manners. 'Business all right with you and so on?'

'Terrific,' said Leon, or rather, 'Triffic. Got permission from the National Parks Commission to expand. I am seriously bloody pleased, I tell you. Going to build six more huts.' Leon's voice was not Pretoria-pure, but he separated his vowels and suppressed his aspirates in a wonderfully imitable – I imitated it all the time – Afrikaner fashion. Six maw uts.

'Are you full right now?'

'Wouldn't be catching a plane if we were full, man. No, we have two days without clients, quite a relief, I tell you, it's been non-stop. Going to Chip to talk a bit of business, couple of big meetings and so forth. Plenty clients coming Thursday, plenty-plenty clients. Party of bloody ten, bunch of people in England you've probably never heard of. Called Wilderness Express.'

After a slightly stunned silence, I managed to say amiably enough, 'Bit of a squeeze on game drives.'

'Nott!' said Leon, another great Afrikanerism. 'Bought a new Land Cruiser. Came in from Jo'burg three weeks back, just cleared customs this week, slow bastards. My partner had to move in and kick plenty arse, get the damn thing free. But tell me, George, what is happening with the Tondo Pride?'

Leon, I knew, had little time for George as a businessman; I suspect that even my poor father could have given him a few tips in that area. But Leon knew that when it came to wildlife, and especially when it came to lion, George was the man to ask. 'George will know,' people in the Valley said when a conversation about lion reached impasse, and George generally did. And lion were also business: if you showed your clients lion, they tended to go home happy.

'They knocked down an old buff this morning,' George said. He gave the location precisely. 'I fancy that they will stay on the riverine strip now until it rains. I know it's early, but the drought conditions have altered things. Game concentrations are higher round the river than I have ever seen this early in the season, and practically all the standing water has gone. I think the pride will stay where they are till the end of the season. The plain after the ebony grove due north of ours is currently their core area. Not that that helps you on the opposite bank.'

'Well, you'd be surprised at what I have in mind, George. But tell me, have you heard any talk about the bloody road? I need information.'

'That old story again?'

'Shit, George, you never hear anything unless it's a bloody bird. It's all started again, man: second strike of natural gas out in Western Province, want to build a road straight through the middle of the park to make the journey time to Chip down to six hours, open the area up. People from the Ministry of National Resources spent a day with the old man, Chief Mchindeni, talking about a four-lane highway.'

'Are you sure?' I asked, not a good question.

'Jesus, of course I'm bloody sure, and I'm going in to Chip to get even more sure.'

'That would be the end of the park,' I said, naïvely stating the obvious. But I was suddenly dismayed: the end of the park, the end of my life in the bush.

Leon shot me a brief look of contempt. 'It would be the end of my bloody business, man,' he said, Afrikaner-tough. 'Bastards don't bloody care. I'm going to shake a few trees down in Chip, I tell you. These bastards are going to get a fight.' Git a faart.

At this point, Helen joined us, boarding pass in hand, and Caroline also arrived, having shepherded her clients into the departure 'lounge'. She placed her elbow on Leon's shoulder, which immensely solid item was located at a convenient height for her. Leon was built on the principle of the cube, with a khaki baseball cap (marked 'Impala Lodge' and bearing a leaping impala logo, nicely made – 'got 'em done in Jo'burg, man, none of the local rubbish') perched on the top.

'I have to go through now, they tell me,' Helen said. 'Perfectly dreadful. I feel like running away, coming back to stay with you for ever at Lion Camp. I don't suppose you'd consider smuggling me back?'

'Of course,' I said. 'Any time.' I kissed her cheek, not without affection, and said, not without truth, that it had been lovely having her. 'Oh Helen, do you think you could be awfully kind and not actually mention to Joyce that we nearly missed the plane? She'll be waiting for you at Chipembere Airport, you'll be seeing her in an hour.'

She smiled. 'All right,' she said. 'And George. Thank you so

much, it really was the most – most wonderful – oh dear –'
and there and then, this stately and self-possessed lady was
overcome by a deluge of tears. She seized George in a bear
hug, kissed him soundly and fled, sniffing, while George and
I said more nice things, wonderful having you, come back any
time, Auntie Joyce will miss you.

'What have you been doing to that poor woman?' Leon
asked.

'Oh, nothing really,' George said. 'Found lion for her this
morning, that's all.'

'It wasn't the showing that affected her,' I said. 'It was
making her walk up and shake hands with them.'

'Tell you what, let's get back to them this afternoon in the
vehicle,' George said. 'We'll drive right into them. I think that
should be possible in this terrain. Worth a try, don't you think,
Dan?'

'Why not?'

'Right into them?' Caroline asked. 'You don't do that, do
you, Leon?'

'Listen, sweetie, what George does with lion and what I do
with lion are two different things. I try to keep my clients
alive. Don't want them eaten by lion, or dying of bloody heart
attacks.' Art attacks. 'You want to have a art attack, sweetie,
you go driving with George.'

'Well, you can if you like,' George said vaguely. 'Very welcome, any time, come now, come with us this afternoon, we've
no clients today either, you know.'

To my considerable surprise, Leon pounced avidly on this
invitation. 'What a bloody brilliant idea. Triffic, brilliant.
Look, sweetie, why don't you do that, go and look at George's
lion, find out where he is hiding them. Look round his camp,
give me a full run-down of their operation. Have a good time.
Look after her nicely, you guys, right, and don't get her bloody
eaten or I'll come across that river with a bloody gun.'

At this point the airport manager approached us. 'Mr Schuyler, the plane is leaving now, all the passengers are on board.'

'Christ, sorry, James, all right, I'm out of here.' Out of year.

32

He kissed Caroline on the lips, the bastard, said, 'Goodbye, sweetie, don't get bloody eaten,' and was gone.

'Are you sure this is all right?' Caroline asked, suddenly a little taken aback by all these arrangements being made on her behalf. 'It's a nice idea, but I don't want Leon to impose me on you, you know what he's like. If it's not really convenient just say – I was planning to spend the day doing the books, anyway, so I'm not being left high and dry or anything.'

'Well, all we've really got planned today is a look at the lion,' George said, 'once I've made a phone call to the office. We've got to call in at Mukango on the way to use their phone. Look at lion, have a few beers, perhaps. No clients till tomorrow.'

'George, aren't we expecting a parcel today?'

'Oh, so we are.'

George and I walked over to the place where the luggage from the planes was unloaded. 'George, they're up to something,' I said. 'Caroline and bloody Leon. I don't like it.'

George looked benign and mildly surprised. 'Sorry, Dan, I thought you rather liked her, I wouldn't have invited her if . . .'

'There's a difference between fancying and liking, George. Not my type. No bloody parcel, of course. Another of Joyce's cock-ups. Oh, well. Let's go and take the bitch to the lions.'

We walked back to Caroline. 'Let's go to Mukango, then,' George said.

'If we've got to go to Mukango, we won't get back till mid-afternoon,' I said. 'So maybe we should take the spot and have a little go for leopard as well.'

'I'd love to see leopard,' Caroline said.

'You haven't seen leopard?' I was amazed. Leopard were rather a speciality of the Mchindeni Valley.

'Well, I don't normally go out with the clients,' Caroline said. 'It's not the way we do things. I tend to be a fixed point at camp, apart from when I go out to get vegetables and so on. There's not much time for game viewing when you are running a lodge full of demanding international clients. I'd love the chance to get out into the bush, actually.'

33

'Come along, then,' George said. 'If you can face it, after Leon's dire warnings.'

'Rather because of Leon's dire warnings.'

I turned to her with sudden pleasure. 'Is there a latent craziness in this apparently sane woman?' I asked George. Caroline laughed. I thought then that there was a chance of reclaiming her for the human race.

'OK,' I said. 'Here's the plan.' This was something I quite often said. This was because it was something George never said. 'We drive to Mukango, both vehicles. George calls the office, talks to Joyce and hears her latest plan for ruining the company. Then we all have a beer. We drive to Lion Camp in two vehicles. Sunday gives us late lunch. Then we drive off and look for lion. Sundowner. Spotlight on, and cruise back looking for leopard. Get back for supper. How does that sound?'

'Admirable,' George said. Caroline smiled at me again, but I coped.

We drove in convoy to Mukango, an hour's journey south. Philip Pocock's lodge had one of the two telephones in the Valley – the other was at the airport but they kept it for themselves – and other camps were permitted to use it for a fee. Philip often pretended that the telephone was his principal source of income; he ran Mukango from a planter's chair beneath a colossal leadwood tree in the Mukango garden. Now in his seventies, he had of late, he boasted, learned the art of delegation. His staff were inclined to dispute this.

I went up to the Mukango Bar, an establishment so grand it had a real barman, and asked for three Lion, Lion being the name of the beer of the country, and it came out a good shade of lion colour, if occasionally a touch cloudy. George was preparing his mind, or perhaps not preparing his mind, for his call. Lion Safaris was a partnership between George and a charming, generous man named Bruce Wallace, and the booking and administration were carried out from Bruce's office in Chipembere. Most generously, Bruce had delegated the day-today running of the company to his poisonous ex-mistress. Her name, as it happened, was Joyce.

George drank half his beer and took the other half to the telephone, which was in reception a few paces away. Joyce, of course, would already have met Helen at the airport, and helped her to make her connection to Palmyra: the standard tourist trip to the country involved a visit to South Mchindeni for the game viewing and then to Palmyra Resort to wind down.

George got through surprisingly quickly, but the line, judging from his bellow, seemed a poor one. And, all too audibly, it was clear that George was in receipt of a royal bollocking. 'No, she liked it . . . Joyce, she may well have been frightened, but . . . Joyce, she said it was the most marvellous day of her life. No, she was not in any danger. She enjoyed it, I promise you. Ah, Heuglin's. What? Oh, sorry, no, a Heuglin's robin has just started singing. No, I know. Sorry. It's just singing. No, of course not, Joyce, it was a great success. Joyce, I'm sure she didn't tell you that she had a terrible time. She said she wanted to come back. Well, next time, don't apologise on my behalf. Oh Joyce, remember Wilderness Express? They're going to stay at Impala Lodge. That was seventy bed-nights you turned down. Oh, all right then, sixty-three. We can't afford those mistakes, Joyce. It *was* a mistake. No, I tell you it was. Oh, never mind. Oh, yes, I knew there was something I wanted to ask you, what about that parcel you promised? There was nothing on the plane. Can you get it to us tomorrow? Why not? Look, Joyce, I *know* cheese is expensive, but so is meat, and this couple coming tomorrow are vegetarians. Oh, not coming tomorrow? Oh God. Not another cancellation, I can't bear it. Joyce, this is ruination. Oh, I see. They've cancelled one night and are coming the day after tomorrow. So we're empty two nights now, oh dear. But we still need the cheese. For Christ's sake, Joyce, I know cheese is expensive, but we'll save money on meat. Do you want to starve them or something? Sorry, Joyce, I know you don't. How should I know why they're vegetarian? Shall I send them to another camp where they'll get properly fed then? Joyce, this doesn't make sense.'

Caroline was listening unashamedly, and to George, not the Heuglin's robin singing strenuously in the shrubbery. More gossip of Rogue Lion Safaris would be spinning round the Valley. Bitch. Bitches both of them. I listened myself, hearing doom in every word George spoke. I had a terrible fear that, one day, Joyce would take the bush away from me. But what could I do?

Philip entered the bar, chuckling to himself. He looked smaller than ever, tortoise neck protruding from the collar of a beautifully pressed khaki shirt. 'Hullo. Is George having problems,' he stated rather than asked.

'George always has problems with that insane woman in Chipembere. And so does everybody else. He's calling the office, you see.'

'Oh, I guessed that. Tying George down, it won't do. George is a free spirit, you do know that, don't you?'

'Of course I do,' I said, mildly nettled. 'I work with him.'

'Not you, this charming – er –'

'Caroline.'

'Yes, of course, and you do realise that George is a great man, don't you? George is bush, you see, pure bush.'

'I see,' Caroline said. 'And you approve of that, do you?'

To my surprise, instead of getting cross, Philip laughed his wheezy old man's laugh. 'I was pure bush myself, once,' he said. 'Then I started being a sort of politician, when we needed to get the park established all those years ago. And then I became an old man running a tourist business. But I was pure bush first. And last too, I think.'

'I see,' said Caroline.

'Yes, maybe you do, and maybe you don't. Humour the old bugger, eh? What do you think of life out here, now you've been in the Valley for – what? – four months?'

'It's been wonderful. I love it. I never want to leave. Can't imagine any other way of living.'

Philip began laughing again at this, and followed with a

36

bout of coughing. 'I'm so sorry, er, Caroline, but your words have a dreadful ring to them. I have known three ladies, each one as lovely as yourself, who said the same thing to me. I can't imagine any other way to live. I never want to leave. And I married them, all three of them, consecutively, not simultaneously. And do you know what else they said? After a while, they all said the same thing. It's me or the bush, Philip. Face facts: me or the bush. And so I faced them; the facts, that is. And I always said the same thing, or maybe I just thought it: awfully sorry, old girl, but that is not really a fair contest, is it? And so I have a wife in Cape Town, a wife in Chipembere, and a wife in Wiltshire. And I'm still here.'

'Is there a moral in this story?' Caroline asked.

'I don't know,' Philip said. 'Perhaps.'

'Perhaps the moral is that you've always been faithful to your true love.'

Philip stared at her for a moment in some surprise; he had not expected acuteness. Nor, it must be said, had I.

George came back, running his hand through the growing-out stubble of his haircut, making himself look rather like a crested barbet. He and Philip exchanged greetings. 'And is all well back in Chipembere, George?'

'Oh, well enough. But I just feel I'm getting a bit old for all this. I spend my life worrying about cheese.'

'Oh no, you're not, George. You're just the same; it's the park that's grown older. It's older and softer and easier, and it doesn't suit you any more. It's not what it was when you first came here, let alone what it was like when I came here, all but fifty years back, and started killing all those poor animals. The park has become a success, and that is not what you are made for, George.'

'Success?' George asked disbelievingly. 'We're going broke.'

'I'm talking about the park, not about your or anyone else's business operation. The pioneering has been done, it's time now for the second-phase people to try and make sure that the work of the pioneers doesn't get wasted. But you're a pioneer; you shouldn't be here any more.'

'Thanks, Philip.'

'George, I'll tell you what you should do.'

'Do, Philip, do.'

'Go north. Go to the North Park. Open it up for tourists. Bring in the first wave. It's a matter of starting all over again up there, no roads, no camps, no tourists. Just the bush. The South Park is too soft for you. Go north.'

'Why don't you go?' I asked. This was a bit cheeky, from someone like me to a person of Philip's eminence, but I thought on the whole that he deserved to be asked.

'Too old. Too stiff to live in a tent, too tired to go where there are no roads. If I were twenty years younger, I'd go. Goodness, I'd go like a shot, because the North Park is now what the South Park was when I first came here. But I'm not. Young, that is. The South Park has kept pace with me. We've grown old together, old and soft. But you're young, George; it's what you should be doing.'

'I don't feel young,' George said, feelingly.

'Have a beer then,' I suggested.

'A good idea. Not totally devoid of initiative, are they, George, the young buggers? Are you training him well? Or does he still confuse the barking of heron and bushbuck?'

This was a reference to a brick I had dropped during my safari guide exam, the examiner being Philip Pocock. In fairness to myself, I must add that it was the only real error: I had passed with an A grade. Philip had given me a tough time during the exam; his principal technique for unnerving a candidate was to respond to a piece of proffered information with the single word 'Elaborate'. But I had elaborated in a most elaborate fashion, and if my botany had been a little shaky, my large mammal stuff had been easily enough to carry the day.

So now I merely gave Philip the brief version of my normally elaborate impersonation of the call of the wood owl, and stood up to wave to the barman, indicating that four more Lion would be in order.

'And what is it you are doing with Lion Safaris, Caroline?

I know – they are abducting you from Leon and making you work for them as the caterer they so badly need.' Philip glanced at George with amiable malice.

'Yes, that's something I've often wondered, George,' Caroline said. 'Why don't you have a caterer? You must be the only camp in the Valley without one.'

'Oh.' George gave himself a vigorous scalp massage, changing the style from crested barbet to hoopoe. 'It was a row I had at the start of the season with the office.' He gestured vaguely in the direction of the phone, meaning Joyce. 'They wouldn't let me employ a caterer, after I had taken on Dan as well as Joseph Ngwei. Said I had too many staff.'

'How do you work it out, then?'

'By sort of committee. Me, Dan and Joseph, and Sunday the cook. He's done rather well, actually.'

'So well you will surely pay me a double bone-arse,' I said, in Sunday's voice.

'He'll be furious about the bloody cheese,' George said. 'I daren't tell him.'

'I'll get Joseph to do it,' I said. 'He'll take it better from him.'

'Excellent.'

'Oh, you should join these people, Caroline,' Philip said delightedly. 'Look at the mess they are making of it all. Join them and sort them out. You're just the person they've been looking for.'

'I should bloody well think not,' said Caroline, sitting up straight, all her primness returning. 'I hardly think a business diploma, not to mention cordon bleu cooking qualifications, is the sort of thing they need.'

'*Exactly* what we need,' I said, with great heartiness. 'Start this afternoon. No, you're our guest this afternoon. Start tonight after supper. From nine o'clock tonight you must do everything I want, all right?'

'*No* chance,' she said. No teasing required today, clearly. Sod you then. How were we going to get through the day without coming to blows? 'I am assistant manager of a properly

39

run tourist operation that offers a luxury safari to top-drawer international clients. And that's how I intend things to remain.'

'We just show our people the bush,' I said. 'Food is not cordon bleu, but we offer the best lion in the Valley. Lion is the principal item on our menu.'

'That's why you get the sort of clients you get, and we get the sort of clients we get.'

Philip was laughing at this exchange. 'That will suffice, children, thank you. Ah, George, I used to put lion before the comfort of my clients once, but not any more. I am old, and my clients are too fat. It seems that this is the way clients want it to be: a taste of wilderness, and a lot of food and drink and lying around, and then off to Palmyra Resort for a rest, that is to say, lying around eating and drinking. That is the way it must be. So if you are not joining Lion Safaris, Caroline, what is this visit all about? A spying mission, no doubt. See what your deadly rivals across the river are getting up to.'

Caroline stiffened. 'They have very kindly offered to show me some lion, since we haven't got any clients in camp tonight. For once.'

'Oh, a visit to the Tondo Pride,' Philip said. 'That should be part of every bush person's experience. To visit the Tondo Pride with George. Are they well, the Tondo buggers.'

'Killing left and right,' George said.

'Is George really as dangerous with lion as they say?' Caroline asked.

'You mean, as dangerous as Leon says,' said Philip. 'Oh yes, I should think so. But the thing is, I've never felt terribly safe with George. Even when there are no lion around. Even when we're not in the bush. Not a terribly safe chap, George. You go with him and see the lion. You'll have the time of your life.'

4

From the moment that I joined up with George, I felt as if I were becoming part of an African legend: a minor character in the great legend that was George. Though in fact there were really two legends about him. Among ethologists, and among readers of popular science, he was a ground-breaking genius. But in the Mchindeni Valley he was a dangerous lunatic. His book *Lions of the Plains*, popular science at its best, had hit me like a shell in my teens. The behaviour of animals, both wild and tame, or half-tamed, had always been the central part of my life; with this book, things acquired a clarity and a purpose they had never before possessed. Hence the zoology degree, hence the study on zebra.

George had produced both the long academic study and the popular work in partnership with Peter Norrie. The academic paper itself was extraordinary; I had wrestled long and hard with it over the course of my studies. Hours of observation, minute cataloguing of detail, and a final analysis in which every insight, every leap of intuition was backed up by a thousand statistics. It was a venerable piece of work, twenty-five years old, and still considered a template for all single-species work. It was a pioneering study, and it paved the way for an ever-proliferating number of similar projects, last and least among them my own.

The people of Mchindeni Valley had difficulty in reconciling the academic legend with everybody's favourite crazy, with broken specs and open-work crochet crotch. It must be admitted they had a point. The lion study was endlessly meticulous: not George's most obvious quality. And it was finished: George was a man with a thousand talents, but finishing things was not among them. In the end, I learned that the organising and completing side of things had been Norrie's contribution, most of the observation and all the insights George's. Norrie was an academic in shorts; after this joint paper was published he never again left his university. George stayed in the bush, and never published another paper.

Lions of the Plains made money, a respectable amount of the stuff if not a fortune. Norrie had laid his share down as the deposit on a house in Cambridgeshire; George had spent his setting up Lion Safaris with Bruce Wallace. Thus he had exchanged the awed respect of academe for the amiable derision of Mchindeni Valley. 'George *knows*,' people would say, especially when talking of lion, but soon they would be swapping George stories. The vehicle that fell into Kalulu Swamp. The vehicle that George drove off the pontoon and into the Mchindeni River with six clients on board. George's fall from a tree, his night in the bush unconscious beneath it, covered in blood, his insouciant arrival twenty-four hours later at the Mukango Bar, ordering a beer while still blood-plastered. There were a million stories.

Mine was, and is, about the best. It concerns the first day we spent together: the day after Philip Pocock's beginning-of-the-season party, when George and I went looking for zebras, so that I could show him how to recognise a stallion within five seconds.

George picked me up at Mukango in the morning and we set off in his terrible beaten-up Land Cruiser. We chose, as a random destination, the distant lagoon where Lloyd had claimed the sighting of his palmnut vulture, and then on, a great loop north to George's camp. We bounced around the park at a great lick, George slamming on the brakes every time we saw zebra. After five seconds I would call 'Stallion!' and point. Then we would clamp our binoculars to our eyes and stare pruriently until we had a firm diagnosis. 'Yes. Definite male.'

'*Definite* male.'

And I was right way above chance expectation, and George asked me again and again about the clues that made instant diagnosis possible, and I rattled on endlessly about my zebras while the African Legend listened with extraordinary humility. It was almost as if I were the venerable, aged-in-the-bush legend, he the young, damp-eared know-nothing. It was certainly as if we were colleagues. A little later I diagnosed not humility but generosity: perhaps the only quality that really matters.

For the rest, we talked endless wildlife shop. George was, I soon learned, a generalist of bewilderingly wide knowledge, but still wider curiosity. We discovered a taste in common for wild speculation. Why not? So often in science, the intuitive leap comes first, the spadework second. George recorded all these pieces of speculation onto his tape recorder, vowing to investigate them further, to seek out evidence. After a long morning of it, we reached the lagoon where the palmnut vulture had, or had not, been seen. We pulled into the shade of a kigelia tree, and scanned about with binoculars. George produced lunch from the inaptly named cool box. We flipped off the tops in the door-latch of the Land Cruiser and drank it.

I found the palmnut vulture too. George fetched his telescope, an instrument which, I was to learn, was forever falling off its tripod without warning, and focused on the bird for a closer inspection. 'It's actually a fish eagle, isn't it? An immature?' The question was a statement. I took a look myself.

'I see what you mean. I'm completely wrong.'

'Well, they do look quite similar.'

'George, do you know what I think?'

'That the fish eagle is the bird that Lloyd identified as a palmnut vulture.'

'I'll give you –'

'Better than even money?'

'Much better. Heavy odds-on. Outrageous stringing.' I then had to explain to George that 'stringing' was birding slang for faulty diagnosis, and so the bogus palmnut made Lloyd a stringer of heroic dimension. Pleased with the thought, we finished our beer, restored the bottles to the 'cool' box, and

George started up. Or rather he didn't. He turned the key, but nothing happened. 'Oh dear, I wish it wouldn't do that.'

'Do what?'

'Well, there's something wrong with the ignition switch. It sometimes turns the heating on by mistake when it's in the off position. And that drains the battery. And sometimes the wires fall off the battery, too. Perhaps it's that and not the heating. I'll have a look.'

He opened the bonnet and discovered that it was, indeed, the detached wire at fault. I passed him, at his request, a wallet of tools from the glove compartment. After a few moments of fiddling, George asked me to try the key again. Success. He slammed down the bonnet, and we drove off again, travelling fairly briskly towards Lion Camp. We stopped a lot on the way, especially for zebra. George was now trying to diagnose the stallions himself and was getting the hang of it fast. But then the vehicle went lame on us. 'Sod it.' Puncture: a routine emergency. 'Give me the wallet of tools again, Dan. I'll get the jack.'

'What tools?'

'The ones you gave me before.'

'You never gave them back to me.'

'Of course I bloody did.'

'You bloody didn't. Anyway, they're not here.'

'Oh dear.'

'Anything vital in there?'

'Wheel wrench.'

'Oh, bugger it. Perhaps we can bodge the wheel nuts loose with a shifting spanner. Have you got one?'

'Oh yes.'

'That's all right, then.'

'It's with the wallet of tools.'

'Oh, arseholes, where the hell is the tool kit?'

'I rather think I left it on the front bumper after I closed the bonnet. After I had fixed the wire back onto the battery. It will have fallen off, probably still under the kigelia tree.'

'About two hours' drive away.'

'About that. Oh well. We'd better walk.'

'*Walk*? It'd take two days.'

'No, no, no, to camp, to my camp, to Lion Camp, you know. It's only about a mile off, and I've plenty of spare tools there.'

It was an iron rule of *The Safari Guide Training Manual* that when in trouble, you stayed with the vehicle. Walking safaris were, of course, permitted in the Mchindeni National Parks, but only in the company of an armed scout. George and I, unarmed, set off into the bush. 'You hardly ever see any game around here,' George said airily.

'Oh good.'

Within five minutes we had walked almost straight into a lioness. She was lying stretched out beneath a tree, as soundly asleep as only a lion can be. She did not move a muscle. I loved her. We swung away from her, altering course to follow the bank of the dry Tondo River, aiming to cross at its confluence with the Mchindeni. That was enough bad luck for one walk, anyway, I thought.

After five minutes or so, my pulse had slowed a little and I had stopped mouth-breathing. I felt extraordinarily exposed: naked. We reached the high bank of the Mchindeni: three hundred yards away, I could see the framework of a couple of incomplete huts, signs of rather desultory human activity. This was my first sight of Lion Camp.

Our path took us to the confluence, the wide funnelled mouth of a river of sand, its banks studded with thick combretum bushes. It was at this point, about ten yards from the first bush and a hundred yards from camp, that there was a small, localised nuclear explosion. The first bush blew up in front of us; with a great detonation of snarls and a rip and snap of breaking twig, there before us was the biggest lion I had ever seen in my life, dark-maned and colossal, with carthorse-huge feet, an eye-filling sight of teeth and mane and yellow eyes. Afterwards, I felt the experience was rather like the playing of a fruit machine, a subject on which I was an expert: a wait for the flashing symbols to settle on a decision and to spell out your fate. For about one hundredth of a second, the symbols seemed to flash through the yellow eyes – fight or flight, fight or flight, fight or flight – before settling on jackpot. Flight. The lion, surprised and horrified almost as much as us, opted for discretion, and with a sudden flick of the hips, revealing balls like footballs, he turned and covered thirty yards in an instant of time, spinning around on an eminence above us to lash his tail and show us the whiteness of his teeth.

There followed one of those lifetime three-second pauses. And then George said quietly, without turning his head, 'Definite male.'

After that, of course, there was no escape. That lion did something to me, you see. I was never quite sure what: only that it was irreversible. That night, as we dined at Lion Camp, George invited me to join him as his assistant for the season, and I accepted at once. I took my safari guide exam a fortnight later and the day after that, I was showing our first clients the bush, talking hard on zebra, swotting hard on birds and plants, badgering George to teach me more bird calls. I took up residence in a hut on the banks of the Mchindeni, and every night, I slept to the sound of lion music.

5

Caroline's first response to Lion Camp almost got her thrown into the Mchindeni River for bisection by hippo. 'My God, it's beautiful,' she said. 'The things you could *do* with this place.' Certainly I flung into the river the thoughts I had been having about reclaiming her for humanity.

It is true that the place didn't look all that much. You hardly even noticed it; from a couple of hundred yards you might pass by without seeing it. Not a drop of paint in the place, not a square inch of concrete. I liked it like that: above all, it was *right*. But as I looked at the place through Caroline's eyes, for an instant I saw a kind of shantytown: a handful of guest huts, walled in weathered and dusty bamboo matting, grass-hatted; staff huts that were little more than lean-tos. The only structure of any solidity was the sitenji: an African term used for a camp's all-purpose shelter, the eating, drinking, reading, talking, writing area: a nicely thatched roof, more elaborate than the roofs of the huts, supported by stout wooden pillars, with a knee-high wall made from tied-together bundles of dried grass. Inside were a dining table and chairs. Beyond the sitenji, on the edge of the bank, a few 'comfortable' canvas chairs were grouped around a small pile of ashes: we had a fire here at night when there were clients in camp.

'I mean, the potential of this place,' Caroline said, looking at the elegant grove of ebony trees to the right of and behind the camp, which let through a dappled sunlight. There seemed to be in her eyes something of the same excitement that George and I felt when we saw a crowd of vultures perched high in a tree, and wondered what we might find beneath. 'Fabulous. Just fabulous.'

'What would you wish to do with the place?' asked Joseph Ngwei politely.

'This could be the hottest camp in the Valley,' she said, ignoring, or perhaps unaware of, the hostility she was inspiring. 'I mean, only six guest huts?'

'Five,' I said. 'Ten beds.'

'But you could double that easily, it's perfect.'

'I know it is.'

'I thought Impala Lodge had the best location in the Valley, but this is better, the views along the river are better, and that wood is unbelievable. You could really do something with this place.'

'Ebony glade,' I said.

'I can't believe you don't do more with it.'

'We thought that improving on perfection was beyond us.'

She turned to me, eyes alight with delight, and said: 'Come on then. What about a guided tour?'

'It won't take long. There isn't much to see here. Only the bush.' I showed her the sitenji; this had a bar at one end, at Joyce's insistence, but no one had ever stood behind it. We used it as a shelf for our natural history books and the spare pairs of binoculars, all intended for the use of clients, and very dusty they got there. Caroline went out to the half-circle of 'comfortable' chairs and stood at the fireplace. She remained there for a long while in silence. A great white egret was fishing in the middle of the stream, beside him a spoonbill working furiously in comensal proximity. After a while, she asked: 'Will you show me the huts?'

The huts were just huts, creaking baskets with light-permeable walls. Each contained two spindly, metal-framed single beds, two mosquito nets, and a small table bearing a Thermos jug of imperfectly chilled water. 'Where's the floor?' Caroline asked.

'What you are standing on is the floor of the planet earth,' I said. 'A light covering of sand from the Mchindeni river bank. What more could anyone want?'

'Well, if you don't know, I can't tell you,' Caroline said. 'I can see why you keep hearing rumours about the National Parks Commission wanting to close you down. Who on earth can you get to come and stay here? Why don't you put concrete down?'

'It's not allowed. We're inside the park here: no permanent structures allowed.'

'Impala Lodge is inside the park, and Leon got permission to lay down concrete.'

'I'm aware of that. We don't actually want concrete, though. We prefer Mchindeni river sand.'

'What about lavatories?'

'Oh, we've got them, don't panic.' I took her to the nearest of the two. 'Long-drop. Sort of a deep pit, an oil drum at the top. But as you see, a real lavvy seat.'

'You didn't think of building them en suite, of course.'

'Not a good idea. They get to whiff a bit by the end of the season, you see.'

'Leon got permission to fit flush toilets at Impala Lodge.'

'Yes, I know, and the water towers are a wonderful land-mark for lost travellers.' The sarcasm washed over her. She seemed to be rather overdoing the casual, professional interest in a competitor's business. I felt like a house owner listening to a tactless potential buyer criticising the wallpaper and talking loudly about dismantling your favourite room.

Caroline asked: 'And showers?'

'Ah yes. *Pièce de résistance*, the showers. Clients love them. Follow me.' I led her to the edge of the river bank, where three oil drums stood. Beneath the central one, a small fire of mopane wood was kept perpetually alight; mopane, hard as diamond, forms small coals that glow for hours.

'Don't tell me,' Caroline said. 'You splash yourselves down out here in the open.'

'Would we be so coarse and unsophisticated? Come.' I led her down a short flight of steps, cut into the river bank. At their foot was a small ledge, its outer edge guarded by a bamboo rail. Behind the rail were the two shower cubicles, each the size of

49

a telephone kiosk, roofed with thatch, three walls and a floor cut from living river bank. The fourth wall was air; each cubicle gave a matchless view across the mighty Mchindeni. And from each, you could see both egret and spoonbill, and hear the grunting and guffawing of a pod of hippo in a deep pool a few yards away. Caroline inspected the shower head and the two taps, which were fed by the oil drums above: hot and cold. A straggling party of a dozen foxy-red puku was coming down to drink on the far side of the river; a pied kingfisher flashed before us, halted in mid-air, hovering hard, before plunging twenty feet into the river, emerging triumphantly fishfull.

Caroline placed both her hands on the bamboo rail, and looked out over the river. I said nothing; nor, for once, did she. A sudden piercing whistle, surprisingly close, cut the air, and she jumped. 'Puku,' I said softly. 'Alarm call. Look, there he is, right below us.'

'Antelope whistle? Is this a tease?'

'Would I do such a thing? I know it's an odd noise for an antelope, but it's what they do.'

Obligingly the puku did it again, and Caroline laughed suddenly. 'You know, there are moments when I see the point of you lot. The shower is lovely. But doesn't all this neo-primitivism upset the clients?'

'Some are a bit taken aback at first,' I said, answering seriously because this was intended as a serious question. 'Especially if they've been told to expect something different. And that happens more often than we would wish.'

'But that's dreadful. Can't you control the way you are marketed? It's the first rule of business, surely.'

'Well, that's our Joyce for you. But the thing is, once we've got the clients – on the rare occasions we get any, that is – it begins to work to our advantage. We tell them this is a camp, a bush camp, the real thing, no half-cocked lodge. This is where the real bush people go. And we give them lots and lots of bush, lots and lots of animals. They mostly get the hang of things. The ones who are nervy at first generally end up the biggest fans. They feel they've achieved something, which they have, and they end up really pleased with themselves. That's great fun for us, when it happens, and it happens a lot.'

'Yes, I can see how that might be a good strategy,' Caroline said thoughtfully. 'If you could market it properly, it would certainly be effective. If you could tap in to the right sort of clients.' She laughed at herself suddenly. 'God, if I stay here much longer, I might even start to see the point of George's insane driving.'

'You're a lady very easily swayed.' I realised that this was a rather risqué remark far too late to call it back.

But Caroline only laughed, and ran up the steps ahead of me.

Sunday coped well with the unexpected guest, producing a quiche from his hole-in-the-ground oven – that too fascinated and appalled Caroline – and putting together a salad. Over the meal, Caroline started to ask how we managed for light. Paraffin. What, no electricity? No generator? Leon had a generator. Yes, we knew that. We knew that very well indeed. We heard it start every evening, and when the wind blew in the right, or the wrong direction, we heard its mutter throughout the evening. We had no wish to impose further din on ourselves, on our clients, on the bush. 'But how do you keep the animals out?'

'We don't.'

'But don't you get animals in the camp? I mean, we use the generator to run an electric fence. So the clients can walk about camp in comfort and safety.'

George broke into the conversation suddenly, with his mouth full of quiche. 'Course we get animals in camp. It's in the middle of the bloody *bush*, isn't it? Where do you think you are, Kew bloody Gardens?'

'I'm sorry, George,' Caroline said, quite humbly. 'I'm not used to the idea of animals in camp. Impala Lodge is sort of a safe area, an island, if you like, surrounded by bush, where the clients feel safe. You look out at the bush from the safety of Impala Lodge, if you see what I mean. You do it differently here, and I'm not used to it.'

'Out here we're awash with animals,' I said. 'Going for a pee in the middle of the night is one of life's great adventures.'

'And the animals really come into camp? What sort of animals?'

'Elephant the other night,' said George. 'Hippo round the edges every night.'

'Heard leopard this morning,' I said. 'Did I say? While I was waiting for you and Helen, right on the edge of the ebony glade.'

'And bloody honey badger,' George said.

'We bear good will to all living creatures at this camp,' I said. 'Except honey badger.'

'What do they do?' asked Caroline. 'Steal honey?'

'They steal bloody everything, and last week they managed to rip open a tin trunk full of food. A tin trunk! They *bit* it open.'

'We had lion in the camp last night,' Joseph said. 'I found tracks after you had left on the walk.'

He had George's full attention immediately. 'Really? How many?'

'Just one. Female, I think, not a full-grown male, certainly. She passed between your hut and Dan's, round the back of the sitenji, and then in front of huts four and five.'

George considered this for a moment.

'But what are you going to do about it?' Caroline asked, alarmed, and no doubt already considering the adventure of the nocturnal pee.

'Not sure. I'd like to have followed her,' George said. 'But it'll be too late now, of course. Perhaps she was going to look for our old friend, the alpha male. Because he wasn't with the rest of the Tondo Pride this morning, was he? Perhaps there's a honeymoon going on.'

'But the rest were all there on the buff this morning, George, all twelve of them.'

'I know. That's why it's interesting. She must have come

from another pride, probably the one to the south of us. Seeking a spot of exogamy, perhaps.'

'Exogamy?' Joseph asked.

'Copulation outside the pride. Very healthy thing, of course. Refreshes the gene pool.'

Caroline said nothing, but you could see that she badly wanted to. She could not understand how lion, rather than the camp, were George's priority.

'I know,' George said. 'Perhaps we could do a little detour tomorrow and look for her. On the way to the airport to collect the vegetarians.'

'They're not coming tomorrow,' I reminded him.

'Nor are they, bugger it. Oh, bugger this bloody season. Bugger everything. Well, never mind. We'll listen out. Maybe drive out tomorrow if we hear anything in the night.'

'Excellent,' I said. 'We'll do it. Now, here's the plan for today. We have coffee. Then we go and see lion on the kill. I'll pack a cool box for sundowners. Beer, everybody? You coming, Joseph? Lion, Coke?'

'Sure. Lion.'

'Caroline, you haven't got binoculars, have you? A few spare pairs on the bar, the small ones at the end are the best. All right?'

And so, half an hour later, we set off. I must confess to a paltry stratagem. Joseph and I conducted a constant, never admitted competition for the front seat of the vehicle. Travelling up-front with George was always instructive; you could never learn enough. But on this occasion, I 'forgot' my hat and went back to fetch it at the last minute, returning to find George and Joseph in the front, Caroline on the back. I swung jauntily into the back alongside, trilby at a dashing angle. Cool in the Bush.

We were delayed on the way to the lion kill by a small group of kudu females, tall, stately and gorgeous, a deep maroon, almost a purple colour, painted with white stripes by a wavering hand. They had ears like satellite dishes, large eyes in faces also picked out with slim white stripes. They stopped motionless at our approach, an utterly characteristic antelope attitude: neither quite trusting nor quite fearful, they gazed unwinking. 'Oh, the lovely, lovely things,' Caroline murmured beneath her breath.

'Surely you've seen them before.'

'Not close. Look at those faces, it's like the hymn; you know, that line about "looked down with sad and wondering eyes".'

'Bateleur,' said George. 'Oh, and hear the brubru, sounds just like a telephone.'

'So it does,' said Caroline. 'I've never heard that before.'

We drove on. 'How odd, to start singing hymns in the middle of the bush.'

'Not so odd. I sing hymns everywhere. My father is a vicar.'

'Oh,' I said, rather inadequately. 'What does he think about you being in the bush?'

'He thinks I'll grow out of it.'

'My mother thought that,' George called from the front. 'A lot more vultures.'

He was right. The umbrella thorn above the kill was now thick with them, motionless, like weird and probably poisonous fruit, as they surveyed the banquet from which they were still excluded.

'All right,' George said. 'Ready for a spot of bundu-bashing, Caroline?' Without reducing speed, he drove off the track and onto the bush-studded plain. This had a drastic effect on the motion of the Land Cruiser: on the road, it rolled like a Channel ferry in mildly inclement weather; the plain imparted a violent pitching and yawing motion that mimicked a sea passage in a typhoon. Caroline, propelled from her seat, made a desperate lunge for the grab-bar. I was already standing high, one foot on the spare wheel and the other on the vehicle's side, holding onto the grab-bar with one hand. Though it looked fairly cool, this position was not, in fact, for Caroline's benefit: good bush-driving in these circumstances is a team job. With the height, I could give George useful information.

The way between us and the lion was blocked by the dry watercourse. 'Left. No, on a bit. Past the bushes. There, you can get down and up here.' George inched the vehicle down, and then took the rise on the other side with a sudden rush. At the lip, the vehicle twisted giddily, one wheel lost contact with the ground, but after a moment it toppled and fell back with a gratifying thump, and we were across. The way ahead was across a wide area of black cotton soil. This is perfectly horrible stuff. The ground, flooded, dried out and baked, cracks into cobbles. It feels like crossing a sea of cricket balls. You can make walking pace at the easy parts.

'Is it legal to drive so far off the road?'

'Oh, I don't know.'

'Leon says you need a fast escape route when you drive near lion.'

We drove on. 'The kill's where it was this morning,' I called from my crow's nest. 'Two, maybe three lion on it. I can see six lying around still under the thorn tree.'

'Two more under the bush on the right,' Joseph said.

'I was just coming to them,' I said with dignity. I hadn't seen them at all.

'Bullshit,' Joseph said. 'And a single female there, that makes twelve.'

'I still can't see them,' Caroline said anxiously.

'Take the nearer of the two thorn trees. Follow the trunk down to the ground. Then left, just a little.'

'*Oh.*'

We drove juddering on, pitching and yawing across the merciless ground. George cut away from the line we had walked that morning, coming back to the lion from a more open area. The bushes fell away: we had an uninterrupted view: sandy shapes in sand-coloured grass, a hundred yards away.

George halted for a moment, looking around, and said encouragingly: 'Perfect. Perfect.' And then, without any more ado, he drove straight into the middle of them.

He drove furiously on at the not quite walking pace that the conditions demanded, and once comfortably and utterly surrounded by lion, he stopped. And, to an audible gasp from Caroline, switched off the engine.

The nearest lion was perhaps six feet away, a young maneless male. His sex was not hard to diagnose: he was lying on his back with his balls in the air, all four paws aflap. I counted eight lion about us: not one had moved a muscle at our approach. We were pretty well surrounded: lion on three sides of the vehicle. But not one among them cared: they were in a perfect ecstasy of digestion. A female shifted her head a few inches, as if finding an even more comfortable spot on the pillow. She lifted a lazy paw and aimed a sledgehammer blow at a fly. 'Even Auntie Joyce is happy,' George said. 'I think I can get a bit closer, you know.'

'Why not?'

George reversed out, fidgeted around, headed back in, like a man fussily parking in a supermarket car park. 'That's more like it.' Beside me, I saw Caroline's hand tighten on the grab-rail, harder than she had gripped when rocking across the black cotton soil. 'Jesus,' I heard her say. 'Oh Jesus.' It sounded more prayer than blasphemy.

The balls-in-the-air male shifted onto his front in a sudden boneless movement, and at once he was on his feet. He then picked his way around the vehicle, moving stiff-legged, belly wagging full beneath him. A long arm out of the vehicle, and you could have stroked him. Awkward and unathletic, because very full, he approached the picked corpse of the buffalo, which was open towards us, displaying an espalier of ribs. He flopped down at the kill and began to feed again, with the self-satisfied air of a binge eater who knows he is going to pay for this later. The two lionesses on the kill exchanged growls and snarls with him, but they were all too full and too happy to quarrel properly. One of the lionesses stood up, and walked back to her companions, incidentally towards us ('Oh Jesus') and, finding the shade of the vehicle a handy novelty, she flopped to the ground as if she had suddenly been denied the use of her limbs.

After twenty minutes of contemplation, silent but for occasional mutterings into the tape recorder, George spoke a little louder. 'Jesus.' This time, it was clearly a blasphemy.

'What's up?'

56

'Switched the bloody heating on.'

'Oh dear.'

'Hope it hasn't drained the battery.'

'So do I.'

'Give it a while to cool off.'

'Best idea.'

'Oh my *God*, has the vehicle broken down?' Caroline asked.

'It's all fine.' George, I am sure, intended this to sound soothing.

'Oh Christ Jesus.'

'It's all fine. Not a problem.'

Caroline clearly did not believe a word of it. We sat there for another twenty minutes. Lions shared and swallowed and dozed; one lioness approached another and licked the blood from her companion's spattered face with an audible scraping of the rasp-file tongue. I kept a wary eye on Caroline. Not from lust, or even aesthetic pleasure, but because I didn't really want her leaping from the vehicle and fleeing with terror across the landscape. But there seemed little danger of this. Mostly, she was staring at the lion with a rapt but absolutely unreadable expression. Well, if terror, it was suitable revenge for her wish to impose perfection on Lion Camp; if delight, then it was a delight I shared. Inevitably, or naturally, I wondered how many men had seen such an expression on her face, and what they had made of it. Ah well. Away to our right, the sun was beginning its rapid descent: a huge red ball, apparently the source of neither heat nor light, floating, not quite gravity-less, down towards the Mchindeni River.

'Perhaps a sundowner,' I said.

'Very well,' George turned the key: the moment of truth. A heart-stopping half-second of pause, but then the vehicle coughed and growled and bit. A lion lifted her head at the sound, and then let it fall heavily to the ground: idleness incarnate. And we withdrew.

We stopped for sundowners at a high cliff that overlooked a wonderful gathering of crocodiles in the river twenty feet below, a sight straight from the Jurassic. I leapt lightly to the ground, and took two bottles from the cool box, opening one nonchalantly with the other. Cool in the Bush: I had spent hours patiently learning the skill from Joseph. I presented a gentle gushing bottle of warmish Lion to Caroline with a flourish. 'Thanks,' she said. 'Do you have a glass?'

No glass. 'Joseph! Fool and idiot, incompetent boy, why you no put glass in cool box for madam?'

All Joseph's Cool-in-the Bush ways fell from him in the face of my rage and he replied in the African's traditional deferential half-whisper: 'Sorry, sah. I forget. Sorry, sah.'

Caroline looked at me: joy! she was horrified. 'You packed the cool box yourself, didn't you?'

'Then Joseph should have reminded me. Joseph, remind me you're fired when we get back to camp.' I swiped the top off another beer and handed it to him; he took it with his left hand, for his right hand was making a traditional non-deferential phallic gesture.

'Thank you, bwana,' he said. 'You kind master.'

I opened a third beer for myself and passed a fourth unopened to George, who removed the cap with the door-latch of the doorless Land Cruiser. I then went to join Caroline, who had moved to sit on the edge of the cliff, her legs dangling into space. 'How did you like the lion?' I asked her, inspecting with care her profile. Her hair had slid forward and there were freckles on the back of her neck.

'Have you ever read the Narnia stories? C. S. Lewis?' I shook my head. 'In all the books, there is a glorious God-like lion, and in one of them, he confronts one of the main characters, a horse, a beautiful mare. And as soon as she sees him, she trots up to him, and she says something like: "Please. You're so beautiful. You may eat me if you like. I'd sooner be eaten by you than fed by anyone else." I'd always loved that. Always been rather haunted by it. But I never understood it before. I mean, I understood the idea. But I understood it today almost as a physical longing.'

I looked at her for a moment in complete disbelief. 'That's wonderful,' I said. 'That's made my day. It really has.' There was even a remote but discernible prick of tears at the back of my eyes.

'The paradoxical gentleness of the lion around something they have killed,' she said. 'The sense of brotherhood, or sister-hood. I wanted to join in.'

'We had one client who said that she never saw lion without wanting to fling herself among them.'

'Yes. I felt that. But it's not like wanting to throw yourself off a high building, or in front of a train. I wanted to join them. Not for the danger. For love, really. I wanted to rub up against them. I wanted to jump in and roll and roll and roll with them. I do hope you haven't read Freud, Dan.'

'It's not just you,' I said. 'It's something lion do to people. You just have to be very close to them in order to feel it.'

'The eyes, there seems to be real eye contact.'

'It's the round pupils that do it. Your house cat at the vicar-age has vertical black slits for pupils. Lions have round pupils, like people.'

'I'm sure you're right, but it's not only that.'

'It's not. It's certainly not.'

'Are you going to spot, Dan?' George's voice called us from the vehicle. I looked back. I could see the glowing end of his cigarette. Night was falling with its usual suddenness.

'Joseph?' I asked, explaining to Caroline, 'He's got better eyes than me, the bastard.'

'Dan, I'm a client today. You do the work. I want to watch today.'

'Yes, sah,' I said. 'Sorry, sah.'

George lifted the bonnet and fixed the spotlight wires to the battery with matchsticks (it used to work off the cigarette lighter, but George had borrowed the plug for something else, and it was currently missing). I climbed onto the vehicle, resum-ing my stance on the spare wheel, one hand on the grab-bar, and took the light. George switched on, and I silently splashed the beam down into the river. Two hundred red lights answered back: the eyes of the crocodiles.

We drove off into the darkness. I raked the bush with the

59

spotlight, swinging the beam from one side of the road to the other, dousing trees with sudden light, seeking reflection and movement. Mostly I sought eyes. The bush at night is, to the possessor of a strong light, a jewel box of eyes, shining out at you, challenging you to comprehend the treasures. You look for small clues: the height of the eyes above the ground, the distance between them, the proximity of one pair of eyes to the next. You skim the light past puku and impala. Mostly, you are searching for nocturnal carnivores: genet, civet, white-tailed mongoose. And mostly, you are searching for leopard.

I was aware that Caroline was now standing beside me in the back; I could see, from the corner of my eye, her hands pale in the darkness, holding the grab-bar. I released my own single-handed clasp and placed my hand on top of hers for a period of, say, 0.25 seconds. She turned and smiled. I felt suddenly wildly intoxicated by her delight. To see lion close is an intense physical experience: to be released from their presence leaves a glow of perfectly resolved tensions. 'Where's my bloody leopard?' she asked.

'Any minute now.'

Sometimes it works like that. Before five minutes had passed, I had one. It was a damn good spot, too, if I do say so myself. I saw a trace of movement a hundred yards from the track, a glimpse of profile, no shining eye: clues enigmatic, to say the least. 'Go in, George.'

'Are you sure?'

'No. Go in.'

'Betting?'

'Two to one against. Go in.'

'I'm going.'

'To the right. Follow the spot.'

A lurch forward, a crash-halt. 'There's nothing, Dan.'

'Go past this clump, swing right – *aaah!*'

'Jesus. Oh Jesus.'

This from Caroline. For it was a leopard all right, well built and male, and unworried by the impertinent spotlight. He was intent on his own business, moving forward with great purpose on elastic stride. A lion is a vision of power, a leopard is all sinuous skill: a different kind of perfection. The long, spotted tail was carried with a loop at the end; the soles of the spotted paws were coal black. George followed him. I kept him in the spot, and we moved, cautiously, cautiously, because his stride implied that he was out on business and a leopard's business is killing. This was, pound for pound, the most efficient killing machine in the bush. His jaw clenched and unclenched as he walked, like a domestic cat as it watches the birds from a window.

Silence. The leopard slunk on. And in an instant I lost him. 'Bugger it. Cut round the clump there, George, we'll catch him on the far side.'

Joseph said; 'That would involve driving off the edge of a cliff, Dan. That's the river through there.'

'Double bugger. I had forgotten where we were.'

'I think he'll have gone down the bank.' A whistle rang out: another: another: a chorus.

'Puku have spotted him,' George said. 'He went onto the long beach down there after puku, and they have winded him. Breeze's the wrong direction for that approach, silly sod.'

We drove back towards camp. I continued to work the spot, Caroline still stood beside me. 'I said I'd find you a leopard.'

'You did. Jesus. That was the most beautiful animal in the history of creation. You do realise that, don't you?'

'I do, as a matter of fact.'

I felt her glance towards me, and I turned my head. I wanted to try another hand pat, but my courage failed. 'Such beautiful things,' she said. 'Lion and leopard, and the lovely kudu. Perfect perfect perfect. I can't think of a single thing that could make this night more perfect.'

'I can,' I said. The remark was out before I could stop it; I hoped that my sudden, debilitating blush would be hidden in the shadow of my spotlight. I added lamely: 'I mean, we could have an ant bear.'

'I'd like to have an ant bear,' she said.

61

6

Sex mad, my staff, George had said, meaning, of course, Joseph and me. Well, it had to be admitted that the subject did crop up now and again. Young bucks in the bush, and all that. Inevitably, we played up to the idea. We were more than friends, we were team-mates, in a very silly, jolly, splendid lads-together sort of way. Phineas, the gun-bearing game scout, was never silly, no longer a lad: he was a man of substance and dignity, headman of his village. But with Joseph, I could mess about.

He was already on the staff when I joined Lion Safaris; I was something of a distracted afterthought. But Joseph, who had lived in the Mchindeni Valley all his life, was a mere trainee safari guide, and so he was not qualified to take drives or lead walks on his own; I had my full safari guide qualification within a fortnight of arriving in the Valley. This was only partly to do with my academic qualifications and the year in the bush with my zebras. The non-blackness of my skin was also a relevant factor.

I had felt guilty about this, though not guilty enough to refuse the qualification and the job. I spoke of this guilt early on; to my surprise, Joseph was sublimely easy company within days of our first meeting. 'Dan, I have my safari guide exam at the end of the season, after a full season as a trainee. I hope it will be a career for all my life. I am happy. I will study hard for my exam, and you will help me with your herbivores, George will help me with carnivores and everything else. With luck, I will pass. That's good, Dan, not bad.'

And pretty soon, we had settled into a jolly bantering competitive friendship: a small football team of two people. I think we were both delighted with how easy it all was: how genuine the affection. For both of us, friendship outside our own race was a novelty: especially this uproarious teasing kind of friendship, never fearful of causing offence. And we had something better than sport to banter about: we had the bush. It was a shared language, a shared culture.

It was brave of George to take on an African as a trainee safari guide. This was not unprecedented in the Valley, but it was not something every camp operator would do. In fact, Joyce from Chipembere had been appalled. 'Africans are not good with clients,' she said. 'They do not like to talk to them.' So George was punished by the lack of a caterer. The clients were also punished, but Joyce did not think that one through. But at least the clients had Joseph: and they all adored him.

Neither Joseph nor I concerned ourselves much with office politics. I see now that this was something of a mistake. More: it was reprehensible: irresponsible: leading to disaster. But the fact is that sex was far more interesting. Power came a very poor second, so far as Joseph and I were concerned. Sex: the soliciting of an oestrus lioness: the never-ending stud-post call of the honeyguide in the ebony glade: the visit of Gianna. Gianna had already provided me with teasing material that had lasted two months and which might well last for the rest of the season, if not for life. 'Did you show this plant to Gianna?' I would enquire sweetly in front of clients, as Joseph expounded on the medicinal properties of, say, the plant *Ballanites*, a spindly bush that carried thorns up to six inches long. It annoyed me that I couldn't make him blush. 'I was blushing mentally, Dan.'

Joseph and I used often to take the morning walk together, to give George a break. We would meet Phineas for coffee at half past five, while the clients woke and joined us, rubbing their eyes. Phineas would lead us away at six, and we would return for breakfast three hours later. It sounds a lot more fierce and hearty than it was; the pace was gentle, and we stopped constantly to show clients different aspects of the bush. Joseph was not of course allowed to lead, but I paid no attention to that. We were pretty much on a level when it came to knowledge and experience, and we enjoyed the teamwork. I was better than him with large mammals, but he outstripped me easily on plants. Plants were a serious weakness: I only knew about them if zebras ate them. Joseph could add human dimensions to all this; he knew all about the traditional medicinal properties of plants.

'Joseph, I've got a good idea. We could halve the time we spend on these morning walks. Why don't you just point out the plants that are *not* aphrodisiacs?'

'Aw, Dan . . .'

Naturally, the pricking *Ballanites* was an aphrodisiac. So was the kigelia or sausage tree, plants that grow huge salami-like fruit. A sausage tree in full fruit looks like the window of a delicatessen. Joseph's explanation of the ritual use of kigelia fruit was a masterpiece: 'And so, if the betrothed lady is unhappy with the size of the fruit her beloved has selected . . .' His innocently knowing explanation had even Helen helpless with laughter: 'Joseph, please stop . . .' 'However, if the couple lose the sausage they have selected, and it continues to grow . . .'

Early on, I had asked Joseph how he had learned so much about the mysteries of the bush, expecting to hear about sitting at the feet of the village wise man, walking the game-trails with athletic tribal hunters, gathering plants with lore-rich and wizened crones. He said: 'I have read a lot of books, Dan.'

I wish Joyce had been able to see the way the clients clustered around him. Nothing showed her lack of judgement of our clients' likes and dislikes more than Joseph. He was an African, and therefore exotic, but no one ever needed to 'make allowances' for that ineluctable fact. He was that rare thing, a man at home in two cultures. On clientless days, he would often take mealie meal and relish with Sunday and the rest of the backroom staff in the kitchen, but the following day, he would eat Sunday's three-course best with the new clients and dazzle them with his charm and knowledge. He moved from world to world without seeming to notice any differences. An African is the least insular person on earth, and moving from custom to custom, language to language has always been the stuff of daily life. Most Africans I met spoke several African languages and English besides. Joseph absorbed languages without trouble. Early in the season, we had an Italian family for five days and Joseph was making fair headway in Italian long before they left. All in all, he was the most colossal asset to the camp: with clients, with the staff. If he had a professional weakness, it was for sudden and debilitating crushes on clients.

Joseph was wonderfully at ease with everyone – apart, of course, from beautiful white women, in whose company he tended to assume what I was soon calling the lost-doggy face. Such women would cause him to be hit by the thunderbolt of love, for which Joseph was in any case something of a lightning conductor, capable of being struck many times during even the mildest of electrical disturbances.

'Well, what about you with that doctor's wife?' he had retorted more than once.

'I deny it absolutely. I treated her with simple courtesy.'

'Every time you spoke to her, it sounded like the stud-post call of the honeyguide.'

And so on. Inevitably, we also speculated about George's arrangements. Left to myself, I would have assumed that George was one of those naturally celibate people. He seldom talked about women, mainly because lionesses were so much more interesting. But after a while, I caught up with Valley gossip. George was supposed to have an African mistress in Chipembere, with whom he stayed on the rare occasions that he passed through town. It was possible, even likely, that he paid for the place, or at least contributed in some way to its upkeep. They were said to have been an item for years; there was a child, perhaps children, some said. She was, according to legend, a lady of great spirit, indeed, of great ferocity. She was said on occasions to 'beat him up'. I did not know how much of this to believe, but the beating-up sounded reasonable enough; it was one of the few ways you would be able to get George's full attention. George and I discussed sex a good deal, but it was always the sexuality of lion.

Lion are what George called Joseph and me: sex mad. Joseph and I had a joke about two lions in a bar. 'How did you make out with that cute lioness last night?' 'Oh, I feel really bad. I'm getting old, man. I couldn't do it the eighty-sixth time.' This was a reference to George's record. He once observed a lion copulate eighty-six times in twenty-four hours, seventy-four times with one lioness and twelve times with another. Pass the *Ballanites*.

Lionesses are slinky, sensuous and sexually demanding. 'She looked like she really enjoyed that,' a client said unnecessarily, when, early in the season, we located a honeymooning pair.

'Why not?' George had asked. 'If you allow them pleasure in food, which I am sure you do, you must allow them pleasure in sex too. One drive is as profound as the other, and I don't think one species of mammal has the monopoly on pleasure in either area, do you?' Over dinner, he had talked ceaselessly on leonine sexuality. The day after the eighty-six copulations, the male had copulated another sixty-two times and still he did not stop. Eventually, he did it 157 times in fifty-five hours. The clients were spellbound.

Joseph also managed to spellbind a client on the subject of sex. The client in question was one half of one of the odder pairs we had that season: perhaps the duffest of all the duff clients sent to us by Joyce. They were odd because they had absolutely no interest in mammals, birds, reptiles, amphibians, fish, invertebrates or plants. They had no curiosity. They had come out, I suspected, free of charge, as the return of a favour they had done Joyce. They were Italian, mother and daughter, and they ran a hotel in Capri. Joyce had spent a holiday there the previous year. They came to Lion Camp out of pure disinterested love of the freebie.

Valeria was the mother, a tough lady. You wouldn't give her hell about your bill, that was for sure. She was one of those women who set out at a certain age to be purposefully unattractive. She clearly relished the power to be unpleasant whenever she wished. The power was always latent rather than actual while she was with us, but I could feel her savage potential in every unsmiling response to a pleasantry. But at least she spoke English – rather well, in fact.

There was a different problem with her daughter Gianna. She was barmy. For a start, she bleated like a wildebeest, or a gnu, gnu being onomatopoeic. Most of her remarks were accompanied by a preludial bleat: 'Gnu, *mamma, è molto caldo, molto molto caldo.*' She was mainly silent, entirely monoglot, and she spoke to no one except her mother. This made her rather heavy going. She was seventeen or eighteen, pretty enough in a rather moon-faced way, but the barminess put me off. She didn't like the heat, but she found a solution. She took showers. She would descend the steps in the river bank, turn on the cold tap, and stay there until the drum was empty. This generally took about two hours. 'What does she *do* in there, Joseph. Can't you find out?'

'Aw, Dan . . .'

'It is a matter of scientific interest. Why don't you build a hide on the opposite bank, borrow George's telescope, keep her under observation . . .'

'You should build the hide, Dan, or maybe erect it. Weave it out of *Ballanites.*'

When she emerged from one of these prolonged soakings (at which point one of us would have to tell Jonas, the room attendant, and he would grumpily go to fetch fresh water from the river) she would invariably be clad in a bikini. The first time she did this, the effect was startling. For she never dried herself. She would march about the camp, or sit down for a meal, dripping, while Joseph and I would try hard not to be caught looking at the outline of hardened nipple beneath the fabric. Her face was moon-like and her manner childish, but her body was extravagantly womanly. Joseph's lost-doggy face was in place at the first lunch, which Gianna took bikini-clad and dripping, beads of moisture trickling into an imposing cleavage.

She didn't go out on the evening drive. She didn't go for the walk the following morning. This seemed rather to defeat the object of staying in a bush camp, but it was *troppo caldo.* For supper, she took only a shard of chicken and a guano-like puddle of spinach. She then helped herself liberally from her mother's plate, four hands and four irons busily at work together. Neither made any comment on this.

After twenty-four hours in Lion Camp, with the post-supper coffee just served by Isaac, the waiter, and accepted by all the company except me, Gianna had still not addressed a single remark to anyone except her mother. The fire was alight, but neither of them showed any sign of wanting to sit around it, discussing wildlife and the sexuality of lion. That left us rather at a loss. After a long and unnerving silence, Gianna said (to her mother, naturally): '*Io volevo giocare a carte.*'

'*Va bene, cara.*'

Valeria produced a much used pack of cards, and shuffled and dealt with alarming dexterity. They played with silent intensity while George and I spoke, a little self-consciously, about pair-bonding and territorial behaviour in the Egyptian geese that were kicking up a racket in the dark on the opposite bank. Joseph meanwhile looked thoughtfully at Gianna's chest, which was covered by a T-shirt though not, I was fairly certain, anything else. Then, suddenly and magnificently inspired, he spoke.

'*E difficile, questo giocco?*'

'*Gnu!*' said Gianna. '*Parla italiano?*'

'*Un po.*'

'*Te'lo insegnero.*'

'*Benissimo.*'

This was a masterstroke. Valeria relinquished her place to Joseph. Gianna started to explain the game. For the first time, she was happy. The rest of us went to bed, leaving the two of them with their heads bent low over the cards. As I nodded off to sleep in my hut, I could still hear the prattle of Gianna's voice; the occasional interjection from Joseph; quiet laughter, shared.

The following morning, at half past five, I was expecting to be, as usual, the first to take coffee, but Joseph, who normally clung to his bed until the last possible minute, was already waiting. 'How was the card game, Joseph?'

'Very good, Dan.'

'Who won?'

'I did, actually.'

'What were the stakes?'

'Aw, Dan . . .'

7

I found no ant bear for Caroline.

But the camp was welcoming. Isaac had forgotten we were clientless and had lit a fire; Sunday had prepared for us a merry meal of Ethiopian curry. This was our standard dish on clientless days. George had acquired from somewhere a ferocious plastic bag full of spices, its predominant colour an unnaturally sharp crimson. 'Ethiopian curry powder,' he had termed this equivocal mixture, and had given it to Sunday for safekeeping. It was not subtle stuff: it had the kick of a horse, or a zebra. And so, when we had no clients, Sunday would gather everything that needed eating up, and create a nose-stinging vat of curry. It was emphatically not a dish to set before strangers, but George, Joseph and I all relished it. It was a pretty severe test, but Caroline sailed through it. She did not turn a leucistic hair. The single paraffin lamp that lit the table picked out sharp shadows beneath her cheekbones.

The talk was all leopard. She quizzed George hard on their way of life, explaining: 'I loved the leopard because he was perfect. That's it, really. I have never seen anything so clearly incapable of improvement. Quite immaculate.'

'Maculated,' George said pedantically.

'All right then. Immaculately maculated.' I cast a covert glance at Caroline's immaculately maculated throat.

'Perfection is a leopard's survival strategy,' George said through a mouthful of curry. 'A leopard is a lone hunter; if it gets injured, it can't hunt, can't eat. Not so with lion, because they hunt team-handed. An injured lion can share a kill; an injured leopard starves. So leopards will always surrender a kill to hyena because they daren't risk getting injured in a scrap. Lions can be as rough and ready as you please.'

'Lion Camps also. Rogue Lion Safaris.' But Caroline was smiling as she said this, smiling almost conspiratorially.

'I resent that,' I said. 'We're hardly ever ready.'

'Talking of readiness, are we doing a walk tomorrow?' Joseph asked, not betraying overmuch eagerness.

'He lost a lot of sleep when we had some Italian clients in camp,' I explained to Caroline.

'Caroline, would you like to do a walk tomorrow?' George asked.

'Well, I'd like to see how Lion Safaris handles the walking side of things,' Caroline said. 'For completeness, you know.' That seemed an odd remark, somehow. 'But I know it's not often you people get a chance for a lie-in, so . . .'

'I'm game,' I said. 'You two take a lie-in. I'll give Phineas a shout in a minute.'

'Can I have some more curry?' Caroline asked.

By the time the curry was finished, George and Joseph were showing signs of flagging. 'Anyone want coffee?' Joseph asked doubtfully.

'Only if someone else is having it,' said Caroline.

'I'm having some,' I said, avoiding Joseph's eye. I never took coffee in the evening. 'George, Joseph?'

Both refused. I went to the kitchen, where a mealie meal and relish session was in full swing. I asked Isaac to make coffee, and Phineas if a walk at six the following morning suited. 'No worries,' Phineas said; we had had a pair of Australian clients the previous week.

George and Joseph went to bed, and I suggested to Caroline that we take our coffee by the fire.

'Perfect.'

I kicked the mopane branches a little to encourage a flame, and Caroline settled onto one of the 'comfortable' canvas chairs, looking out at the African night: extravagantly star-studded: the enigmatic shapes of the trees around us and on the far bank of the river. There was no moon. In our ears the rattle and cackle of the pair-bonding Egyptian geese. I poured coffee and brought it to the fire.

'What extraordinary cups. Where's the cucumber sandwiches?'

I took a place beside her: glanced at her face, in enigmatic profile, as she looked out at the darkness over the grand sweep of the Mchindeni River. In the quiet came a sudden complicated pattern of hoots from the ebony trees above.

'What's that?'

'Wood owl. Permanent resident in camp. Listen, he says, "Now then whooo's a naughty boy?"'

Obligingly, the owl did it again, prompting an immediate reply: the same call, a tone lower. 'Male and female,' I said. 'Duet. Cementing the pair-bond and all that.'

'The basis of their relationship is sitting in a tree saying who's a naughty boy?'

'Correct.'

'I suppose that's the basis of a lot of relationships. Barring the sitting in trees.'

'Talking of being a naughty boy,' I said, 'I have a bottle of Malawian Scotch in my hut. I've been saving it for a special occasion. Do you think this is it?'

'I suppose it could be.'

I went to my hut, and found the bottle by Braille; it was about half full. I heard a distant roar of lion, followed by the much nearer whoop of hyena.

'Sounds like the hyena are moving in on the kill,' I said as I returned to the fire. 'The lion must be pulling out, the hyena going in for the remains. Like so?'

'Perfect.'

We sat in silence for a little while. A loud splashing from the river: hippo leaving the shelter of the Mchindeni for a night's grazing.

'It's not bad, is it?'

'Really quite a lot like whisky.'

We listened to the hippo's progress as he climbed the bank on the far side of the ebony glade.

'Did you ever see the film *Out of Africa*?' Caroline asked.

'No.'

'I got rather a thing about the film. Impressionable age, and all that. So then I read Isak Dinesen and loads of other Africa books. But I think it's only today that I've realised the fundamental flaw in it all. Considering the film changed my life, that is rather a shattering discovery.'

'Elaborate.'

'The hero is played by Robert Redford, and he is a wonderfully handsome fellow who can't bear to leave the bush.'

'Bush fever. It's a known problem.'

'Redford plays him as a perfectly ordinary chap who's just a bit more handsome than the common run of chaps. But I realised today that he can't possibly have been like that.'

'How so?'

'He must have been completely barking. All you bush types are.'

'You mean George?'

'I mean all of you.'

'No, really, Caroline, people call George mad, but that's a terribly simplistic view. I'd face a charging lion with him. In fact I have.' I told the story of the definite male.

Caroline did not laugh, as I had hoped, but she seemed powerfully struck by the story all the same. Instead, she smiled, very long. 'I think that proves my point. Mad. In a sort of deeply sane fashion, but mad all the same.'

I laughed, affectionately, at this description. 'I think you are getting the hang of George.'

'Dan, I'm not talking about George.'

'What do you mean?'

But she wouldn't elaborate, she just sat there smiling, resting her glass against her cheek.

'Leon isn't mad,' I said. As soon as I let the remark go I wanted to call it back. A guffaw came from the river: hippo. Leon's square and uncompromising shadow fell between us, and the holiday mood gently tumbled away. It was as if the invocation of his name were a call to order: as if we had been granted a brief dispensation: a short holiday from daily life, which, through my clumsiness, I had brought to a premature

73

end. Leon's name was a spell; it killed a brief mood of magic.

'Leon loves the bush all right,' Caroline said. 'The tough business talk isn't the whole story. He believes that the only way to save the park is tourism, top-drawer tourism. If we can bring the right sort of clients to the park, put a dollar value on wildlife, then the park will be saved. So Leon brings in clients; that's his way. He solves problems. He likes challenges. He gets things done.'

'How did you meet him?'

'At the World Travel Market in London. I had just joined a small travel firm, as a partner. We did tailor-made safaris, middlemen between clients and camp operators.'

'I know about the World Travel Market,' I said. 'I remember George saying that he wanted to go last autumn, but Joyce – that's our manager – wouldn't agree to it.'

'Good God. If you're not at WTM, you're not really in business, are you? Anyway, Leon was there, and that was that. I had been planning to work at the other end of the travel business, but things changed at a fairly rapid pace. It has been a very challenging few months, but I've loved it.'

I felt very young. 'And things go well, and so on? I mean, are you planning to stay here?'

The mood about us carried on dying. 'I suppose. I am good at running camps. I'm good at running a business. Good at money, actually, a hateful sort of talent to have, but bloody useful. I was doing well in England. People thought I was mad to leave. I had been left quite a lot of money, you see, and I had made one or two quite good investments. Property and so on.'

'I thought everybody who did that got caught by the recession and was left with huge unsaleable houses.'

'I got out early.'

'Smart.'

'Yes,' she said, unapologetically. I had no other answer. That day when I went through the card at Lingfield didn't really compare. The distance between us grew. At the far end of the ebony glade, I heard a barred owlet's glissandi. Despite him, silence stretched.

From sheer awkwardness, I got up, and crouched down to fiddle with the fire, shuffling the mopane branches further into the embers. Caroline got to her feet as well, no doubt to signal the end of the evening. I had cocked it up, had I not?

She walked over to the edge of the bank, and looked at the river a while. 'The quiet waters by.'

'Yes.'

I looked up at her from my crouch by the fire. She was outlined against the sky, moonless and cloudless, a shape spelt out by the constellations and galaxies and nebulae behind her. A terrible sadness overwhelmed me. I stood, and walked towards her.

She seized my forearm with terrible violence. 'Jesus!'

The force of her double-handed grip filled me with alarm. 'What's up?'

'Jesus Christ, there's something in the camp.'

'Oh.' There was a pause, in which we both thought about lion. Then I heard it too, steps lightly crunching the fallen leaves of ebony, as if someone were tiptoeing through a field of poppadom.

'Probably George or Joseph going for a pee,' I said soothingly.

'Why has it stopped then?'

I heard half a dozen more paces, and then it stopped again. I laughed just a little. 'You're absolutely bloody well right, it is something. It's something absolutely colossal. Come on, let's check it out.'

'What are you bloody grinning at?'

She had a point. An unholy delight had seized me: wild curiosity, the wildest possible kind, come to think of it, had me in its sway. Again. As it did every day. The Darlin' Girl Syndrome struck me once again. The sound could mean anything: that was where the delight came from. 'I mean, let's take a look at it. It really is bloody big, whatever it is. Come on, let's go.'

'Stand still, you fucking lunatic.'

'You stay here then. I want to take a look.'

'Christ, don't go.' She let out a small peal of laughter. 'I'm sorry, Dan, but, Jesus, don't go.'

'Come with me then. We can't stay here till dawn. There's not enough whisky.'

She laughed and said 'Oh God' again, but when I attempted to walk back into the sitenji, she did not try to stop me. She did not let me go, either. We passed into the shelter in a kind of comic double-shuffle, Caroline caught halfway between giggle and scream. In the deeper darkness beneath the thatch, I paused to listen again. I heard a sound, as if someone were operating a giant zip. Whatever it was, it was stripping leaves from a tree. Not a carnivore, then. But perhaps elephant. Still, an eating animal is a contented animal: that was as firm a rule as existed in the bush.

I motioned Caroline down into a crouch, and we shuffled behind the bar, then up to the frail knee-high grass wall of the sitenji. I raised my head and looked out. And I started laughing again, pointing outwards, *upwards*. 'There.'

'Oh my God.'

There, its topmost point eighteen feet above us and thoughtfully snacking on ebony leaves, stood the most massive bull giraffe in the Mchindeni Valley, or if not, a close contender. Despite the fact that this was the bush and his home, he looked surreal and utterly incongruous: a giraffe can do that anywhere.

I stood, very quietly, and Caroline stood with me, still grasping, though more gently, my right forearm. So I wrapped my left arm around her: why not? She released and then embraced me for a while. I could feel trembling laughter in her body. It was one of those hugs between people who are not quite sure of their physical relationship: shoulders touching but hips decorously apart, our bodies making a kind of narrow Gothic arch. But like electricity, hilarity flowed between us.

'Isn't he great?'

'Stop bloody grinning at him.'

'I'm grinning at you.'

'That's all right then.' We stood, now half disengaged, which is also half engaged, my right arm about her shoulders, her left thumb hooked onto my belt. 'What are you thinking?'

'They're not normally nocturnal. I wonder what has brought him here.'

She made a small but violent sound of exasperation. 'Look, concentrate on me for a second, Dan. I know it's hard when there're lovely things like giraffes about, but do try and listen for a moment. I said you were a lunatic, and I'm bloody right. But tell me, do you think this still counts as a special occasion?'

'More than ever.'

'Then perhaps a small Scotch? To restoreth my soul?'

'Of course.'

And so we sat, as we had earlier, before the fire, the quiet waters by, glasses in our hands. 'Why weren't you frightened? It could have been a lion. Doesn't the bush frighten you?' There was an edge in her voice again, sharp, but subtly different from the voice with which she had sniped at me at the airport, at Mukango, when I had first shown her around Lion Camp.

And so I thought about this for a while, and made a decision to entrust her with the truth. 'Can I explain to you something I call the Darlin' Girl Syndrome?'

'All right.'

Darlin' Girl, I told her, was a horse owned by Cynthia, my father's most regular mistress. The horse was not, of course, officially named Darlin' Girl, she was Lady of the Lowlands, and she came to us as an unraced three-year-old of not terribly good breeding. The first morning we exercised her, Cynthia was there, eager to see what her horse was made of. She and my father were on foot and horseless, the rest of us, that is, me and the ten or so lads, led our horses into the exercise ring for the preliminary walking exercise. Billy, the smallest lad, was given the new mare, on the theory that she would like as little weight as possible on her back. My father gave him a leg up onto her back. I forget which horse I was riding, but I remember the gratifying thump I heard behind me. Someone was off, and it wasn't me. I turned my head to see Billy on the floor, splayed out like a starfish, and Lady of the Lowlands facing the opposite way.

'Jaysis focken Christ some focker has been beating that little mare!' My father was frothing with anger, but muttering, not shouting. He never shouted around horses. He approached the mare, took her bridle, said to her: 'Darlin' girl, what are you thinking of? Nobody will hurt you here. This is a nice new yard and you'll get fed nothing but caviar and focken champagne.' Without changing his tone of voice, he said: 'Billy, hold Dan's horse. Dan, get down, and jump on this nice little mare for me.'

'What did she do?' I asked him.

'Just a little spin and stand and a little buck.'

So it was just about impossible to stay on. Oh well. I felt a clutch of fear at this; who wouldn't? But my father legged me up, and I lowered myself softly into the saddle, and crossed the stirrup irons over her withers. 'Keep a loose rein, Dan, don't touch her mouth. Now, ask her to walk forward with your legs.' I did so. And bang. She was up, down and around in half a second or less, while I clung on unbelieving.

'Darlin' girl, we're going for a little walk, and there's no harm to befall you. All you other fockers get off your horses, lead them back to the yard and wait. Tie 'em up, don't forget to loosen the focken girths.' Then followed a strange hour. We walked round and round that exercise ring: how many circuits? It seemed hundreds. At first, my father led the horse by the bridle, me just a passenger. Walk, stop, walk, stop: darlin' girl. He talked away, soothed, patted, made much. 'Dan, she spun when you touched her with your legs. So don't ask her for anything.'

Round and round we went. Then he took one hand, then eventually the second off the bridle, still walking beside her, talking away, darlin' girl. Then he stopped. The mare and I walked on. We completed a circuit, he took the bridle again. Stopped the mare. 'Now ask her this time, ask her to walk forward, little squeeze with your legs, soft as anything. Darlin' girl, will you walk a little with me?'

I asked with my legs. We went forward: triumph and relief. Another circuit alongside my father, then another with just me and the mare, a feather-light contact on the rein. 'Ask her to stop, Dan.' We stopped. 'Ask her to walk, Dan.' I asked: a touch of my legs, a feather touch of my calves. A miracle happened, or nothing did. She walked. Completed a circle, stopped at my father's side. 'You darlin' girl, didn't I tell you how easy it all is?' He gave her handfuls of mints. 'Get off that mare, Dan. Darlin' girl, you've done wonderful. Put her straight back in her focken box, Dan, and fill her manger up with focken carrots. You'll do, my darlin' girl, you'll do.'

After that, I had special responsibility for riding the mare. There was no malice in her, only fear, but she was frightening to ride. Whenever she was stressed or perplexed, she would spin, stand, buck, all in one. She had me off enough times. Each morning my first thought was fear, my second eagerness. The trouble we had persuading her to enter starting stalls. I was always a little afraid of the horse: but, of course, she was my favourite; I think now, my favourite ever. And in the end, she won her race, a thousand-quid maiden at Bangor, and Cynthia promptly retired her as a brood mare. 'I never thought it would happen,' Cynthia said. 'It's a triumph. It could have been a disaster, but it has been a wonderful adventure. You are so wonderful, no one else in the world could have done that, with my crazy little mare. And what you do with horses, and the way you live, well, it's just *right*.'

'Shall I tell you something?' my father had replied. 'I'd do it just the same if it was focken wrong.'

Again, as I finished another long story, I expected Caroline to reward me with a small laugh. Again, she listened to the tale in silence. After a while, she said: 'And that's what you feel in the bush? Fear and love?'

'Yes, exactly. But not fifty-fifty. Perhaps ninety parts love to ten of fear, or ninety-five to five, maybe. But the fear is an important ingredient. Like the Ethiopian curry powder.'

'Yes. Yes. I see, now. I don't know if you know, Dan, but there is a prayer about God whose service is perfect freedom.

79

Perhaps there should be a prayer about the bush. Whose madness is perfect sanity.'

We seemed to be sitting in a small, private room, barely big enough for two, but a room which had enclosed within it the entire Mchindeni Valley, the world, the universe: a small room filled with the distant sound of lion and roofed with endless constellations and galaxies and nebulae.

8

Constellations and galaxies. I wish I could remember the number of times George taught me how to navigate by the stars. But it just wasn't the sort of information that stayed in my head. The second night I spent in Lion Camp was just such a moonless, cloudless night, but with an early season bite in the air. George stood on the highest point of the bank, clad in a flapping bush-jacket, pointing out the stars, using a chicken bone from one of Sunday's preliminary Ethiopian curries.

Joseph and I stood craning our necks as George indicated the Southern Cross, and how you could use it to work out the cardinal points. We followed the chicken leg, swivelling and revolving: there was the swan, and there the scorpion. 'And just further round – it's hidden by the branch of the ebony tree – but if we step just out of the way, we shall see –'

I uncraned my neck and turned to George, but he was no longer among us. 'George?' No reply. I looked over the edge of the river bank. There, ten feet below, was the starfished body of George, lying there rather like Billy after his involuntary dismount from Darlin' Girl. I had heard, even by this time, most of the Valley's stock of George stories. I thought, I have known the man for less than a week and I have already killed him. 'George?'

'Oh *bugger* it.'

'You're alive then.'

'Bloody funny.'

'You all right?'

'Of course I'm not all right.'

I knelt on the edge, preparing to lower myself off the bank, which was more or less sheer. 'Not there, Dan,' Joseph said. 'Easy way. Here.' He led me to an ancient hippo gully, a track to and from the river worn by decades of hippo passage, a precipitous staircase. Down we went, and found George now sitting upright in a sea of gluey mud. The river was still high at this stage of the season, and the landing soft, if sticky. It was the best time of the year for swallow-diving from the bank. George was heavily winded, no worse. A Lion beer completed the recovery process, though he remained stiff for a few days. More comically, he also retained a carapace of mud for a few days, because the showers had not yet been installed, and naturally George did not have, or did not wish to waste, a clean shirt. But then George was always immune to the usual discomforts: neither the biting of tsetse fly nor the teasing of sweat-bees impinged on his awareness. This early revelation of George's selective system of awareness, his boundless ability for ignoring things that troubled or vexed a normal person, should perhaps have given me a clue about the nature of the financial affairs of Lion Safaris. But even after George had spelled things out, spelled them out with pedantic clarity, I remained oblivious of the nature of the coming troubles. Selective awareness, indeed.

'I suppose it is appropriate to start the season on a note of pure farce,' I said, as we celebrated George's fall, the mud drying and cracking on his back, with the post-lapsarian Lion.

The tumble had brought out in George an unaccustomed mood of gloom. '*Natura non facit saltus*,' he said. 'First law of biology: let it be a lesson to me. But listen, if you are interested in farce, don't stay in camp. I'm just an amateur. Go to the office in Chipembere if you want to see the real pros at work.'

'How so?'

'You'll meet Joyce when she comes to camp next week.'

'Elaborate.' George, preparing me for my exam, had naturally introduced me to Philip Pocock's principal ploy.

'To be frank, I don't really know if we will still be in business next season,' George said. 'It's the way Joyce runs the company. She hasn't a clue. Not a clue. It's not incompetence. It's madness. We'll not make a profit, we're just not getting the clients. I'll show you.'

He produced the bookings book, though not without a lot of scrabbling about in various bags. 'Not that it's not great to have free time occasionally, a day or so with no clients, but look at all these gaps. A week here. Three days here. Two more there. Another three there. And look at the size of the parties. Two or three seasons ago, the camp was full most of the time. Now look; a couple, a couple, a couple. Party of three. Single person, for God's sake. The only time the camp will be full is when we get a decent party led by a friend of mine, company called Wilderness Express. Thank God for them, anyway. They might just make the difference between breaking even and not. As we stand, for three weeks of the season, an operation staffed by one game scout, two safari guides, one trainee safari guide and seven backroom staff will be looking after single clients. And even if we could afford to stay in business at that rate of occupancy, the National Parks Commission might well throw us out.'

'Can they do that?'

'Oh yes. The Commission grants us the licence to run Lion Camp, and it comes up for review every three years. We have to demonstrate that we are operating the camp well and bringing foreign exchange into the country. And the truth of the matter is that we are not.'

'What's gone wrong, George?'

'Ask Joyce next week. Ha! Remember that one?'

A complicated pattern of notes rang out from the ebony tree above us. 'Barred owlet,' I said confidently.

'Any comment, Joseph?'

'Wood owl.'

'You bastard, Joseph.'

'Listen again. Now then, whooo's a naughty boy?' George hooted out the words with gusto.

'In the villages, they sometimes kill wood owls,' Joseph said. 'If it perches above your hut and calls, it brings death to the hut. People used to abandon their huts if that happened, build another. Still do, some places.'

'Perhaps we should move camp,' I said. 'A death is one thing we can do without.'

The owl called again, followed at once by his mate. 'It's the female that calls a tone deeper, not the male,' George said.

'Here's the plan,' I said. 'We have one more Lion. And then bed.'

'Good.'

I fetched the beers, warm from their crate, since we had not yet connected the gas-powered fridge. This was because we had no gas. But for once, this was nothing to do with the inefficiency of Lion Safaris. No one had any gas. Supplies were expected daily in Mchindeni township; some people even believed the gas would be here before the first clients. Others were more pessimistic, or more resigned, or perhaps they had merely been longer in Africa. But nothing surprises an Old Africa Hand, not even those rare occasions when everything goes according to plan.

We drank. Joseph updated us on the hut-building. This was technically George's job, but even in his first couple of weeks, Joseph had shown a touch of genius with labour relations. The thatcher was still complaining bitterly about the quality of grass, but he would finish the thatching of the sitenji the following day. The guest huts were all now complete save the walls. The next day, we should get from store the bamboo matting with which to make them, also the beds, tables and mozzie nets. Isaac wanted a day off to go to a funeral. No, it was genuine. Funerals came with alarming frequency in Africa. 'Who's dead?' I asked.

'Isaac's older brother,' Joseph said. He added, in Isaac's lilting voice, 'he had a slooow puncture,' meaning that he had AIDS. Joseph explained that Isaac had promised to be sober and waiting at the side of the road by his village from nine o'clock the day after next. He understood that the time would be taken from his leave.

'Now food,' George continued, with unaccustomed seriousness. 'Joyce is sending frozen meat on the plane tomorrow. So one of us must meet the plane –'

'Dropping Isaac on the way –'

'And take it to the deep freeze at Mukango.' Like most camps, we rented freezer space there.

Joseph said: 'Sunday wants to know about vegetables.'

'So do I,' George said. 'I'll do the run tomorrow and call in on Piet.'

'Then better do that before you go to the airport, or the damn stuff will defrost and give all the clients botulism.' We dickered on about the minutiae of running a camp. It was in the nature of things that the smallest matter was endlessly complicated. Any week might bring, say, an egg shortage or, God forbid, a beer shortage. There had been poor rains, the wet season hardly worthy of the name, and everybody in the tourist industry was worried about the supply of fresh vegetables for their international clients. Piet, like Leon an Afrikaner, ran a market garden operation with copious irrigation. He had guaranteed that he would be able to supply all the camps with vegetables right up to the rains; no one was quite sure whether he would deliver or not. Vegetables had become one of the great staples of Valley conversation: 'So if Piet lets us down, we could take a truck up to Nsefu market, stay there overnight, bring it back full.' 'Plenty of stuff in the northwest, I know a bloke who can . . .'

In Africa, the standard conversational fall-back, at least among whites, is fixing things. Arranging: dealing: mending: overcoming shortages. Getting a new part: borrowing welding kit: finding the right kind of paint. Transport: calling in favours: obtaining the unobtainable. A couple of weeks later, when the first Italian clients came out to stay with us, Joyce had moved heaven and earth to find Martini, an item unobtainable in Chipembere. In the end, she managed to persuade an airline steward to bring in a bottle from London. Needless to say, the Italians drank nothing but Lion.

But that is by the by. I finally met Joyce shortly after the huts had been completed and I had passed my safari guide exam. She came out for something approaching a state visit: it was, George said, an annual ritual. She insisted that she was to be treated like a client, so that she could judge the standards we would reach during the coming season.

And so we turned out in force to meet her at the airport. Each camp kept at the airport a wooden sign bearing its name: you stood sheepishly by the sign until your client approached you. Joyce had already fixed us up with the biggest and most embarrassing sign in the Valley, so we stood by LION SAFARIS and watched her walk towards us. By this time, of course, I had built up a picture of what she would look like. Even so, I was taken aback. She was clad in an olive-silk version of a safari outfit: wide skirt, three-inch-wide belt to emphasise her dramatically slim waist, short-sleeved silk shirt with patch pockets and epaulettes. On her left wrist about a hundred gold bangles. She was cadaverously thin, and the skin of her face stretched back from a powerful straight nose. She was perhaps fifty, looked every year of it, and clearly believed she could pass for thirty-five.

George said that she had been beautiful once. She had even done a little modelling. She still expected men to lie down and die for her. She loved clothes and style and design. Her conquest of Bruce Wallace, George's partner, had been effortless, and she had led him a terrible dance. Bruce had spent about ten years perpetually on the verge of leaving his wife and children for her: would pluck up his courage and announce the fact to his family, whereupon he would learn that Joyce was about to marry someone else, someone who really appreciated her. And on and on. Eventually, passions had cooled. But somehow, in the meantime, Joyce had won full control of the day-to-day running of the company. Bruce, I learned, had more or less given up.

'George,' she said, offering him a lined but perfumed cheek to be kissed. 'And you are Dan, yes?' I had her taped at once. Phony posh. She clearly did not believe the pretence could be penetrated; she had lived in Africa a long time. No one would buy her 'upper-class' act in any seriously exacting circle in England, but here she was able to get away with it. These things were written up in neon lights to a fellow-Englishman,

86

particularly one used to the unthinking snobberies of the race-course. Not that either my father or I had ever been welcomed in any seriously exacting circles ourselves, but we knew what the circles demanded. And it wasn't Joyce.

'And this is Joseph,' George said.

'Be very careful with my baggage,' Joyce said to him by way of greeting. 'Especially the cardboard box.'

'Yes, madam,' Joseph's affectation of servility brought an involuntary smirk to my face, but I mastered it before it could be seen.

'Please drive, Dan,' she said. 'I need to get an idea of your competence and style as a safari guide.'

So I drove into the park. See the hippo from the bridge. See the bachelor herd of impala: look, they're all males, see the lyrate horns. See the lilac-breasted roller perched on the dead tree: how pretty. My luck was in: a breeding herd of zebra. 'That is the stallion, the rest are breeding females and foals, apart from that one there, he is a young male. But he is tolerated in the herd, because he has never shown any sexual interest in the mares. The first time he does that, the stallion will kick him out, and he'll go and join a bachelor group. Now this is not strictly speaking a harem you are watching, because the females are linked together not by the dominance of the stallion, but by an intricate web of friendship. Now, see those two mares over there –'

'Drive on. I think we have had quite enough zebras, thank you very much.'

'And there above us is a martial eagle, the biggest bird of prey in the world. It preys entirely on other eagles, though it will also eat vultures. It takes them in flight and tears their wings off.'

'Really? How fascinating.'

'Very big birds. Twenty-foot wingspan.'

'Extraordinary. One can always learn something new when one comes to the bush.'

I caught the faces of the two other passengers on the seat behind. George, to his credit, was quite expressionless. Joseph's eyes were bulging slightly, like a child about to giggle in church. For I was, of course, talking complete nonsense. I told myself sternly not to push my luck any further. I drove on towards camp.

Once we arrived, and Joyce had laboriously 'freshened up', the inquisition began. Why was hut five so close to the river? Why was hut one so far from hut two? Why was the lavatory seat so high in the second latrine? Why was the roof of the sitenji so low? What were those books doing on the bar?

She asked – well, told – Joseph to bring her the mysterious cardboard box, and she opened it for us. It contained, of all things, a dozen bone-china cups and saucers. The cups had delicate little handles, the saucers had delicate little curly rims. Every piece bore a delicate golden tracery. 'There. What do you think?'

'Where did you get them, Joyce?'

'At the Chinese store in Chipembere. They had only one set. I am very pleased. I think they will raise the tone of the business. You will not use the large mugs.'

'Joyce, the clients like large mugs.'

'Clients like elegant living, George.'

'In the bush?'

'Most especially in the bush. That is precisely what you fail to understand, and that is why the business suffers. Use the cups. Call the waiter. Explain to him.'

After supper, and over coffee taken in the absurd cups, George having half a dozen refills to make a point, George and Joyce settled down to a long discussion of the way the season was looking.

'Why are there so many gaps, Joyce?'

'Things are bad, everywhere. Tourism is down all over the world. We are doing *well*.'

'Mukango Lodge is full all season,' I said stupidly.

'You believe that, do you?' she asked pityingly. 'Everyone knows that Philip Pocock is a liar and a cheat.'

'Joyce, where is that big party from England? I can't find

them on the revised booking schedule you've given me. The group called Wilderness Express.'

'They are not coming.'

'Oh shit, did they cancel? They were bringing a party of ten.'

'They are not trustworthy people. Simply not businesslike. They tried to get their tour leader to stay with us for free. I think they assumed that because he is a friend of yours, he can cheat the company. Naturally, I was not having that.'

'But tour leaders are accommodated free everywhere in the Valley.'

'You believe that, do you?'

'Look, these people are all right, can't you get them back?'

'If you wish to be cheated, it would be possible, I think. But I will not do that.'

'Some other camp will take them.'

A pitying expression, as if we were all children, and badly brought-up children at that, spread over her face. 'I think not.'

It was a bizarre evening. I said little. George's behaviour interested me: even worried me. He was plainly convinced that Joyce was incompetent, malicious and probably a liar to boot. But he did nothing. He exerted no authority, for all that he was a partner, she a mere employee. He argued against her, but she won every point. It was an extraordinary, almost Job-like response to adversity, but all it did was to make Joyce worse. The more George gave in, the more she bullied, the more she exulted.

She was not interested in company profit, that much was clear. She was not interested in efficiency. What she liked was her own way. What she enjoyed was little victories. She liked power, yes, but she liked it in bite-sized morsels. She had no grand schemes, no dreams of global conquest. A few small triumphs, the impeding of the path of others: that satisfied her, that filled her anorexic frame to bursting.

'What sort of clients are we getting this season, Joyce?' I dared to ask.

'Top-drawer international clients.' She smiled fondly at her coffee cup.

'But surely we are offering a bush experience. Something that places like Mukango and Impala can't touch.'

'No. You're rather naïve, aren't you, ah, Dan? We must be more elegant. Look after the small things. Yes? It's hard for people like you. And George has simply been in the bush too long. He doesn't understand what international clients want. Let us be frank: it is a matter of class. Really, you know, I sometimes think I am wasting my time. I bring these lovely cups out into the bush, and George sneers at them. I inspect the camp, and I find that the lavatory seat is *nine inches too high*. You people try to destroy everything I do. It is not malice, believe me, I do understand that, but you people do not understand how top-drawer international people like to live. I send you the right sort of people, not rabble like Wilderness Express. I just want you to look after them. Treat them with respect. Don't make things dangerous for them. I will not have them frightened. Ah, Dan, do you have the remotest idea of what I am talking about?'

'Yes,' I said. 'You explain things very well.' I had heard my father dealing with difficult owners often enough, watched him listen with apparent fascination and respect to all their crack-brained ideas. Keep agreeing, Dan. Keep agreeing till they've gone. Then do what you focken like. Yes, Dad. I had been about eleven when he first taught me that rule. But though my father was brilliant with both owners and horses, his business had collapsed while I had watched, or gone to study zoology. I had done nothing for my father; I could think of nothing to do about Joyce. Owners and horses I could cope with, clients and lion. The rest just passed me by.

'Joyce, there is one more thing I must bring up,' George said. 'That is the question of a caterer. There's a girl that Philip Pocock –'

'George. I have said all that needs to be said on this subject. The company cannot pay another European salary.'

'We have always paid three European salaries before –'

'That was before you took on a trainee safari guide without consulting me.'

'Look, Joseph – sorry, Joseph, but I have to explain – Joseph is a trainee, and he is paid the official trainee rate, which is a pittance; he gets the same salary as Sunday. You *know* that, Joyce. And we need a caterer, every camp in the Valley has a caterer –'

'You think that, do you?'

'Of course they do, it's the system, how else are we to –'

'You have brought a problem on yourself, I suggest you solve it yourself. Work it out between you.'

'I'm a whizz at frying eggs,' I said. 'Dozen at a time. What about you, Joseph?'

'Only mealie meal, sah.'

'That's fine. Fried eggs and mealie meal –'

'That'll do, Dan,' George said, almost sharply, for all that my intemperance was a tactless gesture of support. I was on George's side, but no help to him.

'There is nothing more to be said on the subject,' said Joyce. 'Now, if you please, I am going to bed. I will not walk tomorrow. I am catching the eleven o'clock plane. Wake me for breakfast at 7.15.'

She made her stately way to bed. There was a long, echoing silence. 'You bugger, Joseph, you and your mealie meal, sah.'

'I owed you one for your twenty-foot eagle.'

George did not laugh. Instead, he said, 'Do you know what?'

'What, George?'

'I have just seen our hopes of breaking even this year thrown into the Mchindeni River.'

'Can't you do something? Why don't you speak to your partner about it?'

'It's not that simple. Bruce wouldn't think of getting rid of her.'

'But surely if you explained –'

'Bruce believes everything she tells him. He only keeps the company going to keep Joyce in a job.'

'I've got an idea,' I said. 'Look at things from Joyce's point of view. There are two things wrong with this operation. The first is that allowing guests to stay is going to bugger things up, so let's not have any. The second is that the location of the camp causes too many problems. We are a bit cut off. So we should move it into the middle of town.'

'Ha!'

'What?'

'Hear that?' George held up a finger, and fixed me with his eyes, alight and alert for the first time that day. 'Yes! And there, yes.'

'Got it. Lion. Quite distant.'

'Not just bloody lion. Listen, for Christ's sake! It can only be the Tondo Pride. First time they have been this close all season. They are moving towards the river already. Tell you what, let's drive out first thing tomorrow and see if we can find them.'

'You've forgotten Joyce.'

'Oh arseholes. Maybe tomorrow afternoon then.'

'Why not?'

9

'Good morning, madam.'

'Uh?'

'Good morning, madam. Your water is ready.'

'Caro?' I said softly, almost silently. 'Say "thank you, Jonas." Then he'll go away.'

'Uh . . . thank you, Jonas. Jesus.'

'It's all right.'

'Oh good. Hullo.'

'Hullo.'

'Jesus.' She sat up, pushing handfuls of hair from her face: one last vision of galaxies and constellations: immaculate maculation.

'Did I tell you last night how beautiful you are?'

'Yes.'

'Good.'

We both needed to perform an internebullar leap from a night far from the common run of things, into a day full of threatening and disturbing possibilities.

'Dan?'

'Hullo.'

'Thank you for my holiday in the bush.'

'Any time.'

'Perhaps not that.'

'Well, then. The pleasure was all mine.'

'Perhaps not that, either.'

I wanted to sob violently, or perhaps to run naked and cheering into the Mchindeni.

She smiled at me for a while. Then said: 'Look, no regrets, Dan, none at all, no matter what, but can you get out of this hut without being seen?'

'I expect so. Go and wash. Jonas has just filled the bowl outside your hut with warm water. If no one is in sight, cough, and I'll make a run for it. Then we'll meet up over coffee in the sitenji in five minutes, and we'll go for a nice walk. Your holiday in the bush isn't quite over yet.'

'That's good.'

We stood up. However, that made us want to embrace. For a moment, the earth lurched and swayed in its orbit. Then Caro was wrapping a towel about herself. I was distractedly throwing arms and legs into clothes, and Caro was opening the door of the hut. A cough, a half-suppressed laugh. And I was gone, sneaky as a leopard.

A few minutes later, we were hypocritically drinking coffee and exchanging matutinal greetings, though there was no one to hear or to see. In the river, a great white egret and a spoonbill were feeding in comensal tolerance.

'Did you sleep well?'

'Not too well.'

'I hope the bed was not too uncomfortable.'

'A little on the small side – Jesus. Dan, did we drink a lot of whisky as well?'

I went to the ashes of the fire. The bottle of Malawian Scotch lay capless and capsized. 'Rather a lot, yes.'

'Must have been a special occasion, then.'

'It must – morning, Phineas. Coffee?'

Phineas, tall and loose-limbed in his lion-coloured uniform, gun dangling from one large hand, accepted coffee after I had sugared it for him with four spoonfuls, the cup being, of course, small. 'Giraffe,' he said.

He pointed a slender hand with unconscious grace, and showed us a giant and definite male, a stately bull giraffe and almost certainly last night's invader, which made him, of course, the finest giraffe in Africa. He was, quite extraordinarily, in the middle of the Mchindeni, wading purposefully to the far side. Water sloshed around his ankles.

'On his way to Impala Lodge,' I said.

'Ah-yes,' Phineas said in his near-whisper. 'Remember the

place, Dan. We can cross. Take the vehicle. There is a way down, far side of the ebony glade, little bit difficult but OK. Then come back this way, all along the beach. Cross there. Where giraffe is crossing. Head back towards Impala Lodge on far beach. Before you get there, is a shallow bank, very very easy, go straight up. You see the place, by the big sausage tree?'

'I have it.'

'OK place to walk across, too. Very shallow. You can see if there are no crocs, walk straight across. And a long way from the bank; nothing can surprise you. Maybe we take a walk across one morning.'

'The giraffe has done us a good turn,' I said. 'We'll try the crossing after lunch. But where shall we walk this morning?'

'South maybe. To Robin Hood Grove. Back along river.'

This definite answer meant that Phineas had heard something in the night, and thought we might be able to locate it. From habit he did not elaborate: he knew better than to raise false hopes in clients. 'OK, Phineas.'

Bush-walking is a ticklish art, a constant balancing of possibilities. It is a simultaneous seeking and avoidance of risk. You want to get close to large animals, but not dangerously close. A walk is quite different to safari by vehicle. In a reasonably well-visited park, a vehicle is accepted by most beasts as a big, noisy, bad-smelling neutral presence, a stinking irrelevance. On a walk, the animals relate to you as mammal to mammal. Hence the gun. But the weapon that really matters is simple, or complex: bush wisdom. Phineas had worked in the park for twenty years and was as bush-wise as they come. He led us off with, as ever, the gun balanced and useless on his shoulder.

A bush walk can be packed with incident, or alarmingly quiet, as if nothing above the size of a thrush lived there. That was how the morning began. I pointed out birds, footprints, dried turds: all signs of the life that teemed invisibly all around us. A civet midden: the scattered and spattered dung of hippo.

We walked on, following the logic of the country: that is to say, the paths made by the bigger animals, ways that followed no straight line, but which meandered from one good food source to another.

The bush is crisscrossed and crosscrissed with animal roads. As yet another path intersected our own, a smoking football of dung lay before us, three or four footballs in fact, glistening with damp. 'Ha.'

Phineas and I squatted, and we each stuck an index finger into a football. 'Ten, fifteen minutes?' Phineas nodded agreement. I indicated a direction with my thumb. Phineas grinned, lightly punched my biceps, and pointed the opposite way. Wrong again. Never mind. We stood.

'Little surprise for you,' I said to Caro, very quiet. 'Keep close. Don't talk now.'

Phineas was letting a trickle of dust flow from his fingers: mostly towards us, a little from the right. Good. We walked into the insensible breeze; ahead lay the Robin Hood Grove, so named by Joseph, who had a romantic heart. It was a well-spaced ebony glade, smaller than our own. As we walked towards it I counted six elephant, feeding, browsing on the leaves of the underscrub. Five adult females, one youngster, half grown, about ten years old. I looked at Phineas – a facial shrug. We go in.

At twenty yards, we stood still, silent, and to the elephants quite invisible: a feeling of almost God-like privilege. Invisible, inaudible and crucially, unsmellable. The elephants ate: and an eating animal is, of course, a contented animal. We heard the rasp of elephantine trunk against bough, the slap as a trunked hank of grass was bashed free of dirt against a raised foreleg. They seemed, like ships, to drift with the wind: ancient vessels moving idly across the friendly waters of their home port. The munch of leaves: the occasional mammoth, or at least elephantine gurgle of digestion.

Still they drifted, apparently propelled by the tiny wind, pushed towards us with infinite gradualness, towards the invisible and unsmellable party of humans. It was time for a little cosmic courtesy. I looked at Phineas: the rifle butt on the floor, barrel resting against his thigh. We exchanged looks. He made a backwards nod of his head and stayed put, gun between client and danger. I gestured Caro back: eyes entranced, she retreated. I took a step back to join her. It must have been this flash of movement that did it, though there was no escaping the need to move.

For something caught the eye of the nearest elephant. She gave a start, like a nervous spinster finding a man in her bedroom, and at once gave us the charge: ears wide and flapping in an elephant's stumbling run. We let her get within ten yards and then, almost simultaneously, Phineas and I clapped our hands. At the sound, the elephant, almost apologetically, spun round and shambled off, more or less without breaking stride. The rest of the elephant group walked briskly after her.

'You're cool,' Caro said to Phineas.

'Ah-yes, madam.'

'Adrenaline for breakfast,' she said.

'Darlin' Girl,' I said to her, and her eyes lit up, at the remembered story, at the implied endearment. And so she draped an arachnoid arm about my shoulder, in contradiction of her early-morning desire for secrecy. Her face was full of joy: so must mine have been. I secured her with my nearest hand; linked and joyful, we walked back along the river bank to camp. 'Is this the first morning of the world?' she asked.

'Yes.'

Back at camp, we breakfasted massively, while I avoided Joseph's eye as best I could. 'Did you find a *Ballanites* bush on your walk this morning, Dan?'

Conversation drifted inevitably to the staple of fixing. Isaac was owed a day off. There was a parcel of frozen meat coming on the plane tomorrow. The vegetarians would be on the same plane. Was it worth driving to Nsefu market to try and buy cheese? No, it was too far.

Caro interrupted. 'If you need cheese, I've got plenty at Impala Lodge.'

'Would you consider selling us a pound or so?'

'I wouldn't, no. I'll give you some. A good guest always offers a small gift to her host.'

There was nothing to say to that, not in public, so I didn't say it. Nor did Joseph, which showed uncharacteristic restraint. George and Joseph then began to discuss the cheese run. It was a two-hour drive to Impala Lodge, back to the main gate, over the bridge, loop through the villages and back into the park on the far side. 'I believe Caroline and I have the answer to all our problems,' I said. 'It is all very wonderful, and it all began with a giraffe.' I explained about the crossing point.

'Well, if Phineas says it will go, it will go,' George said. 'Just tell us when you want to leave, Caroline, and we'll make the crossing in convoy. That sounds rather rude, doesn't it? Stay as long as you want. You're only fifteen minutes' drive from home. Stay for lunch, if you like.'

'Do you know, I think I will. I'd better get back soon after – but – well – it's so nice here.'

'Ha. Paradise flycatcher. On the bush in front of us.' There was, too, a tiny bird with a tail three times longer than its body.

'How wonderfully absurd,' Caro said. 'The tail looks quite ridiculous.'

'It *is* ridiculous,' George said. 'The tail is an epigamic character: its sole function is to attract the opposite sex.'

'Rather like Dan's trilby,' Joseph said.

Morning was a quiet time in camp. Caro had a shower and returned exclaiming over its delights. She and I sat before the river. I wrote up my notes, a much postponed task; she borrowed from the bar a copy of *Lions of the Plains*. 'Orange-breasted bush-shrike, hear it, Caro? Singing Beethoven's Fifth.'

As lunch was drawing to a close, Joseph raised his head a fraction. 'Vehicle,' he said. A moment or so later, I could hear it too. I felt a curious disappointment. We normally welcomed visitors to break the routine of camp life. This time, even though we were remote from it, I feared the intrusion of the outer world. It was not the flycatcher that had brought a touch of paradise to the camp.

The noise rose, and then, swirling into camp, a brand-new Land Cruiser, and driving it, Leon.

'Definite male,' said Joseph, a trifle maliciously.

'Complemental male, more accurately,' said George, and smirked to himself.

Leon parked with a flourish by our own vehicle, which looked even older beside this apparition. A cloud of dust hung in the still air. He stepped to the ground, stretched, took off his baseball cap and gave his head a good scratch. He turned to us with a grin of pure exhilaration. 'Ullo, you guys. Ullo, sweetie. They didn't kill you, then, these guys?'

By this time we had got up to meet him. He took Caro in his arms and kissed her soundly; he followed this by giving us each a finger-crushing handshake. We walked back to the sit-enji, Leon with his thick arm about Caro's frailer shoulders. 'You find that bloody Tondo Pride all right?'

'They've shown me all kinds of lovely things. It's been quite a stay.'

'As long as you don't run my business like these guys run theirs.'

'I was going to offer you a bottle of Lion,' I said. 'But we only give them to polite guests.'

'Shut up and give me a beer, you bastard.' Give myur byur.

'Yes, sah, sorry, sah.' I went to the kitchen, returning in a detour via the new Land Cruiser. I walked around it. It was perfect. I wanted to steal it: steal it for myself, steal it to give Lion Safaris a better and more mobile future. But what I did was give Leon his beer.

'Thanks, man.'

'You bent your new vehicle yet?'

'Nott! I told you, man, I was so bloody pleased with it, I drove it straight here. Like a bloody kid, I was so happy. Meetings all afternoon, then picked up the vehicle, had a few beers, and set off about 4 am. Cruises like a bloody bird. Suspension over the bad road outside town, you wouldn't believe it. Took the long hill like it wasn't bloody there. Now I want to get my mechanic to fit some game-viewing seats right away; got these Wilderness Express people coming tomorrow, we'll lay on a decent two-vehicle trip for them now. But look, George, I came all this way to see you for a lot of reasons: first, to pay a social call, get a beer off you. Second, to see if you killed my girl, and, if you had, to throw you in the river. Third, I have to pass a letter to you, and I can tell you what it says too. I was in a meeting with some guys yesterday, and the park warden, bloody old Mvuu, was there, and he asked me to deliver a letter to you, sure, Mr Mvuu, only four bloody hours out of my way. He wants to see you, George, you and your number one safari guide. He is coming to Impala Lodge tonight, says will you go and talk to him. Don't know what the bastard wants.'

'Mvuu wants to see us? Why on earth would that be? I haven't spoken to him since the start of the season. And that was only hullo.'

'So I thought if you have to make a four-hour round trip, the least I could do was to have a bit of a braai, make an evening of it, have a few beers.'

'Very kind, Leon.'

'Nott. Mvuu wants to inspect Impala Lodge: what he means is he wants to drink a 'ell of a lot of free beers, and I want you guys to come and take the load off me, otherwise he will expect me to sit with him while he loads up. That man is a full-time drunk, I tell you.'

'And how was town? Learn anything about the road?'

'Ach, talk, plenty-plenty-plenty talk. They are set on building the bloody road, start building next dry season, can't do it in the wet. Send the diggers in next dry season and drive away all my bloody clients. It's disaster. All go bankrupt. Look, I must get back to Impala, get the braai ready.'

'Tell you what,' I said. 'Caro, er, Caroline and I saw a giraffe cross the river just upstream of camp this morning, and Phineas reckoned you could drive across in the same place.'

'Is it? If Phineas reckons it's OK, it's OK. Unless there's a soft patch on the beach. Don't want my new vehicle stuck. Or my old one.'

'George and I planned to drive across anyway. Blaze a trail. You and, er, Caroline can follow in the other two.'

'That's smart. I've got a bloody winch on this new vehicle, too, so if you get stuck, I'll pull you out. No one has to worry.'

So after another beer, we set off, three vehicles in a line. George took the wheel, of course, being the better bush driver, not to mention the owner of the vehicle. Phineas was right about the descent: it was difficult and precipitous. I stood on the spare wheel and called out lefts and rights, and George inched the way down, not smoothly, smoothness was not part of George's way of facing the world, but in a series of dramatic and effective jerks. Braced and gripping hard, I applauded the finding of level ground, looking back to see Leon following George's tracks, and behind him, Caroline, frowning hard but handling her vehicle with a competence that impressed but hardly surprised me.

The procession skimmed along the sand of the beach, back towards Lion Camp, and I spotted the sharp, clear marks of giraffine footprints: twin-toed, massive but exquisitely pointed. 'Follow those tracks, George.' The tracks entered the water and, with fractionally more caution than usual, but not much, we did the same. The going was firm beneath, the water scarcely reaching the wheel hubs. All too simple. We paused on the far side while the others crept across, and then drove on briskly along the beach. I indicated the spot Phineas had shown me. 'I know, I know.' George took the gentle ascent at a great lick, banging me around in the back, while the master and mistress of Impala Lodge continued to follow our tracks, their eyes and their noses filled with the dust of our passage.

We stopped at the top in a circle-the-wagons formation. 'A spot of bundu-bashing, and you're onto the road, and then you're just two hundred yards from home.'

'Thanks, George, very decent of you. Come back any time after sundown, right? Plenty beer.'

'Thanks, you two. Thanks for the stay. It was perfect. Immaculate.'

'Any time, Caro.'

10

It was fifteen minutes after the sun was down – there was no such thing as sunset in the Valley; one minute the sun was up, the next it had gone – when we set off to Impala Lodge, and the night was already dark. I drove as I badly wanted to try out Giraffe Crossing. Joseph stood on the back with the spotlight. Nocturnal bundu-bashing is ten times easier when someone is spotlighting for you; a bright light, steeply angled downwards, gives the best warning of obstacles, lumps, hollows and unexpected beasts. I followed the spoor of our earlier crossing, while George beside me gave me a good deal of useless advice. I negotiated the descent gingerly, but swept through the crossing and made the ascent of the far side comfortably. Joseph, swinging the beam of light, found a white-tailed mongoose, out early for the night's work. Another spot of bundu-bashing – 'Mind the tree, Dan.' 'I'm *minding* the bloody tree' – brought us onto the graded road, and I swung smoothly along its sweep towards Impala Lodge.

I had seen the camp from the road, from the bush, from across the river, but had never visited. I had forgotten the size of the gateway with its two huge pillars of mopane wood, stained red-brown, each topped by a buffalo skull. Between the pillars a huge piece of polished wood, cut in a shallow curve, formed a triumphal arch. It bore the legend 'Impala Lodge'; on each side an impala leapt with controlled grace into the beautifully formed letters. Beneath them, a tall African in a beautiful khaki shirt was opening for us the famous electric fence.

Joseph switched off the spotlight as our reception committee came into sight: two figures, much of a height, one wide and muscular, one lithe and narrow, smiles of welcome on both faces. I felt the application of the red-hot pincers. 'What animals are these?' Joseph asked softly. 'Must be two different species, a comensal relationship.'

'Understandable error, Joseph,' George said. 'But it is simply a case of pronounced sexual dimorphism. Observe the epigamic moustache on the complemental male. Good evening, Leon, er, Caroline.'

Greetings were exchanged. 'Come and have a beer, man, quick, get yourself ready for Mvuu. He is taking a shower, bloody man is drunk already, says he'll see you when he is through. Denis!' This last a roar. 'Denis, beer now-now, beers all round, three four five beers.'

He walked us towards the campfire on the edge of the river, which burned merrily in a shallow bowl of concrete. 'Cheers, everybody.' He took a python-like swallow from his bottle. 'Christ, George, it is worth going to bloody town, man. Because then you come back to the bush, and have a beer in your own camp, and you say, Christ, I remember why I'm in this bloody stupid business.'

'Why did you go? Couldn't someone else collect the new vehicle for you?'

'I had a lot of things to do, lot of things in a short space of time. Evening with my partner for one thing. Tell him to get his finger out.'

'I didn't know you had a partner,' I said. 'Thought you were a sole owner and all that.'

'Nott. No bloody chance. Not how this country works. Just my bloody money, my camp, my vehicles. But my partner fixes things, and you know how much that is worth in this bloody country. I wish he could fix bloody Mvuu for you.'

'You know what Mvuu wants then?'

'Not a bloody clue, man.'

'Did his camp inspection go all right?'

'Bloody bar inspection.'

'I've never been here before,' I said. 'Any chance of a camp inspection for me?'

'Sure. Why don't you show him round, sweetie?'

Caro looked at me, almost shyly. 'All right.' And showed me a different world.

The huts had low brick walls, painted white, and thick, high-pointed roofs of thatch. A concrete apron extended beyond each hut to form a verandah, shaded with a roof of thatch. Each verandah had a pair of genuinely comfortable chairs and a low table for drinks and was arranged to give a spectacular view onto the Mchindeni. In the dark I could see the gunmetal gleam of the river, the silhouette, black against black, of our ebony glade, and the shape of the bend that hid our camp from theirs. Underfoot, in the bright electric lights that shone from every doorway, there was green grass: a short green lawn, no less. Lion Camp was all earth-coloured: dust and poppadom leaves below, lit with spangles of sun in the daytime; the huts brown and dusty as if they had grown from the leaf litter. Here, all was brightness, white walls and green-sward. 'How do you keep the grass green?'

'Water it, of course. We have a full-time gardener.' This, it was clear, was an oasis of civilisation in the drought-ravaged bush.

'Stunning,' I said. 'It really is. No half-measures. Will you show me inside a hut?'

It had a concrete floor, mat-strewn. Each hut was a circular beehive, surprisingly spacious. A wooden pillar rose from the centre to support the roof. At the back was a separate room with flush lavatory and shower. A double bed. Dressing table, mirror, small wardrobe, carved wooden decorations, bad pictures of animals on the walls. There were even windows, insect-proofed with gauze. Each hut was a little haven from the bush. 'Very lovely,' I said.

'A little odd, after Lion Camp.'

She smiled: her manner was friendly, polite. I wanted to take her in my arms then and there, but I didn't do anything of the kind. This was a pity, because there was a little pause in which I might have done so, but I missed it. 'You all right, Caro?'

'Why shouldn't I be?' she answered.

It was this sudden reversion into the distant sniper of the

airport that undid me. As the old dislike of her seized me, I found I had at once seized her: seized her to banish this cool intruder, to bring back the person I had known the previous night, and afterwards, during the first morning of the world.

She found that she had, perhaps unintentionally, seized me back.

'Dan?'

'Yes?'

'I mean, have I just left the real world and moved into an unreal one? Or is it the other way round?'

'Only you can decide that.'

'I suppose that's true.'

'If it needs further investigation, come and investigate. Any time. The Mchindeni isn't as wide as it was yesterday.'

I found I had taken her in my arms after all. We held close, no Gothic arch, no mad lechery either. 'I mean, if you want to leave the noosphere again, just drive across the river,' I said eventually.

'Noosphere?'

'The biosphere altered by the hand of man.'

'Yes. Yes.'

We clasped close a moment longer. 'I'll show you the rest of the camp.' It was a call to order: for her own benefit, perhaps, as much as mine. A call back to her chosen world. The gate in the electric fence was closed again.

'Do.'

We visited the office, and next door, the shop, full of objects of fetish, bright cottons, bad pictures of animals, khaki shirts and khaki baseball caps, all bearing the leaping impala logo. The kitchen would have made Sunday drool. 'Oh, let me get your cheese.' She took a generous two-pound lump from the fridge and found a plastic bag; there was a small store of these valuable items.

'I'll put it in the small fridge in the bar. Don't forget it.'

'Thanks, Caro.'

'Any time. Let's continue the tour.' The generator, the electric fence. Then we rejoined the others in the sitenji. This was a magnificent structure, built around a living leadwood tree and quite beautifully thatched. She explained that Leon had imported a team of thatchers from Malawi, where they have a different tradition of building, to do the job: Malawi produced the best Scotch and the best thatchers. The grass was better quality than found locally: she told me how Leon had brought it in from Northern Province. The bar was a single sweep of wood, brought to a high polish, and behind it stood a real barman clad in a khaki shirt with a leaping impala on his left bosom. Beside the bar, a permanent brick-built barbecue, braai in Afrikaans. A cook, wearing, of all things, a towering toque, was quietly working behind it.

'Leon,' I said. 'I'm impressed. Where are you going to put the new huts?'

'I plan to clear land on the upstream side, man, just up the slope of the bank. Keep all the trees and most of the bushes. Keep it a little bit separate from the rest of the camp, make it a little settlement, separate staff. Don't want to get like a big impersonal camp.'

'I'm still impressed that you got permission to build.'

Leon gave a brief laugh. 'So am I. I tell you, when my partner told me he had got a result, I thought he was bloody joking at first. But I may not build now. If that bloody road goes through, I am bloody ruined. Every cent I have is in this place.' A member of Leon's staff came up and spoke to him quietly. 'Mvuu is ready to see you guys,' Leon said. 'Good luck, yeah?'

We were escorted to one of the huts: on its private verandah Mvuu sat. Our escort set on his table two bottles of Lion and a small glass. Mvuu took these without thanks, and did not look at us while he poured, with loving care, beer into the glass. Condensation bloomed along its sides. Mvuu was large and bearded. I thought then that I had never seen him standing up.

He completed pouring, and set down glass and bottle, the beer untasted. 'Mr Sorensen,' he said. 'Mr Lynch. Please sit down.'

We sat. Two upright chairs had been provided. Mvuu, lolling

back in a client's easy chair, turned his attention back to the beer. He drank: a series of small sips, no python-like swallow. Then he topped his glass up again: he seemed to like the sight of a full glass.

'I have had complaints,' he said eventually.

'I'm sorry to hear that,' said George. 'What sort of –'

Mvuu raised and lowered the flat of his hand for silence, making not a sound as he did so. 'I have had complaints,' he said. He sipped, poured, watched the liquid settle. We sat in silence for a period.

'You have put clients in danger.'

'I don't think that's true really. I don't think that's true at all –'

'You have put clients in danger. I don't want tourists to be put in any danger. Do not do so again.'

'But look, I say, I mean, we haven't put any client in danger, who says that we –'

'We have not come here to discuss my sources of information. We have come to discuss the information itself. You have put clients in danger. It must not happen again.'

This time George had the wit to remain silent.

'How is business?' Mvuu asked, with elaborate nonchalance.

'Oh, not too bad, nothing to grumble about –'

'I hear you are having a poor season. I hear you are running at fifty per cent capacity and below. I hear you are not bringing very much foreign exchange into the country.'

'Well, really I –'

'You. Mr Lynch.'

'Er, yes?'

'You are not shaping up as a safari guide.'

'I –' But I fell silent. I was mortified: mortified to my soul. I showed clients the bush: and they loved it. How could he say this terrible thing to me?

'I have had many complaints about you. You are off-hand and rude. You are a frivolous person. You do not have much knowledge. Your qualification was rushed through at the start of the season. You will be required to re-take your examination, with a different examiner. This will happen at the end of the season. It may be that I will examine you myself.'

'Oh, really –'

'If you do not pass, your safari guide licence will be withdrawn. Now, Mr Sorensen. You will be happy to know that your safari guide licence is still considered good.'

'Oh, good.'

'The situation with regard to your camp operator's licence is less good. As you know, your three-year licence comes up for renewal at the end of this season.'

'Yes.'

'There has been pressure to have this licence taken away. Listen. I have fought against this. I have put my reputation on the line for you. This is because you have an international reputation as a scientist. I have effected a compromise. It is now quite likely that your licence will be renewed for next season. But it will only be valid for one year. After that time, it will come up for review again. We want to see evidence that you are operating near capacity.'

'Oh, er, thank you.'

'Not at all. Your reputation in the world is very good, Mr Sorensen, and we are proud to have you in the Valley. But your reputation locally is very bad. You need to pull your bloody socks up.' The menace in this banal phrase was extraordinary. A long pause developed.

Eventually, George said: 'Is that all, Mr Mvuu?'

'Yes.' His glass was empty, he began to fill it very slowly from the second bottle of Lion. 'Ah, no. There is one more thing. You have a very excellent scout, Phineas Banda.'

'Oh yes, I can certainly say that –'

Again, the big, flat hand was raised and lowered silently on the table. 'It is the opinion of the South Mchindeni National Park Executive Committee that Scout Banda would be better employed in a camp that had more tourists.'

'Phineas has been with me for six years –'

Once again the hand. 'We will make a change in seven days. Scout Banda will report to my office. Please give him this instruction.' He handed George an envelope: George tucked it obediently into a shirt pocket. 'I have not decided who I shall assign to you for the rest of the season. He will be a competent man. That is all.' He sipped, poured. 'Send the waiter to me.'

Shaken, George and I retreated. We were silent. There was absolutely nothing to say. I seemed to be out of my depth: so did George. This was a trouble beyond Joyce's capabilities. I felt a terrible fear. Beyond anything else, I feared that the bush could be taken from me. So I took action at once. I drank. George too. What else to do? Why not?

My memories of the rest of the evening are a little swirling. I talked a good deal, though nothing, so far as I recall, that I had any serious reason for regretting. That was something. The food was good and plentiful, which must have helped. I recall the constant dipping of hot meats into a bowl of slightly sweet, playfully spiced sauce, and Leon shouting across the company: 'Hey, Patrick, where did this sauce come from?'

Africans, in the main, do not do much shouting. Denis, the waiter, being much closer, answered for Patrick. 'He made it himself, sah.'

'On whose instruction? Did you tell him to do it, sweetie?' Caro shook her head.

'He just made it,' Denis explained.

'Patrick!' Patrick, beneath his toque, looked up again from his sizzling braai. 'Patrick, you are a bloody genius, man. Bloody well done, all right. You make this every time we have a braai, I can't get enough of it.'

Conversation got seriously swirly after that. I remember delivering a tremendous scolding to Lloyd, Leon's birding or stringing assistant, on the subject of wood doves. 'Buggered if I'm going to get excited just because some poor bird got fucking *lost.*'

Mvuu did not join the party. He remained on his verandah, though I noticed that Denis was kept busy walking up and down with plates of food and bottles of beer, the bottles always in pairs. 'How did Mvuu get the bloody job?' I remember asking Leon. 'What are his qualifications?'

'His principal qualification is that his sister married Jacob Njiri.'

'Who he?'

'Ach!' Leon, not for the first time, was appalled at my lack of grasp. At a soberer moment, I might have wondered if he did not have a point. 'Njiri is the Minister for Tourism and National Parks.'

Caro I avoided, or perhaps vice versa. Later and swirlier still, I got involved in a rambling conversation with Leon about morality. Leon had been knocking back the Lions pretty seriously himself. 'Morality is a simple matter in the bush, Dan, and that is my morality too. I am talking about the survival of the fittest. And I intend to be the fittest bastard you will find in the whole bloody Valley.'

'A classic error of Darwinism,' I said. 'Fittest does not mean strongest. It means the most suitable. A porcupine doesn't thrive because it is fierce and strong. It survives because it can stick its prickles up a lion's nose.'

Leon dismissed a century and a half of evolutionary science with a brusque gesture of the beer bottle. 'I'm a carnivore, Dan. A predator on the herd.'

'Then I had better tell you a truism of ecology. The prey population controls the numbers of the predator, not vice versa.'

'Nott!'

'Then read George Sorensen, among many others, on the topic. I mean, God, it was his figures on predator–prey dynamics that made his work famous.'

At some point a decision was made to leave. It seemed that Joseph was offering to drive us home. This was an excellent plan. Joseph had a taste for responsibility. The entire party, though not of course Mvuu, all highly hilarious now, went out to the vehicle to see us off. I shook hands formally with everyone in sight, solely that I might take formal leave of Caro. Chastely, I kissed her speckled cheek.

The climb up the bank on the far side of the river seemed to have got a little trickier, but Joseph managed it better than

George or I would have done. I stood high in the back with the spotlight, lighting the way for Joseph, and then dizzily sweeping the beam through the trees. Rather to my amazement, I caught a genet in the beam just outside camp: small, speckled and cat-like, high in the fork of a sausage tree. We watched him for a few minutes: he was drinking nectar from the scarlet flowers, biting them off at the base and allowing the juice to trickle into his mouth.

'What's up, baby?' Joseph asked him. 'You just turned vegetarian?'

'Shit!' I said. 'I forgot the bloody cheese.'

I was tired enough when I got to my spinning bed, but the thought of cheese obsessed me. I could not sleep for the cheese that was lying on the far bank of the Mchindeni River. In the ebony glade, a wood owl commented on my thoughts. Whooo's a naughty boy?

11

The sudden discharge of a bushbuck bark, deep-throated, roaring, as un-antelope-like a sound as a puku whistle and infinitely more startling, and then the crash and crackle of its panicking escape brought long-unsaid words to my mouth.

'Jaysis,' I said aloud. 'I'm strung up like a focken banjo.'

This was a pre-race favourite. It might even have been my father's last words; though come to think of it, he normally said, if ever a horse of his hit the front, 'He'll get beat. They'll catch him. He's tiring. He's not got the focken legs.'

I giggled nervously at this thought, and then told myself sternly to pull myself together. That was easy. At once, hilarity was replaced with terror.

George and Joseph had driven to the airport to collect the vegetarians and to post a letter to Gianna. I had stayed in camp pleading a hangover. Actually, I didn't feel too bad: better than I deserved, anyway. Now I found myself irrevocably committed to one of those gambles that had so characterised my father's way of doing things. 'Why am I doing this, Dan? I don't have to do this. I must be focken crazy.'

This was deeply focken crazy. For I was, of course, on my way to fetch the cheese from Impala Lodge. There were a number of points arising from this decision. I had gone through them again and again in the course of the previous night's beery half-slumbers, making lists of reasons as to why I should or should not be doing this. The hut and the thoughts had revolved in sweeping arabesques, the mad list lengthened and curved and spun, and all the time, even as I debated what to do, I knew I was going to go. That was what frightened me. The main points of the swirling list were these.

1. Walking alone in the bush was so ludicrously illegal that if I were caught, I would lose my safari guide licence on the spot.

2. But if I restored full legality to the enterprise by asking Phineas and his gun to accompany me, the trip would become a formal visit, with witnesses.

3. On the other hand, Leon and/or Lloyd might be there. That would be disaster.

4. But they should be collecting the Wilderness Express party in two vehicles.

5. In which case, Caro might have decided to join them. But I recalled to myself a fragment of conversation overheard last night: Leon, darling (Darling! Ha!), if you can pick up the vegetables from Piet and three crates of beer on the way to the airport, I can stay in camp and get the books up to date. Not a problem, sweetheart, or swee tart.

6. However, Caro would almost certainly have given the cheese to Leon, to hand over to George at the airport.

7. And she might be furious at my unscheduled arrival.

8. And she might not.

9. Why was my Land-Rover with beer-bottle-opening shelf locked up at Mukango Lodge rather than awaiting my needs at Lion Camp? Well, all sorts of good reasons, and there was no possibility of shipping it across the park by sheer willpower.

10. Caro might be impressed at my intrepidness in making the journey alone.

11. She might not. It might be the revelation of total insanity that would convince her of the folly of her night at Lion Camp, the perfect rightness of her life with Leon.

12. I might get devoured, impaled, bisected, flattened or vivisected en route.

It was point 12 that was increasingly occupying my mind as I scrambled down the steep path made by the wheel ruts. I needed to use a hand for support: it was amazing that a vehicle could handle so steep a descent. I walked out onto the beach, eyes slithering about as if I had never seen the bush before, expecting crazed beasts to leap out at me from every thicket. This would not do. For months I had strolled at my ease in the bush. My senses were sharp, my understanding good. I knew what I was doing. But Mvuu had told me I was a bad trail leader. Maybe he was right. Maybe I was utterly ignorant, and my chosen path led directly to a hippo's mouth. But come on, I told myself firmly, Phineas said I was all right, and winning his respect was not a matter of course. I was *good*. I was Cool in the Bush, was I not? I was also focken crazy. I didn't have to do this. Strung up like a focken banjo. I had thought or muttered the same words to myself, several times, when, caught up in the madness of grief, I had set out on the trail to Africa, suffering various crises of doubt and fear in the departure lounge, on the plane, in immigration, in my hostel in Cape Town as I began the search for my Land-Rover. Now, in the madness of love, I was doing something still more crazy. I didn't have to do this.

It is a different matter, being Cool in the Bush when you are walking beside a man who is not only cool to the point of genius, but carrying a gun to boot, and walking alone. I stepped onto the long sandy beach, from which the Mchindeni River had retreated as the dry season progressed. A pair of white-crowned plovers circled about me, making mobbing cries, distraction behaviour to lure me from their nest. This would be in some unfindable scrape of sand along the beach. Upstream, almost beneath Impala Lodge, I saw a small band of puku coming down to drink: they stood, foxy statues, watching a nervous and embarrassed biped coming to join them. It was for them the most dangerous time of the day.

I reached the river's edge and sat to remove my boots, staring hard at the water's surface. I saw no croc. It is always amusing to watch baboon cross the river. They assume, for a few panicking seconds, a mad bipedal gait, jumping double-footed with long arms aloft, until they reach a sandbank and can descend to four-pawed arrogance again. Once there, they hunt for plovers' eggs. They love eggs but are mortally afraid of crocodiles; every now and again, you see a baboon that fancies eggs for breakfast become breakfast himself.

I wanted to cross the river in the same mad panic, but kept a grip. I waded with an appearance of calm. The water was less than knee-deep. On the far side, I dried my feet ineffectively on my socks, wobbling comically on one foot as I tried to keep my bare foot from the sand. Farce and fear were fast linking hands. Booted again, I followed the truck spoor on towards Impala Lodge.

I reckoned that the next part was the tricky bit: the climb, and then the brief walk along the bundu-bashing track to the road. There was a lot of vegetation here, enough to hide . . . well, anything. Also, I didn't care for the humps and hollows of the terrain: any one of them could hide a hippo, and getting between a hippo and water was supposed to be certain death. Then I remembered a morning when Phineas and I had walked almost on top of a lone buffalo, lying in a hollow much like one of these. Single buffalo are reckoned the most dangerous animals you could meet on a walk. Phineas organised a retreat while the buffalo staggered unwillingly to its feet. 'He is sick, that one. He goes there to die.'

Shut *up*, I told myself. Cool in the Bush. Use your senses, use your eyes, use your *sense*. You *know* this place. And the road was surely just ahead, beyond this fig tree.

And then there indeed was the beautiful, blessed road, and as I turned right, I could see the grandiose gateway. Relief shot through me. Then it stopped, and went into sharp reverse. Facing me on the opposite side of the road was an elephant: a big bull, an old one, beautifully ivoried; with him a second, also respectably armed.

I stopped instantly. The leading elephant reached out a non-chalant trunk and ripped leaves from the tree above him. An eating animal is a contented animal, I told myself, repeating for my comfort that ancient rule. Besides, the elephant had not noticed me. Didn't think anyone would be that stupid, perhaps. I took a handful of dust and trickled it, Phineas-style, from my own less graceful hand. Quite briskly, it drifted my way. All well and good. I knew exactly what to do now, so I did it. Absolutely nothing.

I dropped into a crouch and prepared to wait. The thought that the elephant might nonchalantly cross the road to sample my fig tree was a concern, but I can't say that it worried me. I was aware that if the worst came to the worst, I could try and shin up the fig tree: its reasonably accessible branches and a jolt of adrenaline might well be enough to get me to safety. But the matter hardly concerned me any more. I knew where I was now. I just sat, or crouched. Fear had mainly gone: a sort of delight had taken over. I felt a grin crawl onto my face. I was all right now. And I was going to be cosmically courteous for as long as it took. This, I thought, was focken grand. The two elephants had, as it were, put me in my place. A new and more contented sort of love filled me. My place.

It took long enough, but time had long ceased mattering. The elephants continued to feed, and to drift away from me. After a while, they were maybe two hundred yards off, and I decided to move. Quietly I stood and I walked. Impala Lodge lay before me. It was then that fear came. Partly it was a reaction to the walk, and the elephant. I stopped by the pillars, beneath the leaping impalas, and waited for my pulse to return to normal. A minute's wait was enough to tell me that this was a waste of time. For I now began to see where the real folly of this trip lay: not in the journey, but in the destination. And so I ducked under the electric fence and passed through the gateway, walking into safety, or danger. This was real insanity: and real terror, too.

Impala Lodge was deserted. Azoic. I did not call out. I saw no one in the sitenji. Ah. Doing the books. Office. Where the hell was the office?

By the shop. So behind the huts. Yes, there. Through the gauze of the window I saw her. And after the intimacy of the

117

elephants, I saw a stranger. An alien being, not of my world. Head down, left hand on head, tangled up in leucistic hair, right hand tapping, on a calculator, no doubt. She was absorbed in books, in her business, in her world, and for a second, I wondered if I liked her at all, if I had ever liked her. There seemed no trace in that preoccupied figure with the busy dancing fingers of the person who had loved the leopard, who had been undone by the giraffe. Not my world: how could I be in the middle of the bush, yet not in my world?

And yet my heart achieved one of those exotic movements you can sometimes see performed by a spooked racehorse.

I walked to the open door of the office; my shadow fell across her books. 'Jesus.'

'Morning, Caro, I forgot the cheese last night –'

'Jesus, Dan.'

'Yes.'

'I mean, that really is the lamest excuse I ever heard for anything.' She was angry.

'Is that the way to talk to someone who has just risked death simply for the pleasure of seeing you smile?'

'I didn't hear your vehicle.'

'Gone to the airport. I walked.' Pride swelled within me.

'Oh, with Phineas.'

'On my own.'

'On your *own*?'

'Yes.'

She put her head on one side and looked at me. A small switch of hair followed the movement. 'You must be fucking *mad*.' But then I saw a smile climb unbidden to her face. She liked the idea.

I considered this. 'Yes.'

'Do you often do this sort of thing?'

'First time.'

'Did you run into anything?'

'Couple of elephant outside your camp.'

'I mean, this is all deeply mad, Dan.'

Pause. 'I suppose so.'

'I think perhaps we should have a little talk.'

I would not lay claim to any exceptional wisdom in the ways of women and of love, but I knew better than to have little talks. I commenced repeated kissing of her spangled neck. By insensible degrees, 'no' modulated to 'not here'.

'Where?'

'Shop.'

And so, among objects of African fetish, spears, shields, coloured clothes, impala-bearing khaki shirts, bad pictures of animals, pith helmets and Impala Lodge baseball caps, none of your local rubbish, we had our way. 'Joy and triumph everlasting,' Caro said joyfully, 'hath the heavenly church on high.'

'You're right, you're so right.'

'No, you're right, Dan, you're right.'

And so on. And later – not much later – 'Dan, I'm not one of those people that relishes the thrill of imminent discovery.'

'Is that a compliment?'

The emergencies were over, and we were restoring appearances. 'I mean infidelity. Some people have a taste for it, you know. But it makes me feel odd. I don't like it. I mean, I have never been technically unfaithful before.'

'Caro, I never want you to be unfaithful again.'

'Dan. Elaborate.'

But I was wise enough, I think, to say nothing. I held her: infinitely valuable, infinitely fragile, though not her, not her body anyway.

An odd memory assailed me. I thought not of love but a wood. The wood was gone now: a copse not far from our stable yard. It had been a local *cause célèbre*. I had been peripherally involved in petitions and protests, but a road-widening scheme swallowed it up. I had paid a dawn visit to the copse in the last week of its existence, alone, in early spring, and had sat, well-wrapped, beneath a tall oak. I listened to the sharp sibilance of a nuthatch and wondered if I, alone in the world, understood? Was I alone aware of the fragility and the perfection of this place? A melancholy sense of privilege overwhelmed me.

If you sit long enough in such a wood, life reconstructs itself around you. I sat there, as I was to sit for many hours in the ebony glade, still and silent. A small fox, probably a vixen, tiptoed delicately along the fringes of the wood. Run for it, darlin' girl, I radioed silently to her. They're after you. Find another copse before it's too late. If there is one.

They'll soon know how perfect this copse is, or was. As soon as it is gone.

I felt infinitely knowing, infinitely sad. 'I must go, Caro. Go another round with those elephant.'

'Lunatic. Serious, dangerous, certifiable bloody lunatic. Don't forget the cheese.' There was affection in her voice, but it seemed to me then that it was the wrong kind of affection.

No one saw me leave. I had blown it, had I not?

II

North

It was Phineas who had the idea. He was devastated by the news that he was to leave George, after sharing six seasons and more lion than you could count. 'I *know* George,' he said to me. He had joined me for a beer in the sitenji, in itself unusual. 'I don't want to work for a new man. And I don't want George to work with a new scout. Many scouts say George is crazy. I say no. He is better in the bush than anybody. But they laugh and say he wears crazy clothes with holes in, crazy glasses, so he is a crazy man.'

Once again, we had a late cancellation, and four clientless days were to follow the departure of the vegetarians. 'I don't think this season can actually get any worse now,' George said gloomily one morning during the vegetarians' stay. We had completed the walk and the breakfast, and the vegetarians were in their hut, sleeping or making love or whatever clients did during the heat of the day. 'I half suspect Joyce was lying about that booking all along. That's another twenty bed-nights gone.' However, it gave him the chance to offer Phineas a final favour: four days of skiving. For it was also four days before Phineas was required to report to Mvuu's office to be re-assigned. We had to collect our new scout, whoever he was, from the airport that same day, when we picked up a new batch of clients. 'Go and see your family, Phineas,' George had said. 'I'll fill in the time sheet for you, say you were with us all the time.'

'I don't want to leave like that, George.'

'It's very nice of you to say that, Phineas, but we have four clientless days, and there is really not a lot for you to do.'

'Then we go somewhere. Maybe we track lion one more time.'

'Phineas – that's rather a nice idea.'

'I'm game,' I said. 'Any idea where?'

Phineas placed his chin on his hand: long, black and dusty forearm extending from lion-coloured sleeve. 'Last wet season, very late, just before I came back to Lion Camp. Remember, I was tracking the rogue lion after he kill the schoolboy? We followed him north, into the North Park. Never find him. But we find a very good place to camp. Very nice. Many many trees. Very nice area all around. Much game, many buffalo, many-many buffalo. And lion, George, many-many-many lion. At night, we can't sleep. Big fire, big flames to keep them away. Sit up all night, keep the flames high. Best place I have been in the Mchindeni Valley.'

'You know, George, I think that Phineas –'

I stopped talking. George's eyes were looking hard at an infinitely distant point. I waited. Normal service would be resumed as soon as possible.

About five minutes later he began. 'Jerry cans, I've got some. Philip will lend us some more. Food, we can raid the stores here, Joseph can get new supplies. All this contingent on your Land-Rover, Dan. Will it go? And will you lend it to Joseph?'

'Should do. Not a problem.'

'Maps I have, and anyway Phineas knows the way. What else? Mozzie nets from the huts, and we have bedding. Water container, what to use, bugger it. Or no, we can wash that big paraffin container. I knew that would come in handy. Might make the water taste a bit, never mind. So: get the vegetarians onto the plane tomorrow. Go to Mukango, steal Pocock's jerry cans, maybe steal some of our own meat from the deep freeze as well. Back to Mchindeni township. Fill up the vehicle and the jerry cans with fuel, we'll get through a lot. Then bugger off.'

And that, give or take a few small emergencies of George's devising, was how we set off. Joseph was half pleased at being left in sole charge, half miffed at missing the trip. The vegetarians, actually a charming couple, both of them good birders and on their third trip to Africa, had enjoyed their stay with us. We found them lion (the Tondo Pride turned up trumps and knocked down another buffalo) but missed leopard. 'We'll just have to come back to the Mchindeni Valley. This has been the best trip ever. Nothing we've done matches this.'

We set off in mid-afternoon, which meant we would have to camp on the way. The journey could be done without a stop, Phineas reckoned, but there was no point in waiting until the following day to prove it. There was a cut road that led north, but it was hard going; it had been graded, but only with a single cut. The main game-viewing tracks got three cuts. And it was not much travelled. Occasionally, trees had fallen across the road: we bundu-bashed a way around them. 'Traffic-calming measures,' I said.

We camped on the northern boundary of South Mchindeni Park. The boundary was a river, tributary to the Mchindeni, and the crossing looked a bit special, certainly a little too special to do in the half-light of the rapidly falling dusk. So we tried, instead, at sunrise: an invigorating start to the day. Both banks were precipitous, and the flow still deep, even at this stage of the season. The descent was the most exciting part: at one stage I seemed to be standing to attention on the lid of the glove compartment, but George, operating on some private theory of gravity, eventually re-found level going without losing any passengers. In the middle of the river, water rushed into the doorless cab, but that was no matter. Most of it splashed out during the ascent, and at the top, we bailed out and drove north.

The going was now startlingly different. The grader did not cross the river, and the road was marked only by a truck spoor. This gave out after a while. We were in a country without roads and the maps meant very little. For long periods, Phineas ran ahead of the vehicle, finding the way, and George followed. When the country opened up, he swung aboard again.

Eventually, we hit the Mchindeni, narrower here than in the south. We paused for a moment to try and get our bearings. Phineas's face had clouded over. 'Can't you find this camping place, Phineas?'

'It is north.'

'We have cut off an awful lot of the river. Are you sure? Maybe we've gone too far, and it's back south.'

'I think the river comes in very very steep, short way ahead. Then it goes away again. We let the river go, and pass on straight, across a big plain. The river comes back, and that is the nice place.'

'Are you sure?'

'Very sure.'

And so we let the river sweep away, and it was here that the going went from bad to appalling. We hit black cotton soil and our progress was jarring and dreadful. 'Eats the bloody diesel, this stuff,' George shouted above the square-wheeled judder. 'Hope we've got enough.'

'So do I.'

Miles across the plain, a distant thin black line. 'Buffalo!' Phineas called; he was standing high in the back. 'Big herd. Maybe one thousand.'

Ahead, I saw a belt of trees, almost as far away as the buffalo. It was a classic Mchindeni riverine glade. 'There?'

'The river. The nice place.'

An age or so later, the black cotton soil relented, and the trees rose up before us. Phineas dismounted and led us again. 'Can we get the vehicle through the trees, Phineas?'

'No worries.'

He ran on tirelessly into the trees. We followed, bumping over tree roots and spinning out in a series of serpentine turns. I heard the sudden bark of bushbuck.

The trees did not form a solid line along the river's edge. At one point, they stood back courteously, making a little arena. The banks here were high and precipitous, the river flowing beneath. The space had been claimed by the most enormous fig tree I had ever seen, its branches growing an impossible distance from the main trunk: another private theory of gravity. We stood on the crown of a horseshoe bend, which gave us an immense double panorama of river. Beneath the fig tree, I saw five black scars of fires: the scouts build fires in that pattern when they sleep out in alarming country. A goliath heron fished with statuesque majesty in the river; simultaneously, George and I pointed to a tiny blue arrow. 'Malachite kingfisher!' Phineas was smiling as if he had personally created the place, which in a way he had.

'This is all right, this spot.'

'Black egret.'

George was right. There, making a black umbrella of its wings was one of the Mchindeni's more eccentric fishers. 'Eland,' I riposted. There, on the far side of the river, the benign eland: huge antelope that weigh a ton and more, and will never permit you any closer than four hundred yards, unless there is a river in between. There were a dozen of them, male and female, all horned. In a bush full of innocents, these always seemed to me the most innocent of all. I never saw eland without some confused thoughts of Eden: beasts incapable of looking after their own interests in a fallen, much changed world. Lightly, a needle pricked my heart as I thought of sharing such a sight, such a thought with Caro.

'You like, George?'

'This is the nicest of all nice places, Phineas. Thank you for finding it.'

'No worries.'

'Perhaps we should have a cup of tea.'

Phineas and I took the stove and gas cylinder from the vehicle and connected them up, and I set about tea-making. George commenced shuffling about the place, face screwed up, presumably in thought. I wondered what Caro would make of all this. Half of her would love it: but I didn't think that was the half that constituted a majority. Phineas unloaded the three infinitely ancient ammunition boxes that George used for stowing his kit. Tea made, we sat on these, elbows on chest-high knees. 'I don't suppose Joyce will catch us this far north,' I said, passing George one of the old banned mugs, tea-laden. I handed a second mug to Phineas, adding six sugars before I did so.

George did not answer. I looked at him. He was sitting half turned and in profile, watching the river. The sun of late afternoon slanted through the trees and caught him in a cross-light: his face, cross-hatched with lines, looked suddenly weary, suddenly old. It had been a long and hard two days, but I had always thought that George was beyond the normal physical constraints. Now with the Sellotape join in his glasses sagging a little, he seemed nearer sixty than fifty. The self-inflicted crop was growing out fast and uneven. He appeared quite incapable of taking care of his own interests.

He dug into the pockets of his shorts and rummaged about without success. Sighing, he took from a shirt pocket his cigarette machine. He rolled a cigarette, and handed it to me without comment. George was adept at anticipating the occasional moments when a cigarette of crackling bush tobacco was appropriate. He rolled another for himself, lit it, threw me his lighter. I caught it, lit my own, tossed it back. George missed, bent down to pick it up, and an avalanche of stuff: rolling machine, tape recorder, papers, pens, spare tapes, batteries and notebook schussed to the ground.

'Arseholes,' he said gently. 'Honeyguide, stud-post call.' He gathered up his fallen treasures, re-lit his cigarette, stood and walked off into the bush. Phineas and I had another mug of tea. Behind us, the honeyguide implored the world to send him some female company. Phineas began to play I Spy With My Little Ear, a game about putting a name to every sound of the bush.

'Greenshank.'

'Red-billed oxpecker, must be on some hippo in the river.'

'Puffback.'

'Where the hell is George? I thought he'd gone for a pee.'

'Maybe he find something.'

'Do you think we should go and look for him?'

Phineas just laughed, and then said, 'Long-tailed glossy starling.'

The sun sank lower before us. Together, Phineas and I called 'fish eagle' as the triple scream rang out – the last acclamation of territory until the new dawn. We gathered some small sprigs of firewood: we had picked up a useful collection of fallen mopane branches on the way, but we needed kindling before it got too dark. We had, after all, a long night of lion-frightening ahead of us.

'Where the *hell* is George? Do you think I should switch on the spotlight as a beacon, Phineas?'

'Maybe. If he is not back and it is dark.' But Phineas was untroubled, trust in George undented. George was not, in the main, a master of working relationships. Sunday and the rest of the backroom staff were a little wary of him: Joseph's sympathetic ways with the staff were perhaps his greatest asset to the camp. The staff did not really understand George and his preoccupations, and they found it hard to come to terms with his utter lack of dignity. The eccentricity, the vagueness, the glasses put them off. But Phineas saw George in the bush, not in the camp, and he knew George for what he was.

I had got as far as extricating the spotlight from the rest of the kit when I heard George's voice. 'Any chance of a hand, anyone?'

'George?'

'I'm down here.'

Eventually I found him, halfway up the river bank. Phineas and I gave him a hand each and hauled him to the top. 'Thanks.'

'Where have you been, George?'

'Down the river bank. Along the beach. Found some tracks, followed them a bit. May have found something.' He had that irritatingly smug smile that meant he was not going to tell us what he had seen, but whatever it was, he was pretty pleased about it.

'Do you think we should investigate tonight?'

'I thought right now, as a matter of fact.'

'Why not?'

George wanted the vehicle down at the bottom of the river bank. Phineas, after a fair amount of chin-rubbing, remembered a place where the bank flattened out into a series of wide, shallow steps, about two miles downstream. 'Perfect. Then we can cut back up the river, and there we are.'

'Where?'

'We shall have to see.'

We recrossed the Hateful Plain of cotton soil, but on a different course. It was quite dark. But we found Phineas's staircase and the descent was no problem, with Phineas guiding us from the back with the spotlight. Once down, George cut back upstream and north again, asking Phineas to keep the light on the blackness at the bottom of the bank, now rising steep and lofty again. 'Yes. Here.' George halted and switched off the engine. 'Would you pass me the spot, Phineas?' He splashed the beam silently about the bank. 'Nothing. Good. So we wait.'

So we waited, the sounds of the bush all around us: the tinkling of crickets, the bleep of epauletted fruit bat, the scream of a lunatic.

'Pel's fishing owl,' I said. 'Immature.' The sound was described in one of the bird books as 'a lost soul falling down the bottomless pit'.

We waited. I felt my head nodding more than once, for it had indeed been a hard two days. But George was re-invigorated, re-inspired. He played the spot around restlessly, commenting on every sound. 'Scops owl.'

'Yes.'

'Lot of bats.'

'Yes.'

'Why is there never a break in cricket chirps? Does every cricket chirp all night or does one take over the instant another is silent?'

'I don't know.'

'I suppose the thing to do – ah! Good evening, everybody.'

George had caught in the spot a distant shape a couple of hundred yards away, a shape moving, walking beneath the overhang of the bank. It was at the limit of the spot's effectiveness, but there was no problem in diagnosis. Lion. Of course lion, inevitably lion. No mistaking that purposeful slouch. And then behind her, a second lion. And then, behind again, not slouching but bouncing and stumbling, four more. Cubs, two bouncing and two stumbling: they drew level with the vehicle and one of the bouncers flew at one of the grown-up slouchers in a daft ambush, and the two rolled briefly. And onward they walked towards us. At twenty yards' distance, they stopped.

It appeared that there was a small waterhole at the foot of the bank; we could hear clearly the sound of lapping as one of the lionesses crouched down. When she had finished, she lay beside her grown-up companion, and watched as the cubs began their play. And so we watched with them. 'The two small ones are about two months,' George said. 'The other two maybe five months.'

It was a show that went on, it seemed, for ever. They played Ambush and Hunt, they ganged up on each other and then shifted allegiance to betray each other in a new burst of wrestling and tumbling, batting each other mercilessly with their fubsy, cubsy soft paws, hissing and bleating. At one point, one of the lionesses initiated play – George commenting delightedly to his tape recorder – by picking up one of the smaller cubs and tossing him (definite male, George assured me) into the air, to land on her upturned chest. She was promptly submerged beneath a tidal wave of paws.

'I don't think lion can bear the thought of life without physical contact,' George said.

For a second I wondered if I could myself. And then, as if a referee's whistle had blown, the game was over. One of the lionesses stood and led the rest of the group away, up a steep hippo staircase to the top of the bank.

'George,' I said. 'That was too bloody good. I mean, that was genius. How did you know they would be there?'

'Thought I'd go down the bank and have a look after I'd had my cup of tea. Just check for tracks on the riverbed, you know. Cast about for a while. And then I found lion tracks, really fresh, and so I followed them. Came across this place, the ground all stirred up, and a few clear cub prints among them. So I wondered if they would come back. You know how lion have favourite places, unlike leopard, and that's especially true, or at least, it *seems* especially true when they have cubs, and they're restricted to a smaller range, of course, because less mobile. I have often known them visit the same place each night. It's not absolutely reliable, but then that's lion for you, isn't it? Never terribly good at keeping to rules. But I thought this place was worth staking out.'

He turned the key to start the engine, but it didn't. 'Oh dear. I suppose the spot has drained the battery. We have been here rather a long time, haven't we?' Phineas and I jumped off and gave the vehicle a shove. It started after the briefest of efforts, for it was a very willing beast.

Back at camp, I cooked a large curry, not as good as Sunday's, but the location added a certain savour. Phineas built a fire, and we sat around it afterwards drinking tea.

Eventually, I spoke about the matter, or one of the matters, that had been on my mind for some days. 'George?'

'Yes?'

'Am I really a bad safari guide?'

George looked shocked. 'Who says so?'

'You know. Mvuu.'

'Oh yes, I'd forgotten about him, silly old sod.'

'Well, it worried me. Did you hear about that, Phineas?'

'I hear you had a big telling-off. But Mvuu is not with you in the bush. And I know. No worries. With you there is not a problem.'

'Thanks, Phineas. Because Mvuu – well, he worried me.'

'I don't see why,' George said.

'I'll tell you something. I really like trail leading. I didn't think I would. It was just an excuse for staying out in the bush. But I really enjoy taking people into the bush, getting them excited, making them understand. And when they get the point – well, it's great, isn't it? But am I really all right at it?'

'Well, you took the vegetarians out more than I did. What sort of a stay did they have?'

'They said they loved it.'

'There you are then. And they were birders and you showed them a lot of birds; you've come on a whole lot there. You've always had pretty good knowledge of large mammals. You've learned a lot about plants from Joseph, well, so have

I, for that matter. You'll re-pass your exam with any fair examiner, even if you don't do a scrap of work from now until the end of the season.'

'Thanks, George.' A silence, filled with the sounds of the night. 'What about the rest of what Mvuu said?'

'What about?'

'About you losing Lion Camp.'

'Oh, I don't know that he was very serious. Throwing his weight around. All blow over.'

'He sounded very serious to me.'

'I shouldn't worry about it.'

I laughed monosyllabically. 'If the worst comes to the worst we could always move out here.'

'Ha.' George made a cigarette, then gave it to me, rolled another for himself. 'I did a little calculation on that. It is perfectly possible, you know. But we will need a second vehicle, and it will have to be a good one. Then we will need a new licence to operate in the North Park, and we shall have to find staff prepared to work out here. That will probably mean untrained staff, so we will have to train them. We will need three months to build a proper camp. And we will need to put the clients up somewhere in the South Park, as far north as possible, so we can break the journey from the airport. So we need some kind of a concession from one of the other camps. And after *that*, the only problem is finding actual clients. Joyce won't stand for setting up in a place like this, and that means Bruce won't. So that means I would lose my partner and the office in Chipembere, and all the contacts with the travel trade in London and so on.'

'You've thought about it then?'

'Oh, thought. Thought. You remember what Philip was saying. And it is possible all right; all we really need is the goodwill of everybody in the Mchindeni Valley, a completely new organisation and about a million kolwe. Couldn't do it for less.'

'Oh.'

The lion-frightening fire was by now a thing of beauty.

Phineas slept beside it with his gun close. I woke twice in the night to find him feeding the flame with more wood.

I had never known such a night for lion music.

III

South

I

Vultures.

In the crown of a thorn tree surveying the thirsty country.

George Sorensen, emaciated, more markedly senescent, as ever leotropic, pointed them out to our last paying clients of the season and spoke the word: 'Lion.'

'Oh boy.'

Vegetation the colour of lion, scarcely a decent mouthful to be had for a herbivore, and even my zebra looked, like George, a little careworn. Only carnivores prospered now, lazily knocking down the weakened buck and buffalo as they skulked their frightened way down to water.

The eating was good for all non-vegetarians, the bush seemed to be heaving with round-bellied carnivores, and pleasing clients had never been so easy. We were dealing with a pair of old boys engaged, like striped kingfishers, in a constant cross-talking duet. They had never before been out of Europe, and we had them spellbound.

'Have you got your camera, you silly old man?'

'I'm taking a picture right now, you blind old fool.'

The heat and dust were prodigious now, but the old boys had walked well, without complaint, constantly stirred by the wonders we found for them. The thermometer hit 40, or if you prefer, 104, by eleven each day. But Bill and Dougie, parched and dried-up characters themselves, took these discomforts in stride. 'This dry heat has taken ten years out of my bones.'

'So you feel like you're only ninety-two, you senile old dodderer?'

The calendar claimed that it was the end of the season, but the skies gave no sign. Not a threat, not a hint of rain; each morning brought only another day of shimmering, eye-baffling heat.

The vultures were plainly visible, despite the hovering heat haze and the dust-laden air. 'We should walk a little closer to the lion, don't you think?' George asked.

'Holy Dinah,' Dougie said, addicted as he was to some eccentric Americanisms; we learned that he had lived most of his life in Canada.

'We'll go in, shall we?'

'Ah, George?'

This was Aubrey, our scout. He had been with us two months and more: ever since our return from the North Park and the Nice Place. Short and round-faced, he had none of Phineas's insouciant ways. 'Well, Aubrey?'

'Is very dangerous.'

'No, Aubrey. It's potentially hazardous.'

'Very very dangerous.'

'I suggest we move as far as the termite mound. That is two hundred yards from the tree with the vultures, therefore at least two hundred yards from any lion that may lie beneath it. So let us go as far as that and assess the situation.' Of the company, only I knew that George was in a towering rage. With George, pedantry was temper.

Out-faced in front of clients, Aubrey worked the bolt of his rifle to put a round up the spout. Then, a caricature of stealth, he led us towards the termite mound. George strolled after him, talking about vultures and scavenging behaviour in ringing conversational tones. 'It's a waiting game, of course, and a very long wait, because hyenas wait for the lions, so the vultures must wait for the hyenas, but there's a huge feed at the end of it all . . .'

George walked to the top of the termite mound, outlining himself against the sky, to Aubrey's hissed disapproval. 'Something bloody big,' he observed. 'Don't think it's buff. My God, I think they've got a hippo. We'll go in, shall we?'

But here, Aubrey put his foot down. Not a step further would he go. Very very dangerous. George descended, and while he and Aubrey debated humiliatingly, I took Bill and Dougie up the termite hill and pointed out the distant group. To those who lacked bush-accustomed eyes, there was nothing much to see. A black shape, like a small grounded Zeppelin, and some lighter, smaller, sand-coloured shapes all around. Even through binoculars, the riddle was hard to read.

'Well, Aubrey advises against it, and a scout is responsible for our safety, of course,' George announced. 'Very experienced and wise in the bush, Aubrey is, so we must do as he says. After lunch we will come back here in a vehicle, which is quite a different matter. We should be able to get some pretty remarkable views. The National Parks Commission doesn't require a scout to accompany a party in a vehicle, because it is so much safer, am I right, Aubrey?'

'Yes, George,' Aubrey said sulkily, not quite having the nerve to say 'not the way you drive, George.' He led us back – in point of fact, he should have asked me or George to lead, and kept the gun between clients and danger, but Aubrey was incapable of asking us anything – at a brisk pace, away from the hidden lion. Covertly, so that only George could see, I made a pistol of two fingers and shot Aubrey in the back.

We walked back to camp for breakfast.

As the four of us sat around the table in the sitenji eating mealie-meal porridge with honey, Dougie and Bill glowed with the delight of it all. They were unaware of our disappointment, unaware of what they might have seen that morning. They were not only new to Africa, they had never looked at or even thought much about wildlife. Curiosity and ignorance fought for priority at every meal. 'And all Africa is like this? Full of huge animals?'

'Well, it's not, actually,' George said. 'An awful lot of it is cattle-farming country. But you can't raise cattle in the Valley because it's full of tsetse flies, so the place got left alone. So it kept its big animals. But it's a ghetto, really. We're surrounded by civilisation. There are very few places left for animals to go. They are running out of places.'

'But this place is safe? Safe for ever?'

'Of course it is, you silly old fool, or we wouldn't be here.'

'It might not be safe much longer,' I said. 'It certainly won't be the same. The Ministry of Transportation and the Ministry of National Resources confirmed last week that they will build a road straight through the middle of the park. They start work in six months, at the beginning of the next dry season. It'll have a big effect. Settlers, poachers, disturbance, disruption. Enjoy it while it's here; you might be the last people to see the park as it was meant to be.'

'How much danger were we in? When we saw those lion?' Dougie asked. It was clear that he wanted to hear that we had been in terror of our lives.

'Seems to me that we weren't in any danger from those lions,' Bill said. 'It is not as if the lions are building roads and carrying guns, is it? It seems to me that the ones in danger are the lions.'

'Very astute, that,' George said.

I didn't tell the story of the definite male; George and I had decided that this was a not-in-front-of-the-clients story. Nor, for the same reason, did I talk about my own solo crossing of the Mchindeni. I had not repeated the adventure. In fact, I seldom thought about doing so any more: no more frequently than, say, a dozen times a day, anyway. The crossing, shallower and narrower than ever, can scarcely have been ankle-high. Never had Impala Lodge been so accessible.

'Is it really just you and George that run this camp?' Dougie asked. He had a persistent curiosity about domestic arrangements, and needed to know how everything worked.

'Oh yes. Very compact operation, this.'

'It must rain soon,' George said. 'I mean, it must. It was 38 when we got back from the walk, and barely gone nine. It'll beat 40 today, I think.'

'I'll take six to four,' I said. 'But listen, chaps, we're going to show you some very hot lion after lunch. Don't worry about that, they'll still be there all right. That kill will keep them there for a couple of days.'

'Well, I hope you remember to take the lens cap off your camera this time, you old fool.'

'Hell, did I leave the camera in the hut?'

'It's on the bar, Dougie.'

'Holy Dinah, I thought I left it out on the trail.'

Eventually, the Old Boys fussed their way to huts and showers and matutinal siestas, leaving George and me to discuss the eternal practical problems. We were low on vegetables, low on beer. We were also low on meat; even in gas fridges, meat went off fast at this ferocious time of year. We still had a chicken and some beef in the deep freeze at Mukango. 'Maybe we should take the Old Boys for an all-day drive across the park tomorrow. Visit Mukango, buy them a beer. Lunch on the way. Sundowners on the way back. Plenty of game. Night drive, back here for supper.'

'They'll get well roasted.'

'We can take it easy, plenty of stops, plenty of shade. But if they don't fancy it, I'll drive in first thing tomorrow, if you like, while you take the walk. Or vice versa, if you prefer. But one of us better call the office and see if there's news about those bloody journalists.'

Joyce had mentioned casually during the last telephone call that she 'might' have a party of ten journalists to visit us at the end of the week, a possibility that left me reeling. 'Don't worry too much. Joyce threatens me with journalists at some point every year. They've never turned up yet.'

'That can only mean it's a certainty this time.'

'Oh God. I really think that would be the worst thing that could happen.'

'Never mind. At least we've got some certain lion to show the Old Boys this afternoon.'

'*Bloody* Aubrey.'

'Constipated owl.'

We set out for the afternoon drive Aubrey-less. I put Dougie on the front seat; it was easier on the spine than the back, and we wanted the Old Boys to last out. George drove straight for the thorn tree and the vultures. Bill, beside me on the back, shouted: 'I suppose your camera's back in the hut.'

'No, it isn't, it's right here. Did you remember your bus pass?'

'Here are the vultures again, chaps,' I said. I was now standing high on the spare wheel. 'Lion beneath. Lion everywhere. The whole pride's here – hello! George, stop for one moment while I use the glasses.' I climbed onto the seat, focused, and grinned. 'We have an alpha situation,' I said to George cryptically.

'How splendid.'

George turned off the track and bundu-bashed towards the kill. We found an uncrossably deep watercourse winding across our line of advance, and the bushes began to grow thicker. It was a little like driving through Hampton Court maze. We drove on until we found a crossing place, and made it with the usual clang and rattle, the Old Boys holding on gamely. I stood high, to make sure we didn't accidentally drive over a lion. Not quite *Manual*-conscious bush driving, this. Lord knows what Aubrey would have said.

I smelt, rather than saw our objective: a terrible black stench of death and corruption. I called George to slow down and to ease past the next clump of bushes. The manoeuvre brought us a sight straight from hell.

Caro had commented on the paradoxical gentleness of lion on a kill. But there was nothing remotely gentle about this. Blood-blackened skull of hippo, buzzing with flies in the appalling heat of late afternoon. And there, lolling beside it, was the alpha male of the Tondo Pride: a huge and self-willed beast who came and went as he pleased. Already, round-bellied, he had withdrawn from the kill. No lion keep to their own rules: this one broke the lot. A black-maned monster, he stared into the vehicle with implacable yellow eyes, pupils tiny round dots in the glare of this ferocious light.

There was no leonine circle of amity at this kill: the lion had made an entrance at the neck, which only two animals could share. The skin of a hippo is too thick for a lion to deal with comfortably. Lion, *vide* Sorensen and Norrie, have no peck order, and so must snarl and slap for a place to feed. The ground was black with blood. Most of the pride, lying around uncomfortably full, had eaten already, but there was a colossal amount of meat left: a great stinking bomb of flesh.

We sat there for half an hour, roasting, enthralled. One of the lion pulled herself reluctantly to her feet and defecated liberally. Scarcely had she walked away when a vulture, descending from the tree with a sound like a falling umbrella, was devouring the steaming globes. The air was thick with the buzzing of flies.

I heard a new sound: an engine. 'Not again,' I said softly. But yes. There, bouncing over the broken terrain and faithfully following in our wheel tracks, came a shining new Land Cruiser, its driver, baseball-capped and epigamically moustached, was inevitably Leon, van der bloody Aardvark. 'Every bloody time,' I muttered into George's ear in front of me. 'I can't bear it.'

'You must take the broad view,' George said, inaudible to our absorbed, though still bickering clients. 'Look on it as comensalism.'

'I look on it as klepto-parasitism,' I said, as the shining vehicle sidled coyly up to our own.

'Afternoon, you guys. Quite a sight, this.'

'Hello, Leon. We'll be off in a minute.'

'Suits us.' He grinned amiably back at his truckload of eight clients, all gazing raptly at our private vision of hell. 'Hope all's well with you lot.'

'Fine.'

Leon could hardly be friendlier. He turned to me. 'Caroline said to say hi, if we saw you.'

'Say hi back.'

'She said to say something. What was it? Some crazy thing. Yes, asked if the wood owl was still calling at your place.'

I felt as if I had been struck lightly in the solar plexus. 'Nope. Died out. Gone extinct, tell her.'

'I'll do that.'

'Bye, Leon.'

We bundu-bashed back to the track. I leant forward and muttered to George again: '*Bloody* van der Aardvark.'

'Dan.'

'Well. He comes over the river every other day now. Every time we find a kill, he comes trundling up behind us with a lorryload of fat rich bastards and a million quids' worth of camera equipment. We've become his bloody bird dogs.'

'You can't blame him. This is the best area in the park, better than anything on his side. What was he saying about wood owl?'

'Nothing.'

'Oh.'

'And don't bloody "oh" me, either.'

'Of course not, Dan.'

But what was I to make of this message, enigmatic, to say the least. Was it a coded summons to leap across the Mchindeni? I thought not. It was probably a piece of meaningless banter, a token of 'friendly' relations. Or perhaps a tease, friendliness spiced with a token of malice. A subtle relishing of power: that was it.

Ever since Caro's visit to Lion Camp, I had been a martyr to peritonitis. But it was an odd version of the disease. It struck for periods of about, say, 0.25 seconds. By one of those rum coincidences, the attacks of this brief but utterly debilitating illness occurred at the same time as the casual mention of Caro's name by another, or by the unpremeditated thought of her. Of late, I had imagined the condition had improved, but the mention of wood owl did me no good at all. What did she mean? *Bloody* van der Aardvark.

Over sundowners, George gave a lecture on lion to the Old Boys, proceeding to their antagonistic relationship with hyena. Darkness fell with its usual startling promptness. I gathered up the empty Lion bottles and attached the spotlight to the battery. George stretched. 'Why don't you drive, Dan?'

'Do you think your eyes are still good enough to spot?'

I asked. The conversational habits of Bill and Dougie were catching.

'You just make sure you don't get the vehicle stuck.'

'Boy oh boy,' Dougie said. 'I just loved that night drive last night. Will we see leopard tonight?'

'With George as spotter, it's a certainty,' I said, and let in the clutch with a jerk intended to throw George off his feet. Behind me, I heard him laugh.

An hour later, George had a leopard bang in the middle of the beam.

'Holy Dinah.'

'Shut up, you old fool.'

A male, this, broad-headed and gorgeous. There is nothing quite as much fun, in a purely sporting sense, as following a leopard hunt. The secret is teamwork between spotter and driver. 'Far side. Stop. Left. Come back. Stop. There he is again.'

The leopard vanished and reappeared, melting down impossible gullies, flickering through the trunks of trees in a glade, us following, roaring and clumsy, making wild circles and detours as the leopard passed where we could not follow. 'It's thinner ahead. Go round and cut him off.'

I followed the beam. A roar from the engine, a fight with the wheel. 'Can I get through here?'

'Try.' Scrapes, clatters and clangs. 'Down everybody! Down! Well done, Dan, now go!'

We kept in touch with every twist and turn. Brilliant work this, nothing less. And then we had him, belly-down and a statue. Ready to charge.

Observe. Never interfere. Cardinal rules. Rules of the park, but more than that, rules that George and I believed in, and invariably followed. You don't interfere in a hunt. George shone the spotlight away from the leopard: but we kept him faintly in view, at the far edge of the beam of the headlights. Ahead, I could make out something else: small patches of whiteness, a pattern meaningless to non-bush-accustomed eyes. But I saw impala. And so did the leopard.

We waited in silence for maybe twenty minutes. Then the leopard was gone. George re-found him in a moment, and this time the charge was on: blinding acceleration, and then he vanished. A moment later, he sprang *through* the beam of light: and it was a leopard's death spring.

I had the engine on in an instant – the kindly vehicle started at first touch for once – and crawled, discretion in every revolution of the wheel, along the length of George's beam of light. At the end of it, at the bottom of a long slope, holding an impala in loving embrace of spotted immaculate paws, leopard. I halted at a discreet couple of hundred yards, engine still on, intending a closer advance if the leopard permitted.

And then, from the left flank of the vehicle, from where, in fact, it had been using our passage as cover, a single hyena, breaking into a sloppy hyena's gallop, grinning hard and heading straight for the leopard. The leopard saw this at once, and with a bound he was away, leaving the dead impala behind as he made a single gravity-defiant leap into the tree behind him. The hyena, as always, had won without a fight.

'Bastard!' I found myself yelling. 'Bastard!'

And I was driving like a crazy man, bucketing down the slope, straight through bushes and eradicating a small tree, and the hyena, seeing this demented roaring dragon bearing down upon him, he – more likely she, I observed, even in the midst of this madness, this being as large and as solid a hyena as you would find in the Valley – turned to snatch something from the carcass and was gone.

I stopped. George steadied the beam. I saw that in the instant of realising her theft was to be interrupted, the hyena had reached into the belly of the impala and snatched from it a small and perfect foetus, dashing into the bush with the soft and floppy thing dangling from nutcracker jaws.

Back at camp, I apologised at length and humbly to the Old Boys for this madcap run. I was deeply ashamed. For this was perfectly appalling behaviour, towards clients far from young, and towards the bush. 'No, you had to do it,' Bill said. 'I would have done the same thing. The leopard did all the work. He deserved his kill. You had to drive the hyena off.'

'The hyena will have gone straight back to the impala as soon as we pulled out,' George said. 'Dan knows that as well as I do.'

'I got a bit carried away,' I said. 'I really am most dreadfully sorry.' I didn't say what I really felt: a kind of cosmic rage at the unfairness of life: a fury that the leopard should lose out to a cleverer but less lovely creature.

'I'm rather glad you did it,' George said. 'I've never seen anything quite like it. Not just your driving. I mean the way the hyena worked out, in a fraction of a second, that the impala ewe was pregnant, that there was a real threat, and that the quickest way of salvaging anything from the carcass was to remove the foetus – and then to perform the, ah, Caesarian in about a quarter of a second ... I'd like to do some serious work on hyena, what do you say, Dan?'

'Why not?'

'They really are rather wonderful things. That was the most perfect example of klepto-parasitism I have ever seen.'

2

George, Phineas and I returned in great content from our trip to the North Park, the Nice Place and the fubsy cubs. I drove all the way back, a journey which we did in a single long day, setting off before dawn and arriving shortly before dark. We had dropped Phineas off at his village before hurrying back to the park and home. The worries provoked by Mvuu's interview at Impala Lodge had perceptibly sloughed away. We would manage, surely. 'God, I need a Lion,' I said, as I turned into camp and halted beside my own battered vehicle, switching off the engine with a pleasant feeling of finality. 'Joseph!' I roared. It was odd that he had not come out to meet the vehicle, but I saw him emerge from his hut, blinking. 'Ah, good evening, Joseph, you must have had a new letter from Gianna. I can see the bags under your eyes.'

'Hullo, George. Hullo, Dan.' There was trouble in his face.

'What's up, Joseph, have you bent my Land-Rover? Jesus, I need a beer before you break it to me. Is it salvageable? Will it ever go again?' It stood, tall and boxy, its hideous yellow mercifully muted by a thick covering of dust.

'OK, I will get some beers.' Joseph vanished into the kitchen.

'Something's up,' I said. 'Do you think Joyce has sacked him?'

'She can't do that. Anyway, how could she have been in touch? Perhaps he's ill. Maybe he's got malaria. I don't suppose he's got prophylactics.'

'Not for malaria, anyway.'

I took a brief stroll around the Land-Rover. It seemed to have no new dents, the lights were all unbroken save the off-hind, which I had broken myself on a Zimbabwean tree, and there was no ominous patch of fluid on the ground beneath.

That was good enough to be going along with. I kicked one of the tyres affectionately, and walked into the sitenji in search of George, Joseph and Lion.

'How was your trip?'

'Brilliant. Phineas took us to a perfect campsite, saw lots of game, brilliant views of lion cub. How's things here?'

Joseph's face was almost a cartoon of anguish. 'George, you gave me the chance to work in the Park. I owe you everything.'

'Hardly. But – er, elaborate.'

'I have been offered a job, George, and I don't know what to do.'

George cocked his head to listen to the dusky chorus of cape turtle doves in the ebony trees behind us. He seemed to have no interest in Joseph's distress. I half expected him to start counting the doves. Eventually, he recollected himself, and said amiably: 'Well, Joseph, I should take it, if I were you. I expect it pays a great deal more money than you get now; it could hardly pay much less, after all.'

'But I am letting you down.'

'You've worked awfully hard and awfully well all season. You know you are officially on trial at a week's notice either way, that's the standard National Parks contract for a trainee, and it is supposed to work both ways. So there isn't really a problem, is there? Ah, there's a red-eyed dove among them, isn't there?'

'But, George, I don't want to leave this company. I don't want to let you down. I owe you so much.'

'Well, that's very flattering, thank you, but you owe me nothing that you haven't repaid already. I can't afford to pay you any more. The company, as you know, has certain problems, and I can't guarantee anybody a job for next season. We're not a good bet for an ambitious young man. You must do whatever you think best.' George turned his head away altogether at this and stared piercingly at the canopy of the ebony glade. In the distance, I heard the triple scream of fish eagle. Then silence.

'What's the job, Joseph? Trainee safari guide somewhere?'

'No, Dan. Personnel manager. Dan, it's many times the money I am getting. It's a European salary.'

'Bloody good. Well done. Joseph, you have to go for it.'

'I don't know, Dan. I want to be a trail leader. They say they will make sure I get my qualification, but I don't know if I will still take clients out into the bush. But it's money, Dan. It's a lot.'

'I know, Joseph, and you've got ageing parents to look after, and that has to be your first responsibility. We understand that.'

'I don't want to do it, Dan. But I have to.'

'You've got to do what's right, Joseph,' I said. George now had his binoculars out, and was looking in the opposite direction. A thought occurred to me. 'Who's offering you this job then, Joseph?'

His face fell again, and he would not meet my eyes. 'Leon.'

'Jaysis, I should have had a bet!' I stood, consumed by rage. 'I should have put the focken mortgage on it. *Bloody* van der Aardvark. And how did he *know* you're so good with staff? That's what I want to know. How did he find out?'

'An academic question, Dan,' said George. 'But surely a hypothesis springs to mind. We did, after all, have a representative of his organisation in camp for twenty-four hours. The grey-headed bush shrike is quite close, shall we take a look at him? It's still light enough, just about.'

After a short while I found I was capable of speech. 'Why not?'

Over the evening meal, a better curry than I had cooked in the Nice Place, George told Joseph that he was free to leave whenever he wished. 'I know you have a week's notice. But in the nicest possible way, there's nothing to keep you here. The sooner you start earning that nice new salary, the better. We won't get in your way.'

In the end, we decided that Joseph would drive my Land-Rover back to Mukango the following morning, and we would tell any of the Impala Lodge people we met at the airport to pick him up there. That night, Joseph and I stayed up late, sitting on the 'comfortable' chairs on the river bank. Isaac had made no fire, since we were clientless. We sat around the ashes and drank Lion. George and I would miss him, I said. So would Auntie Joyce. And what would I do when I needed a *Ballanites* bush in a hurry? We talked on, and talk got more serious.

'I feel so bad about leaving George, Dan. Business is not good. I want to help him.'

'So do I.'

'But you *can* still help him.'

'I wish I could.'

'Why don't you do something, Dan? Sort the company out? You know George can't do it.'

'If you can think of anything I should do, tell me, and I'll do it.'

'Yes. You and George. Too similar. I wanted to be like you and George. But now I am going to Impala Lodge. And it will all be different.'

Eventually, Joseph reeled off to his bed. He was happier than he had been earlier in the day, assured that we bore him no ill will. I sat up a while longer myself, listening to the passage of the night. Not happier.

George and I took the Land Cruiser to the airport the following morning. We had to meet a family of three off the plane; also we had to find our new scout, replacement for the departed Phineas.

George and I set off, me anxious to discuss the situation, George apparently quite untroubled as we bounced our way through the park to the airport. I was all for swearing eternal vendettas myself. 'Joseph's a good man, an exceptional man. So what could we do? We could hardly hope to hold on to him for ever.'

It was, I suppose, inevitable that we walked straight into Leon as we arrived at the airport. Lloyd the Stringer was with him; there was no sign of Caro. Left to myself, I would have cut him dead, or maybe made a scene. George merely greeted them, no more or less vaguely than usual. Leon, however, stood foursquare in front of us both.

'George, I have some words to say.'

'It's all right, Leon, it's not necessary.'

'It is necessary, man. I don't want any bad feelings. I made an offer to one of your staff, but I don't want to do it behind your back. I don't want this to be seen as an act of poaching. There is too much of that in the Valley. It is unacceptable if one camp has a good barman, and then another camp offers him a job as a bloody barman. I have asked Joseph to join my company as an executive, not a trainee safari guide. He will be the first African in the Valley to work in a tourist operation with executive status. That is an opportunity you could not give him. And the boy has earned the opportunity. He is too bloody good to waste.'

'Leon, it's perfectly all right. He goes with my best wishes for his future.'

'Listen to the point I am making, George. I don't want you to think I am being deceitful. I do nothing behind any man's back. I am an upfront guy, you know that. And I want you to see that I am not doing a bad thing, I am doing the right thing.'

'I'm sure you are, Leon.'

'All right then, George. Let's shake on that.' He offered George a big, meaty paw.

'Oh . . . ah.' George eventually got the hang of what Leon wanted, and had his hand wrung for him in Leon's fearfully virile clasp. I remembered, as George did not, to tell Leon that Joseph would be waiting for him at Mukango. Eventually, we got away.

'It's one thing poaching our staff,' I said. 'But I draw the line at considering him a hero for doing it.'

'Well, it's quite a brave thing, actually,' George said. 'I don't suppose anyone else in the Valley would do it. Ah, they're coming off the plane now. You get the sign and round up the clients, I'll try and find the scout.'

'I'll round them up, unless bloody van der Aardvark gets there first,' I said.

'And God forbid you should try and take anything of his.'

George padded away, leaving me without an opportunity of replying. I gathered the embarrassing sign, and took my place alongside the other safari guides awaiting clients. This was a routine time for some serious banter. Lloyd, as it happened, was beside me. He had seen a grass owl the previous night.

'Quite sure it wasn't a barn owl?' I asked provokingly, and received a flood of self-justifying detail.

'Christ, look at those two fat bastards,' said one of Philip Pocock's star guides, standing by his Mukango Lodge sign. 'Won't get anyone else in the vehicle if they're ours.'

'They'll need a hut each if they're coming to your camp, Dan,' said Lloyd.

'Oh my God, look at the babe!' said Pocock's man. 'Come to Mukango, baby. Come and see what I can show you out in the bush.'

'She's ours,' Lloyd said. 'I can tell these things. She has that Impala look in her eyes.'

'Forget it,' I said. 'Once Joseph moves in, you'll have no chance. Do clients lie down for Joseph, or what?'

The procession of tourists wound its way across the tarmac and in through the open double doors, and we all put on our best professional faces and prepared to greet. Friendly but with a background of seriousness. Cool in the Bush. Lloyd got the fat bastards.

'Lion Safaris?'

'Hello, I'm Dan Lynch, welcome to Lion Safaris, Mr and Mrs Gould? And party?'

'I'm Michael, my wife Jean. This is my daughter, Louise.' Well, well, well. A young lady of serious lost-doggy potential. Small, dark, composed. I took her hand and received an unexpectedly assertive response. 'Let's get your luggage, and then we'll be off in the vehicle . . .' I managed at the baggage claim to mutter briefly to Lloyd: 'Tell Joseph we have a client more beautiful than Gianna.'

'Gianna? Right.'

George had found the scout, too, which gave us a win-double for the trip. Or perhaps not. The scout turned out to be the round-faced Aubrey. I felt from the first meeting that there was something amiss. He was an odd mixture of deference and defiance: of cringing and stroppiness. He lacked the self-assurance of such emancipated Africans as Phineas and Joseph; he had none of the know-your-place sycophancy demanded of Africans in colonial times. Aubrey was caught for ever halfway between the two: as it were, an awkward adolescent caught in a prolonged fit of the sulks.

It took, as it does, about ten minutes on the trail to discover that Aubrey was not Cool in the Bush. He walked hunched over his gun, eyes slithering about the place, a palpable air of tension about him. For him, enemies lurked behind every tree and every brake, in every hollow and behind every rise. He was not restful company on a walk. He was not only quite absurdly wary, he was also perfectly useless at spotting genuine sources of potential danger as well.

George and I took the first walk with him together, with Michael, Jean and Louise, and, as I walked behind Aubrey, I remember wondering if he had actually seen the three elephant that stood ahead of us, mostly hidden in a small stand of trees, all contentedly munching on leaves and certainly quite unaware of us. Perhaps, I wondered, I had done him an injustice, and he was about to reveal himself as Cool in the Bush after all. But perhaps he had simply failed to notice them. Rather naughtily, I decided to wait and see; call it a controlled experiment. When we were about thirty yards away, Aubrey saw them. He performed a glorious Chaplinesque double-take, and led us away in an absolutely massive diversion, with me giggling objectionably behind him at every step. 'We must go, we must go now. Is very very dangerous, very very dangerous.'

'It's potentially hazardous, Aubrey,' George had corrected. We were to learn Aubrey's catchphrase: 'unworried'. This was his highest form of praise for any living creature. 'The buffalo are unworried,' he would say, as well they might be, considering they were so far from us they were virtually in North Mchindeni National Park. Whenever a remotely dangerous animal appeared – and Aubrey spotted it – he would jack a round into the breech and make a huge circle away from it. 'Aubrey, we're supposed to show our clients the bush. That's what they're here for. That's what they're *paying* for. They want to see big animals, not avoid them.'

'Is very very dangerous.'

On Aubrey's second morning, we saw a plume of smoke rising above a stand of trees. It was clear that we had run across a group of poachers. Very foolish, or very inexperienced poachers: to build a fire in daylight, and so near a tourist camp was asking for discovery. Aubrey, very het up, decided he had to go in and sort them out. He set off on his own, leaving me with Michael, who found a certain agreeable dry humour in the situation, and Jean and Louise, sitting on the river bank for thirty minutes. It would have been an uncomfortable period in which to meet a hippo or an angry elephant, but we did not. Then I heard three rifle shots fill the bush with their din and echo. 'Jaysis, the focken Russians have landed,' I said, reminded of my father's irritation when shotgun blasts spooked his horses.

Ten minutes later Aubrey reappeared, grinning in great delight. 'They have gone, all of them. We must capture their equipment, the fish. Everything.'

He led us to the poachers' abandoned camp. Pathetic enough: there were just a couple of baskets of fish, which they had been drying over the fire, and a few nets. This was a simple operation, a few men from nearby villages, not a big syndicate financed from Chipembere. Just a few unarmed fishermen who had run like rabbits from Aubrey's rifle. 'Shot in the air to frighten them,' he explained happily, and several times.

'*Three* warning shots?'

'Yes, of course.'

'Of course.'

Aubrey and I carried the fish and the gear back to camp, and all the backroom staff came out to inspect and to pass comment. 'Bad net, not good.'

'Basket is nice.'

Aubrey told the story of their seizure once again.

'Hey, Aubrey,' said Sunday, in English so that I would understand. 'How come you did not catch the poachers? Did they have guns too?'

'It is my job to fire a warning only. It is the instructions of Mr Mvuu. Now I must take the captured items to Mr Mvuu as soon as possible. I must be driven to Mr Mvuu as soon as possible.'

'How come you didn't catch the poachers, Aubrey?' asked Sunday again, roaring with laughter. 'Maybe you are worried they will attack you. Hit you with a fish maybe.'

Sunday laughed as if he would never stop. Aubrey was utterly outraged. 'My job!' he said. 'It is my job to do what I have done.' And he turned and marched off in stiff-legged anger.

'Quick, Sunday,' I said. 'Grab some of those bloody fish. Grab a lot, quick, before bloody Aubrey gets back. Take some for your relish tonight, and make a nice fish supper for the clients.'

Sunday was entranced at the beauty of this officially sanctioned piracy, and plunged his arms deep into the nearest basket. 'Bloody Aubrey,' he said, starting to laugh again.

Over lunch, the incident was, of course, discussed in detail. It was then that Michael came up with what inevitably became Aubrey's secret nickname. 'What's the difference,' he asked, 'between Aubrey and a constipated owl?'

'I don't know.'

'One hoots but can't shit.'

3

Eland were one of the few large mammals that did not bring
Aubrey to a crisis of personal courage. The morning after my
mad charge at the klepto-parasitic hyena, I found a herd for
Bill and Dougie. I had volunteered to take the rest of the
season's walks, and George had gratefully accepted the offer.
After the walk when we found the hippo kill, he had reached
a state in which even the sight of Aubrey was enough to induce
silent rage.

As I was to tell George later out of the clients' hearing, I
suspect that eland were Aubrey's favourite animals, since they
never let you come closer than four hundred yards. So I showed
Bill and Dougie the small herd – I counted eleven – and lectured
them on flight and safety. I observed them through my binoculars; they returned my distant gaze with sad and wondering
eyes.

'If they don't like us why don't they just butt out?' Dougie
asked. 'How come they stay there?'

'If an animal in the bush ran off at top speed every time it
caught a whiff of danger, it would never stop running. The
smart thing to do is to watch your enemy from a safe distance.
Keep your eye on him.'

I really was a great safari guide, was I not? The Old Boys
were entranced by the eland, and excited by my explanation.
Hear that, Mvuu?

'I see,' said Bill. 'Know your enemy.'

'Exactly,' I said, pleased. 'And if we move forward ten yards,
the eland will almost certainly retreat another ten. We'll try it
in a minute, but let's watch them while we have such good
views. Another point, of course, is that if they ran off at top

speed, they could run straight into a pride of lion. So they're doing the sensible thing.'

'Are they really so smart?' Dougie asked. 'If I had a rifle, I could pick 'em off one by one.'

'If you had a rifle you could make a bloody racket and shoot your own silly foot off.'

'Dougie has a point,' I said. 'Men and rifles change the whole system. That's where it all breaks down.'

The eland made the walk a success. Back at camp, George was at the table, getting up to greet us. He had, he said, been writing up his notes. Yesterday's? The previous year's? No matter. Perhaps it was the notes on the klepto-parasitic Caesarian-performing hyena, come to think of it. George and I sold the idea of the all-day drive to Bill and Dougie, and I went to ask Sunday to prepare a picnic. He agreed after a permissible amount of sighing and shoulder-shrugging; as an artist-cook of considerable talent, he was entitled to the occasional mild display of temperament. 'For this I get a bone-arse, yes?'

The Old Boys withdrew after breakfast to shower and bicker; George and I stayed at the table to have an arrangements conversation. 'Good walk?'

'Aubrey was – unworried.'

'Much game?'

'Eland. Very very dangerous. But we were cool. Aubrey let them get to four hundred yards.'

'The Old Boys seem to have enjoyed it.'

'They think Aubrey is Cool in the Bush.'

'You're obviously working very hard out there. Any idea of the route to take today?'

'Go straight to the dead hippo. Loop north. Back along the river to the main gate. Hit Mukango. Beer and phone. Back to the park, head south. I talked to Pocock's main man at the airport yesterday, he said Fish Eagle Lagoon hasn't dried up yet, and it was heaving with stuff. Could be a nice fishing party. Park up in the shade for a good while and see what turns up. Drive on when it begins to get a bit cooler. Find a nice place for sundowners. Spotlight home. I'll put plenty of water and soft drinks in the cool box.'

'Sounds like a good day.'

'If we can't give the Old Boys decent walks, we can give them the best drive anyone ever had.'

'Precisely.'

So we started with a trip to hell. The dead hippo was immensely horrible. The stench, impossibly, was a good deal worse. More vultures had gathered: all four species represented, and in very impressive numbers. There were a dozen lappet-faced monsters among them. Everywhere you looked, there were lion with smeared and bloody faces. This was as brutal a scene as I had ever witnessed: black blood, black and bloody bones, blackened skin. Yet more blackness as a trio of ground hornbill scavenged on the peripheries: black birds the size of turkeys with two-foot meat-cleaver bills. The nearest lion lolled six feet away from us, yellow eyes on mine.

We drove off, to get some moving air, for everyone but George was troubled by the heat, George being essentially eurythermic. The vision of hell quietened the Old Boys for a little while, but a gathering of zebra brought them back to form. I said my piece.

'So the basis of their society is friendship. That's kind of encouraging.'

'You don't suppose they want the friendship of a stupid old man, do you?'

'Never mind him, Dan.'

'Never mind *him*, Dan.'

At Mukango, I fitted the Old Boys with beers, and, their heads being both filled with wonders and blasted by the sun, they found them fairly sizzling down. As George went to phone Joyce, I took them to a shelter Philip had built by the river, telling them there was a chance of racket-tailed roller. I found them the bird, too, and then tactfully left them in the shelter for a snooze.

'All well?' I asked George back at the bar.

'No more clients.'

'Good news and bad news.'

'But Joyce says the journalists are definite.'

'Oh God. How many?'

'Ten.'

'Ten? We'll not get ten in a vehicle.'

'Joyce says we must use your Land-Rover.'

'Must? Anyway, what if it doesn't start? Perhaps it won't, it hasn't had a run since Joseph took it back to Mukango the day he left. Besides, it hasn't got game-viewing seats. The back doesn't come off, and it's got no bloody windows. All in all, it's not the ideal vehicle for game viewing.'

'I did try to tell her this, Dan. But she said we must do our best.'

'Ah well. We can only finish focken last, and God send nothing worse. But it's not as if we will be able to give them decent walks.'

'Ah, here's Philip. Hullo, Philip, how are you? I haven't seen you for ages.'

'Hullo, George, Dan, yes, I keep missing you. Been a bit under the weather, fine now. But I've been hearing a great deal about you two.'

'Beer?'

'I think I had better buy the beer today.' He waved to the barman. 'Three Lion.'

'Are you describing the company or ordering a drink?' I asked.

'Ha. One alpha male in his prime, one old bugger gone in the tooth with his mane falling out, one young nomad still bearing spots on his hide, without a proper territory to call his own.'

'In my prime?' George said. 'God help me when I'm old then.'

'Crocodile tears from a lion, George? Lord, I wish I was as young as you.'

'Oh yes?'

'I'd move on. Tear up. Rather than wait and see the park cut in half by the damned bloody road.'

'More news? It's all still happening then?'

'Very much still happening, alas. My life's work, and so on. Made a call to a contact in the ministry this morning, very depressing news. I have been grouching around all morning, trying to comfort myself by saying that perhaps I gave the park thirty years' extra life, and that's something. But if I were young, I wouldn't stay to see it happen. I'd be down in Chipembere fighting. Harrying people, camping out in ministers' anterooms, haranguing civil servants, talking to newspapers. I did all that thirty years ago, and it was the breath of life to me. I care, now more than ever, about the park. But I'm tired, George. I'm too tired to do anything about it.'

'I never thought of that,' George said. 'Going to Chip, I mean. It never even occurred to me.'

Philip laughed. 'George, I don't mean that you should do it. Heaven forbid. Not what you're made for. You need to be nasty and devious, just as I was. I took on the politicians and I outdeviated them. I was wonderfully nasty then. But I don't get angry any more, that's the trouble, that's where age gets me. I just get sad, you see. Age, George, age. But I wish I could be in Chip to fight for the park, to run a damage-limitation exercise at the very least. But these days, I sit in my chair under the tree and wait for people to tell me the news. And then I get sad. Plenty of news, anyway.'

'What else have you heard?'

'Well, George, I hear you run the finest bush camp in the Valley.'

'That's news all right,' George said. 'News to all the clients that didn't come this season. News to the office in Chip, as well.'

'I had a visit the other day from that girlfriend of yours, Dan.' I turned my head unconcernedly, dislocating no more than three vertebrae in my neck as I did so. I tried to think of a remark somewhere between 'oh, really' and 'what did she say about me?' but I failed. 'Girlfriend' was surely no more than a mildly malicious Pocockian tease, but I wondered how much he knew, or guessed, and how much was common knowledge. 'Yes, she came here to use the telephone and so on, and we had quite a talk. She wanted to know everything about you lot. Every biographical detail. She seemed very taken with you all. Kept talking about lion and leopard, too, as if you two had invented the bloody things. Bushfever, I call it. Remember when you were first struck with bushfever, George?'

'Well, of course I do,' George said.

'Remember that day after the definite male, George?' I asked. 'And how there was a full pride chorus that night, when I slept in the open, under the mozzie net, before the huts were built? I felt it then. Same thing.'

'Well, Dan, your girlfriend had the same sort of feeling when you showed her the Tondo Pride and the leopard. I felt it when I shot my first elephant, a couple of centuries or so back. One shot, what they call a classic kill, between the eyes and down he went, poor bastard. I thought then that there couldn't be anything better on earth than killing an elephant. One shot and down he goes. Little you and big him. Down he goes.'

'You heard about Joseph?'

'I heard. Very promising young man. I am pleased for him really.'

'I suppose I am too,' George said. 'Though it was a blow to lose him.'

'And you both had a run-in with Mvuu.'

'You heard that too?'

'Very odd, that, you know. That was my thought. Uncharacteristic, you see. Mvuu doesn't make trouble. One for the quiet life, Mvuu.'

'I've got to re-take my safari guide exam,' I said resentfully.

'I heard that as well. I wouldn't worry about it. You'll sail through. No one can stop you passing.'

'Thanks for that, Philip. It's been on my mind a lot.'

'But then I heard, you see, that Mvuu himself is in trouble.' Philip produced this additional piece of news with an air of relish.

'We hear nothing out our way,' George said, not particularly interested in Mvuu, and perhaps getting a little tired of Philip's gossip.

'Then perhaps you should listen a little harder, both of you.' Philip turned his tortoise neck from one of us to the other, savouring the moment. 'There was a story in one of the London papers about meat-poaching gangs in the North Park. Priceless wildlife asset ruined by government neglect – that sort of thing. Diplomatic questions arose. There was another piece in one of the big American magazines. It was nothing new to us, the usual story, but it had a bit of extra bite because the Americans picked up on the business of the road, and married the two stories together. Neglect, destruction, a backward nation that knows nothing of conservation. The government got a bit of a pasting.'

'Does that sort of thing matter very much?' George asked. 'I'd have thought they were hardened against such things by now.'

'Ah, well, George, it caused pain. Caused a lot of pain in Chipembere. Caused double pain for Jacob Njiri, the minister, who's supposed to be such a forward-looking chap. But he's very clever. He has a new scheme. He's not actually going to do a damn thing, but he will *look* as if he is saving Africa single-handed. The Chipembere papers are full of it, anyway. He has taken personal responsibility for the North Park, taking it away from Mvuu, and he will appoint a new full-time warden for the North Park alone in time for next dry season. So Mvuu no longer has any control over the North. Terrible loss of face and all that.'

'Oh.'

'George,' Philip said reproachfully. 'This is more interesting than you realise.'

'Oh.'

'You mean we have a bolt hole in North Park, where we can escape from Mvuu?' I said. 'The last pocket of wild country left, where the wild bushfevered few live on. *Homo pococki-ensis*, surrounded on all sides by roads, holding out under siege conditions in the north until the last lion goes?'

163

Philip laughed wheezily at this fancy, and said: '*Homo soren-senia*, I think. But listen, George. Think about all this.'

'I do all the time.'

'That, George, is exactly what you never do. Can you make him think about all this, Dan? Or are you as bad as he is.'

'I try.'

'I waste my time. You're *exactly* as bad as George. But you listen to me, Dan. I don't want George to leave this Valley. I don't even want to see you leave the Valley. But keeping you both is going to take a bit of doing. And neither of you are helping one bit. I expect that of George, I have known him for a long time. But I had hoped for a bit of help from you, Dan.'

Eventually, with yet another rebuke ringing in our ears, George and I continued the all-day drive. My head spun; I wanted to do all that Philip suggested, but all I knew was how to give the clients a wonderful day in the bush. It wasn't enough: although the drive was a beauty. Fish Eagle Lagoon was visited by a party of elephant, wallowing, drinking and messing about: a sight to fill hearts and empty cameras. After that, the success of the rest of the day was guaranteed. For a safari guide, there is always a great release of tension at a really marvellous sight. The pressure is off: everything else you see is a bonus. You have pleased your clients, they believe you know what you are doing. And you can all, client and safari guide both, relax and enjoy the bush.

I drove home in a great northern loop via roads little travelled by, and found various quotidien splendours. Just as the sun was sinking, I made a detour back to the dead hippo. I knew it would be horrible, but I had to take a look. It was even nastier than before. The tormenting flies had gone, but they had left their mark on the hellish scene. The entire exposed side of hippo flesh had changed colour, from black to a pale and dirty grey. Maggots. Every square inch was asquirm. Lion lay around their horrible booty, mainly on their backs, paws aflap. At the neck entrance, the black-maned alpha male lay alone, gorging anew.

4

I opened bottles, each one with another save the last, Cool in the Bush as I was, and handed sundowners to Mr and Mrs Gould and party. They all seemed untroubled by Aubrey's excited shooting-up of the fish poachers that morning. George was talking hard with the parents; Louise had taken her Coke with thanks, and had withdrawn to sit alone on the edge of the bank. That, I decided, as I opened my Lion, the last, on the doorcatch of the doorless Land Cruiser, let me off any immediate social duties. I walked to the bank myself, ten or fifteen yards upstream of Louise and noticed a small fishing group of no less than five species of bird. Interesting, that.

I turned my head slightly to observe Louise, dark hair drawn back for the heat, a young, full-lipped face, a well-filled T-shirt. As I did so, she lowered her eyes, the smallest fraction later, a matter of hundredths of a second, but there was no doubt about it.

Had she been, I wondered, looking with anthropological interest at a hitherto unencountered form of human life, the bush person of questionable sanity? Or was she thinking, who is this intriguing young fellow, with his dusty trilby and his epaulettes and his insouciant ways in the bush? I was inclined to think the latter.

'Yellow-billed stork, hammerkop, great white egret, African spoonbill, grey heron,' I quipped dashingly, and strolled over to her. 'Sharing the same resource. Comensalism. Like *mensa mensam*. Sharing fish in comensal amity.'

Louise looked up at me and smiled, not shyly. 'So no fighting?'

'Occasionally they get fed up with the spoonbill dashing

about,' I said. 'But they only ever give him a Paddington Bear hard stare.'

'Can't say I blame them. Your spoonbill looks like my father doing the hoovering.'

'But apart from that, it's a very tolerant situation.'

'It's not like I thought. I thought it would be all dog eat dog.'

'It's completely different to what you thought, and also exactly the same. It's dog tolerate dog, again and again. Life could not go on if that weren't true. Herbivores tolerate the proximity of lion. But you must remember that everything gets eaten in the end.'

'That's dreadful.'

'It's only death. And nothing gets wasted.'

She paused for a while at this. 'I see. I do, actually, see.'

'Well – I'll try to find you something special in the spotlight.'

'Are you the flasher tonight, then?'

'Don't worry. I shall expose nothing but my ignorance.'

I wanted to impress her, or the clients, with a wonderful or important leopard, of course, but no luck that night. What I found was a lioness. She was walking with great purpose, in a dead straight line. This was slightly odd, because lion are not strictly nocturnal, apart from when they feel like it, of course. We bundu-bashed after her for twenty minutes or so, but she was not hunting. In the end, we left her to it and George drove back. He couldn't find the road. The plain was rather featureless, and we had lost our incoming wheel tracks in the dark. So we stopped and switched off all the lights, and when we had regained a little night vision, George worked out due south by the Southern Cross and followed the line. 'We'll hit the river sooner or later,' he said.

'Not too hard, I trust.' This from Michael, Louise's father.

We found the riverside road before we reached the river and headed back to camp. I produced a pair of honey badger for them, a sight that brought out George's tape recorder, for these beasts are almost always seen alone. And then I caught a giant eagle owl on top of a guinea fowl it had just killed, all of which made it a pretty fair night's spotting.

The evening meal was merry, and Sunday's cooking much praised. 'Have you ever had poached salmon?' I asked. 'This is poached barbel. Sunday and I liberated it from the poachers' haul this morning. What we are eating is a traditional Mchindeni dish called illegal fish pie.'

'Eating in comensal amity,' said Louise, and cast a brown-eyed glance at me.

When coffee came, I encouraged a move out to the fire, but only Louise took me up on it, bringing her coffee to the edge of the river and a 'comfortable' canvas chair. I, coffee-less, joined her. 'Hyena.'

'What a sound. How do you manage to sleep, with all these ferocious animals everywhere?'

Because I'm Cool in the Bush, I thought vaingloriously. 'Because I'm Cool in the Bush,' I told her after a moment. She laughed.

It was at this stage that Michael decided to produce his duty-free malt whisky, and he gave us all hefty shots of Glenmorangie. This did not unify the party; we remained in two groups, one of three in the sitenji, another of two by the fire. But I seemed to have run out of conversation for a moment. After an awkward silence, Louise took up the slack. 'How long have you worked out in the bush?'

I told her about this season and about my year with zebras and friendship, and the resulting paper.

'I thought you must have done some studying somewhere along the line.'

'That's roughly what my supervisor said when he got my paper.'

'But you passed all right?'

'Oh yes. They bullied me to cut out some of the speculation, and it went OK. Why, are you studying?'

'Just finished my A levels. Going to university this autumn. That's why my parents are taking me on this trip. Partly as a reward for getting my place, and partly a sort of last family holiday. Well, they said actually a last family holiday before Louise goes to the bad and takes drugs and sleeps with at least half a dozen students of assorted gender every night.'

I laughed. 'What are you reading?'

'Law.'

'*Law*?' I failed to keep incredulity from my voice, and Louise was rightly nettled.

'What's wrong with law?'

'Er, nothing, I'm just surprised that you er . . .' Oh shit.

'You've been telling me about laws of the bush. There are laws you must keep out here; you can't escape them. There are laws that affect those five birds you showed me, you explained all about it. Laws are the essential framework that keeps things together, in London or in the Mchindeni Valley. You need to keep the laws in order to survive out here.'

'All right then. I'll tell you some good laws. You don't walk towards lion in thick bush. You treat a cow-and-calf-elephant group with more circumspection than a group of bulls. You keep clear of a lone buffalo. You always keep between clients and danger and, in any tight situation, you never never run. Those are real laws and we all obey them. But there are other laws too. Don't drive more than a hundred yards off the road, don't drive down the river bank in case you erode it, don't cross the river, never let clients stray more than ten yards from a vehicle. The last lot, they are paper laws, and I pay them no attention.'

'That's a good point actually. But all the same, you can't ignore laws, paper laws or the other kind. You can break them, but you can't stop them existing. And you can't complain if you fall foul of them.'

'Do you really need to bother with this law course? Why don't you start practising right away?'

'I'm sorry. I like arguing. Naturally adversarial.'

'It's a frightening thought though, isn't it? Deciding on your career at what, eighteen, and that's it for the rest of your life?'

'Aren't you a bit young for all that hippy stuff? Turn on, tune in, drop out?'

'I'm not dropping out. I work in the bush. That's a positive choice, not a negative one.'

'It's not a career, though, is it?'

'If it isn't a career, I'm working in the bush and that's enough to be going on with. But working in tourism in the bush is satisfying, challenging and a decent living, especially if, or when, you start to run your own operation. And I suppose that's a long-term aim.' I thought then, with dreadful guilt, of my father's business skills, of George's business skills. 'But the fact is that I like working with tourists. Even with cranky adversarial ones, as long as they learn to love the bush.'

'Well, I qualify there all right.'

'You'll do, then.'

It was then that the party of three elected to go to bed and 'leave you to it' as Michael said, a trifle lubriciously, or teasingly, I thought, but generously adding the blessing of more Glenmorangie as he left.

'I must say, the idea of working in the bush is rather tempting,' Louise said. 'It's as well for my career that no one is going to offer me a job here in the next couple of days.'

'All right then. Would you like a job here? You could work for us as a caterer. We've a vacancy. Just stay on, simply don't get on the plane, don't go to Palmyra Resort with your parents. Work a half-season here, and start again next April.'

'Are you serious?'

'It depends what you mean by serious. Yes, there is seriously a vacancy, we recently lost a member of staff. And yes, if you wanted to fill it and were capable of doing it, which I am sure you are, then I expect we would take you on. If you mean do I seriously expect you to take it up, then no, I'm not serious. But the possibility seriously exists.'

There was a pause. 'I wish you hadn't said that.'

'Why not?'

'All the time I'm reading law books, I'll think, I don't have to be doing this, I could be living at Lion Camp.'

'I expect it'll make your resolve all the steelier.'

She laughed. 'I expect you're right. That's the sort of person

I am. But because of your offer, I'll sometimes wish I was somebody else.'

'Would it help if I were to withdraw the offer?'

'Oh no. I'll enjoy thinking of it. In libraries in February.'

We sipped Glenmorangie in a long silence. I was aware of the possibility of making a lunge for her, of course I was, the air was full of it. But I did not. I didn't know how such a thing would have been received, either. The point is that I didn't try.

Eventually she went to bed; I kissed her cheek in acknowledgement of the intimacy of our discussion. Perhaps she read it as the sad token of admiration from a man who was forbidden by the laws of the company to make a pass at a client. Who is to say?

I sat up for a while, looking at the narrowing Mchindeni. What I needed, of course, was a cigarette.

There was still a light in George's hut, so I called his name softly.

'Oh, hullo, come in, yes.' He was sitting on one of his ammunition boxes, writing in a large stiff-covered notebook that rested on a tin trunk almost as low as the ammo box. The fact that the position looked both deliberately chosen and extraordinarily uncomfortable suggested the self-mortifying rites of a fakir, an impression heightened by the fact that George wore nothing but a towel. The single paraffin lamp cast odd shadows and exaggerated the almost Gandhi-like appearance of his ectomorphic frame.

'Could you roll me a cigarette, George?'

'Certainly. I'll come to the fire, shall I?'

'Why not?'

At the still-glowing coals of the mopane wood fire we took our seats. I kicked the branches nearer to the centre to encourage a flame or two. George passed me a *Guardian-Weekly*-wrapped smoke and prepared his own. He had added a khaki shirt, unbuttoned, to his ensemble. 'Seems a rather nice chick, that Louise.'

'Nice *chick*, George? What do you mean, "chick"?'

'Don't you say "chick" these days?'

'I don't think so, George. Not to that one – anyway, not to her face. She was lecturing me on ambition and career and things like that.'

'Not very idiotypic of her.'

'Not very. But she's going to be a lawyer, so perhaps it's obligate behaviour.'

'Well, if so, it's a purely hologynic phenomenon, at least in my own observation of lawyers.'

'And mine. Rather unsettling of her, don't you think?'

'Are you talking about sex or careers? I'd like to be sure before I commit myself to a reply.'

I relit my cigarette by thrusting the end against a coal of mopane, for George's roll-ups tended to need a lot of attention.

'I wonder where that lioness was going,' I said.

'I was thinking the same thing. There was a sense of purpose about her, wasn't there?'

'I was wondering if she wasn't an oestrus lioness looking for a male.'

'Well, if so, she knew exactly where the male was, didn't she, because she was walking in a perfectly straight line, she wasn't *looking*. Perhaps she was heading for the alpha male.'

'Or maybe a nomad.'

'Or perhaps a kill. She might have picked up a call before we saw her. I wish we could have followed her.'

'So do I. But just following a lioness walking through the bush is a bit short of action for clients, isn't it? I mean, we might have walked into a fabulous interaction round the next clump of bushes, but on the other hand, she might be walking still.'

'Precisely. If so, I wish we were still following. That would be some drive, wouldn't it?'

'So what do you reckon she was up to? What are your bets, George? Sex or food?'

'Sex or career, you mean?' George asked, smirking to himself and pausing awhile to get full value from this tease. 'I'd take two to one on sex, and better than even money, career. I mean food.'

'Well, if you're going to sit there giving me a hard time, you might as well tell me something useful as well. Because I've been thinking a bit.'

'Bad move.'

'Certainly. I don't deny that for a second. But all the same, can you tell me about where I stand?'

'You mean vis-à-vis sex and career?'

'Precisely.'

George, snuffling with laughter at his teasing, proceeded to roll more cigarettes. I lit mine from the fire, drew fiercely to get the end glowing, and then, more gently and more seriously, took in acrid smoke, a hint of grass fire. Exhaling, I walrused smoke.

'What I'm really asking, George, is: is there any point in talking about next season?'

'Not much,' George said, and lit his own cigarette with a disposable lighter that had not been disposed of. Jonas, the room attendant, had the skill of restoring these items to life. Africa is not a place where the concept of disposability has much relevance.

'Because I'm only on a contract to the end of the season, of course.'

'So you are. And I suppose it needs saying. Of course I'd like you back next season.'

'But I keep worrying, George. Will there be a next season?'

'Probably. I haven't really thought about it.'

'You've said the company is in trouble. And Mvuu was talking about closing you down.'

'A lot of talk. And, frankly, who else would take this on? That's the point of it all, you see. A real bush camp isn't to everyone's taste.'

'But if the company does go wrong, what will you do?'

'Bruce will probably bail us out for another season. Always has done before. Perhaps he won't. I don't know. If not, I'll do something or other, I suppose.'

'What do you think I should do? If the worst comes to the worst?'

'Oh, that's the last thing you need to worry about. One of the other camps will take you like a shot. Mukango, maybe. Philip will be able to help you get fixed, anyway. He likes you, thinks you know your stuff.'

'So in terms of career, I am absolved from making a decision tonight.'

'That's a fair summing-up, yes.'

'That seems good enough to me.' A complex series of hoots from a tree above us. 'Pearl spotted owlet,' I said accurately. 'We'd better get to bed or we'll pass out on the clients. Walking tomorrow?'

'Certainly. You needn't get up.'

'No, I'll be there. See you tomorrow. Thanks, George.'

'Sleep well.'

But I didn't. The thoughts of career that Louise had brought into being were now quiescent, but I was thinking instead about sex. Well, why hadn't I made a lunge at Louise? I liked her, didn't I? No law prevented me. Did it? But the trouble with the thought was that it attracted to my mind another thought. It did so rather like a candle flame attracting a pterodactyl. Caro.

But I wasn't keeping myself pure for Caro, was I? I owed Caro nothing. So what stopped me? I couldn't bring my thoughts of Caro to any kind of order, and I had tried a few methods. Was she the most wonderful woman in creation? Or was she irredeemably deceitful? Had I been, albeit briefly, beloved? Or had I been casually exploited? I tended to oscillate from one view to the other, hour by hour, and at times when the pterodactyl got loose, minute by minute, a form of self-torture that paralysed thought processes and jammed every analytical function the brain possessed.

I heard a lion roar, startlingly close, and wondered if it was the bee-line-walking possibly oestrus female. Then I realised that she had been heading in the opposite direction. Miles away by now.

5

Aubrey had acquired a knack of truncating walks. No matter what route he and I agreed on at the start, we always found ourselves walking back into camp about half an hour before breakfast was ready. This was partly the result of Aubrey's instinctive laziness, and partly his taste for giving me a hard time. Aubrey was able to do this quite effortlessly, with everything he did. For a start, he acted as if everything in the bush was beneath his notice. When George set up his telescope to look at a distant bird, Phineas would always take a look. He was also pretty keen on bird call, a skill he had mostly acquired from George. But Aubrey never looked through the 'scope, never pointed out a bird. Nor did he point out a mammal, for that matter, unless it was one he wished to avoid.

So, the morning after our trip to Fish Eagle Lagoon, I took Bill and Dougie out for a quick pre-breakfast drive after a brief but not exactly incident-free walk. The famous dead hippo was just in range for such a foray. The trip was worth making, too, because in the night, the lion had moved out, and hyena had moved in. Not leisurely feeders, these, they had shifted an extraordinary quantity of meat. They had not needed to use the single entrance at the neck for they were capable of ripping apart the skin, and indeed, devouring it, hyena being designed primarily not for hunting but eating.

The hyena themselves now lay around the carcass, bloated and distended, and far too full either to walk away or to protect the kill. The patient vultures had at last the stage: they had descended to the kill and now surrounded it in a hissing, seething, squabbling crowd, white-backs to the fore like a swarm of jabberwocks.

'That will give you an appetite for breakfast,' I said, as we headed back.

'Don't worry about that, Dan, you should see what I normally have to put up with over breakfast.'

'Don't pay him no mind, Dan. Most mornings I get to face this expression like one of them buffalo we saw on the trail this morning.'

'Ah yes,' I said. 'A fine encounter, that one.'

I was not exaggerating. Bill and Dougie had been close to watching the first instance of a game scout battered to death by a safari guide with the butt of his own rifle. My personal feeling was that I deserved a medal for the way I handled the situation. I even managed to keep Aubrey's dignity, a precious and delicate thing, more or less intact.

Walking with Aubrey was hard work, because I had to do it all myself: all the spotting, all the route-planning. There was never a suggestion of teamwork. If I asked him for his opinion, as I did constantly, at least in the early days, all I got was a contemptuous shrug: fancy not knowing that. All Aubrey did was carry his rifle and walk at the front.

His air of constant contempt irritated me all the more because he was completely useless in the bush. Phineas was able to read game trails like the morning newspaper: Aubrey was always elaborately noncommittal. 'Kudu?' I would say.

'Maybe.'

He was dogmatic on only one aspect of tracking. Lion do not leave tracks that you can confuse with anything else. Aubrey never found lion prints, or at least, never pointed them out.

'Ha! Aubrey, lion!'

'Very old. No good to follow.'

He would say this even when the spoor was palpably clear and new, its outline uneroded by wind. 'Very very old.'

That morning with Bill and Dougie, if Aubrey had had his way he would have killed us all. He really was that useless.

We had been following a broad game trail that led to a slight rise. I was increasingly aware that a decision had to be made, and was dismayed that Aubrey had not taken it. I had thought it was the one kind of decision he could be trusted to make. So I halted the walk beneath a sausage tree. Aubrey sighed: he sighed every time I called a halt to show anything at all to the clients. He was always just the safe side of insolence, but it was a thing narrowly achieved.

And so Aubrey sighed wearily, while I looked ahead at a thin veil of dust hanging a few feet above the ground. I could hear, clearly enough, contented grunts and mutterings, and the sharp click of horn against horn. I could even, the breeze blowing gently towards us, smell the pleasant farmyard smell: a deceiving smell of cattle. It was about as obvious as it possibly could be that there was a large herd of buffalo just the far side of the rise, perhaps a hundred yards in front of us. This was not, in theory, a dangerous situation, but all the same a hundred and more well-armed beasts weighing in at a ton a time deserve a little respect.

'Left or right?' I said to Aubrey. This was very much the scout's decision, client safety being his responsibility. I was not supposed to act unilaterally in this area. 'Or maybe back and loop around,' I suggested.

Aubrey looked at me contemptuously. He pointed straight ahead. 'Camp is that way.'

'Ah yes, Aubrey, but that's not really the point, is it?' Diplomatically, I turned to Bill and Dougie, raising my voice a fraction. 'There's a nice herd of buffalo just over the rise in front. I would guess around a hundred animals from the sound, but it's impossible to say until we get a look at them. Listen, and you will hear them, and see ahead the dust cloud they have thrown up. Maybe you can smell them too. We are going to skirt around them at a distance and then cut back to camp. That way we should get some great views. Just remember to stay nice and close behind me and keep your eyes on Aubrey. All right then, are we set?'

Aubrey shot me a look of polite hatred, but he could not get out of it. He actually did a fair job, taking a reasonable course around the buffalo and making sure that our clients had some very good views, ears filled with the grunt and rumble of the herd. We kept comfortably on the edge of their flight distance, Aubrey always between the herd and the clients, and the buffalo stopped to watch us go by, standing shoulder to shoulder to shoulder, as buffalo will.

In this manner we got back to camp without losing a client. I thanked Aubrey: 'Nice walk, Aubrey, you did a good job with the buffalo.' But not even hypocrisy could dent him; he turned on his heel and walked off.

Just before dark, the Old Boys asked if we could make yet another visit to the hippo kill: both had acquired a macabre fascination for the process of death and digestion.

The vultures had gone, the hippo was picked clean, the skin, inedible to all lion, devoured. All that remained was a black skull, black vertebrae, a black cage of ribs. A single hyena lay in the shade nearby.

'I could get to hate those guys. Too goddamn ugly.'

'Don't you use a mirror when you shave, old man?'

'I always try to act decent with all ugly things, but maybe some folks don't notice.'

'You must take a broad view of hyena,' I said. 'Just an essential part of the economy of the bush.'

'I see,' said Bill. 'These hyena see a gap in the market and exploit it.'

'Got it in one,' I said, delighted with this leap of understanding. 'Just people trying to earn a living.'

The hyena got to his feet and trotted up to the last remains of the kill. He threaded his way into the cage of ribs and lay down there on his belly, teeth bared cheesily. There was an expression of idiot satisfaction on his face.

6

The state of my temper was not improved when I learned that Phineas had been seconded to Impala Lodge. I heard this from Lloyd the Stringer. We had met by chance as I returned from the pre-breakfast visit to the dead hippo, and stopped our vehicles to exchange news, as was the invariable custom of the Valley. Lloyd had a party of clients, and he had taken them across the river for a look at the Tondo Pride on the kill, and had been disappointed to find only vultures and hyena. They had taken a sweep along the river, to see if they had gone to drink, but he had been disappointed again. I was able to take his disappointments in stride, however. Not so the news about Phineas. It had come 'completely out of the blue,' Lloyd said. 'A whim of old Mvuu's, apparently. Phineas will be with us next season now.'

'Send him my best,' I said. 'Tell him I haven't forgotten the Nice Place.'

'Sure,' said Lloyd, adding the birder's traditional enquiry: 'Much about your way?'

'Heard Klaas's cuckoo this morning. Wet-season birds are beginning to turn up.'

'Don't need it,' Lloyd said. 'Tell me if you get a striped crested. Anyway, best to George.'

'Mine to all your lot.' I wanted to send a coded message to Caro, about wood owls, or maybe in-camp giraffes, but I wasn't really in the mood for roguish asides. I didn't feel roguish in the slightest. It wouldn't really do to say, 'Tell Caro I will love her for ever.' For a fraction of a second I thought of sending exactly this message, passing it to Lloyd beneath the disguise of a facetious smirk. But I did not. 'Bye.'

'See you around.'

* * *

There was an odd, restless feeling about the whole day. This was not entirely to do with the shifting of Phineas, nor with the admittedly disturbing vision of hell down at the hippo kill. It was also a matter of meteorology. The weather was changing. The clouds had built up dramatically since dawn, but then they were rapidly replaced by the merciless if bone-healing sun. The rains were coming, but the rains are ever a great tease. The cloud brought with it a great burst of birdsong – how odd it was, I thought, that in an English spring, birds sing up when the sun comes out, but in Africa, they sing when it goes in. Well, I reasoned, sun plus water equals life on any continent, it is the priority that varies. When the sun returned, song shrivelled up in an instant. They would breed when it rained, not before.

A capricious wind struck up over breakfast, not the usual welcome, still-warm breath, but something more like a sharp draught, as if a door had been left open in an over-heated house. George got sharply to his feet and stared upwards: 'Weather front passing,' he said, mouth full of porridge. 'Listen! European swift. That's the rain bird, they ride in on the fronts. First of the season, can you hear them?'

By this time, we were all standing beside George on the bank, and, following his finger, I saw high, high above, the sickle shapes of the birds surfing the big wave of the weather, as if towing a skyful of clouds behind them. Even at such a distance, I could hear faintly their impassioned scream. 'Season is over,' George said. 'European swifts signal the end.'

'Today and tomorrow,' I said. 'We'd better find you chaps something good to remember then. You fly out tomorrow, midday, yes?'

'Oh God, I'll have to check the tickets, but I think so.'

'If you ain't lost 'em. But, Dan, we've had something to remember about every ten minutes. Don't you fret about us.'

The pair of them returned to the breakfast table, while George and I watched the passage of the swifts, riding hard into the new season.

'All over,' George said.

'Unless the journalists come.'

'They won't. But then we'll have to find something for the wet season.'

'I've been trying not think about that.'

'Have you visited Njovu National Park?'

'No. They say it's not as good as the Valley.'

'Not for game viewing, it's all much too spread about, too much water about the place; it's the river that makes for the high concentrations here during the season. But there's a lot of game there, you just don't see it so well. Anyway, the point is, there's an all-weather road that goes through it. It's supposed to be just about passable in the wet season. Still, if we get stuck we get stuck, don't we?'

'What are you telling me, George?'

'Now I think of it, we haven't really discussed this, have we? In fact, we haven't discussed it at all. I thought we had. Never mind. Thing is, I was wondering about trying to get some idea of lion numbers in Njovu.'

'Seems a fun idea.'

'That's settled then.'

'What is?'

George looked at me, amazed at my obtuseness. 'The expedition to Njovu.'

'Is it?'

'Aren't you coming?' he asked, a trifle irritated.

'Oh, I see. You're asking me to come.'

'Well, of course I am.'

'Oh, I see. Why not then?'

'It'll take a bit of setting up. But we'll go as soon as we have closed down the camp.'

'Sure.'

The front passed, but the cloud that followed hurried across the sky as if anxious to be gone. The sun returned before noon, the wind dropped, the temperature climbed. We hit 42 at midday. That evening before sundown, another bank of cloud rolled over, and we had a sudden squall. Actual rain fell, but this was not the Rains. The humidity shot up, lightning slashed, thunder cracked, the wind raged briefly and sent a few large, stinging drops of rain into our faces. But in ten minutes the sky was clear, and the vast sun was resting briefly on the horizon before departing. The night was warm and close.

In bed that night, I felt a sudden, unaccustomed pang of loneliness. The wind was busy, the bush quieter than usual. And where would I go, after a trip to Njovu? Home? Where the hell was that? I was happy when the morning came.

The day was sharp. I stepped out of my hut and found that the wind cut unexpectedly. I poured myself coffee, then returned to my hut to fetch a jacket, a rather fine item, covered in pockets and epaulettes, donated to me by a termitologist when he left the field research centre to return home to England. The sky, it became apparent as it grew light, was cloudy and threatening. Perhaps promising was a better word. I was not thinking with an African mind. I sipped my coffee, waiting for Bill and Dougie to emerge, and for Aubrey to make his appearance. As a horseman I had often longed for rain. 'Need the sting taken out of the ground,' my father would say, cracking a heel into the turf. 'Hard as a focken bookie's heart it is.'

The Old Boys appeared, faces pink from frantic morning scrubbing. I poured them coffee.

'Are you going to find us anything good for our last morning?'

'Do my best. Aubrey!' I called. 'Aubrey!'

A short while later, just long enough to show that he was coming in his own time, Aubrey arrived, his rifle on his shoulder. As always, I offered him coffee; as always, he refused. 'Any ideas?' I asked him. He shrugged. 'How about following the river south,' I said. 'Then cut inland, moving across to the Tondo, and following the Tondo watercourse back to camp?'

'I think it is better we go the other way. Walk along the Tondo first. Then we come back north along the Mchindeni.'

I had suggested this route half as a tease, knowing that

Aubrey hated to walk along the river bank at dawn; it was the time and place where you are most likely to meet hippo, and this was never a peril Aubrey was likely to underestimate. Phineas had had no qualms about early-morning hippo: if you could spot them far enough in advance, they were not a problem. Aubrey, no doubt wisely, would not stake very much capital on his own bush skills. 'OK, Aubrey. Whatever you think best.'

I wish now, more than I can say, that I had insisted on the riverside walk. Or perhaps a walk to the Robin Hood Glade. Or any walk: any other walk in the Valley would have been better. Over and over again, I have replayed to myself that walk along the Tondo, with its wide loops and its broad, sandy floor. And, always, it concludes with the same encounter beneath the fig trees.

We crossed and recrossed the Tondo, holding to a straight line while the dry river curled and curved across the landscape. At one crossing, I stopped. 'Ha! Aubrey, what do you make of this?'

I was squatting on the river floor, delighted.

'Ah, lion.'

'Bloody big lion. Bill, Dougie, you see the print here, a very good one, four toes, and then the three lobes on the pad at the rear. No claws, of course.'

'Is very very old.'

He meant the age of the track, in days, not of the lion in years. 'Very very big, too. It's certainly a male, and I would guess it is the black-maned alpha male we saw at the hippo kill. We don't know exactly when he left the kill, but this track –' Here I remembered my manners. 'What do you think, Aubrey? Yesterday?'

'Older.'

'It's been very windy, so even a fresh track will have eroded quite a bit.' It was yesterday all right. 'He might well have gone down to the Mchindeni to drink, and then come back up the Tondo to lie up somewhere. He could still be pretty close.'

'Maybe we go back to the bank.'

I would have preferred to follow the tracks myself, but I did not care for the idea of tracking lion with Aubrey, any more than he cared for doing the same thing with me. Or with anyone else, for that matter.

The next bend brought us to an open plain area, on which we found a wonderful gathering of impala and puku. The numbers were astounding, but they were widely scattered; and the broken terrain and the impossibility of finding any kind of eminence made counting impossible. George would be disappointed when I told him that. I explained quietly about 'a typical late-season congregation', and how, with the rains, these large groups would scatter across the park. Meanwhile, the animals gazed back at the intruders with sad and wondering eyes, Bill and Dougie for once silent, caught up in the Edenic qualities of the morning. I heard the triple note of red-chested cuckoo: another rain bird had arrived. A long moment of shared contentment.

'I'd like to come here to die,' Dougie said softly. 'Kind of a peaceful way to go. And it's the only place I've been where dying is any use to anyone. Mostly you die, you are an embarrassment. You're just a hundred jobs for people. But here a dead body has a purpose, don't it?'

'Scrawny old man, who'd want to eat you?' asked Bill, not without tenderness.

'It feels such a waste, the idea of dying,' Dougie said. 'But I guess I might feel different about it, if I knew I'd be a meal for a lion. Kind of like when they say in the movies, I'm dying, get me a priest. I'll say, I'm dying, get me a lion.'

'You like this place,' I said. 'I'm glad. It's been great having you both for that.'

'Best thing we ever done.'

'Don't mind him, Dan. Just a maundering, sentimental old man. He'll be all right tomorrow.'

'Not if he's got bushfever,' I said. 'There's no getting rid of that affliction. You'll have to come back every year.'

'Yeah,' said Dougie. 'Or maybe every six months.'

'You should be so rich.'

'What else is worth spending money on?'

'We'll walk to the group of fig trees, shall we?' I suggested.

I had always liked that area: flat, open, studded with a dozen widely scattered fig trees. These are strange things; they start as vines, winding themselves lovingly around some unwilling host tree, and then they take over and become a tree themselves, thrusting out their enormous branches mighty distances from their borrowed, parasitised trunk. They fruit at irregular intervals, every few years, but when they do so, they fruit in magnificent superabundance. They become a magnet for fruit-eaters for miles around. It is a kind of saturation-bombing technique, a bonanza of food designed to spread the seeds over a huge area. Even had I not known from previous visits that one of these trees was in full and exuberant fruit, the crazed shriek of Meyer's parrot would have told me. 'And green pigeon, there in the top,' I told the Old Boys.

We ascended a shallow slope, bringing the trunk of the fruiting tree into sight. Seventy yards away – I know, because I paced it out later – it was a truly magnificent tree. 'Aubrey. Elephant. On the far side of the trunk.'

He jerked as if I had poked him with a sharp stick. 'We stop here.'

'Sure.'

There were two of them, both bulls. The first was as impressive an elephant as you could find in the Valley, massively ivoried. This was unusual. Most of the really big-tusked animals had been killed by poachers in the eighties. The second animal was not much smaller, and also respectably armed. It occurred to me then that they might have been the same two elephant I saw on my terrified solo crossing of the Mchindeni, on my secret cheese-gathering jaunt to Impala Lodge. They had been walking towards the tree, one behind the other when they became aware of us, or of something, as we breasted the slight rise. Both of them raised their trunks and aimed their nostrils at us: snorkelling at our scent. The lead one dropped his trunk, and then raised it again. Then, as if shrugging his shoulders, he reached up into the tree and pulled at a branch. With a crash and a rip, a great fan of greenery descended, and, delicately fixing it with his front foot, he began to feed, devouring a salad of leaves and sweet fruit.

The second elephant followed this lead, and took a branch for himself. An eating animal, I repeated to myself yet again, is a contented animal: as a horseman, I knew this long before I came to Africa. The elephants were aware of our presence, and were prepared to tolerate it. They were, as Aubrey would say, unworried. They were continuing with their lives as if we were not there: this is the ultimate privilege of bush-walking. They would continue to do so unless circumstances were radically altered: unless we did something stupid. So we stopped and watched. Bill and Dougie sensed the privilege, and stood there in silent joy. The elephants ate their figs with much the same feeling.

I turned in a slow circle, scanning the area all around. There were two reasons for this: firstly to see if there were any more delights to show Bill and Dougie, and secondly as a routine precaution, one I could not trust Aubrey to take. This, I thought happily, was turning into one of my better post-Phineas walks. I turned back to my party. In one terrible moment I found I was alone.

I jerked my head left: nothing. Back right: Bill and Dougie, running for their lives. A voice I did not know I possessed rose up within me. 'Walk!' I shouted, the voice of a mad sergeant-major. In the tail of my left eye, I was aware of movement. One of the elephant was coming fast towards us, or rather, towards me, since I stood alone. 'Aubrey? Aubrey!'

No sign of him. I had no idea where he had gone. He should have been with the clients. So should I, according to the *Safari Guide Training Manual* and to what seemed at that moment a moral imperative. They had left my side, but I would rejoin them: first putting myself, as the *Manual* demanded, between clients and danger. They were walking now, but like people hurrying for a train. I moved towards them, trying to impress them and everything around me with a sense of ease: with a feeling of serene inevitability. I wanted to spread calm all around: to calm the clients, calm the elephant, calm Aubrey. I walked in a kind of trance of nonchalance.

Or rather, I *strolled*, glancing casually over my shoulder at the elephant. I had it half in my mind to turn, to stand my ground and clap, but, after a view lasting no more than a fragment of a second, every bush sense I possessed told me to do no such thing. When an elephant performs a mock charge, like the one Caro and I had encountered, he concentrates on size. The idea is to look good: to look *big*. When the charge is meant for business, the ears are not spread, but carried close to the side; the head is not held high, for show, but low, for use. This elephant did not want to impress me. He wanted to kill me.

Elephant cannot run. They adopt a sort of Groucho Marx shuffle. It is always much faster than you would think possible, and once it has been adopted, whether from panic or from anger, it takes a good deal to stop it.

'Under that tree!' I heard myself roaring in my new voice to Bill and Dougie. 'Stand there! Don't move.'

I continued to stroll towards them. All this, from the realisation that I was alone to my last roared instruction, took two, maybe three seconds, but everything passed with the curious elasticity of time that you find only in moments of crisis.

To this day, I wonder what it was that panicked or angered the elephant. I think it is possible that Aubrey had run, and set him off. Perhaps Bill and Dougie had run first, though I doubt it. It was possible, maybe even likely, that the elephant had taken unilateral action. There are a million bush tales about the perfect unpredictability of elephant, and some of them are true. For an elephant to turn in a fraction of a second from contented eating to maddened charging is against all normal behaviour, but the abnormal is the daily business of the bush. There was a procedure for dealing with it, too: and it was not running off in all directions. It was to stand behind the scout and obey his instructions. It is an advantage, then, if the scout does not go missing.

Why, against all accepted probabilities, was the first charge, a charge out of nowhere, meant for business: not to frighten but to destroy? I suspect that it was the flight of Aubrey that turned the problem into a crisis. The ancient axiom of the bush is that nothing inspires pursuit so much as flight; everyone who has watched a cat and a dog knows that. By the time the elephant was coming towards me, he was in an ecstasy of pursuit.

As for me, I was utterly calm. When I think back on that calmness, I shiver. It was the calm of madness, the calm of self-destruction. I was a man possessed: but possessed by what, I have no idea. I was locked into my nonchalant stroll, a gentle amble towards Bill and Dougie's tree. I looked at them, read horror in their eyes, and glanced mildly over my shoulder. I don't know how close the elephant was then, but I remember the view vividly. I still see it sometimes. Quite often. I had an impression of greyness: greyness filled my entire field of vision. I shall not forget that I had to look *up* in order to see the animal properly. Big: grey: massively ivoried: but I walked on without breaking my stride. If I walked, I would be all right. It was that thought, a very foolish one, that filled my mind as the elephant had the sky.

I measured the distances afterwards, on a return visit, for the dusty surface held the tracks well. The final distance between me and the elephant was three paces: a little under ten feet. That was when the shot rang out.

I turned around fully then. As I did so, the elephant turned also, swinging away at right angles to the line of charge. He covered another ten yards and fell. Or rather crumpled. Deflated. Dead with one shot. Hit, as I discovered a few minutes later, in the *side* of the head.

Aubrey appeared from a clump of bushes far away on my left: about sixty yards from the elephant, more than one hundred yards from the clients. My long, slow walk had been a small miracle of self-mastery, but it was at this point that I abandoned control. 'You shot him! You shot him!'

Aubrey came towards us, his face completely blank. 'Why

didn't you fire a warning shot?' I asked him frenziedly. 'The *Manual* says you must fire a warning shot. Why did you shoot him? Why did you shoot him?'

Tears rivered unregarded down my face. It was at this point that I was seized by the urge to grab Aubrey's gun and to batter him senseless with the butt. I could have done so easily enough, so hotly did the adrenaline run. I think Aubrey knew that, for there was fear in his face. But I turned away, dropped into a crouch and sobbed unashamed.

I looked up to find Bill and Dougie standing over me, white-faced. Dougie extended a hand towards me, in an unresolved gesture of sympathy. I opted to take this as assistance to rise, so I accepted his weathered paw and stood. 'I'm so sorry,' I said.

'Don't talk about it, Dan.'

'No.'

We walked back towards camp. It was going to be a very long day.

7

Thunder cracked drily, not so much above as all around us. In the ebony glade, a black cuckoo called, triply sibilant, yet another rain bird, like all the cuckoos. A swift swish as the wall of a hut fell, bamboo matting unpinned. The huts were now mere thatch-roofed frames, though George's and mine still bore suspended mosquito nets and bedrolls.

The weather was cool, and working was pleasant enough. Rain was expected almost hourly. The Mchindeni was a narrow ditch, the ford to Impala Lodge all but leapable. Save for the short and almost dry squall, not a drop of rain had fallen, but with each moment the skies grew more threatening, or promising. Birdsong filled the air, a torrent of sexual excitement. The end of the season, the beginning of the season, it depended on your point of view, but no matter where you stood, or perched, this was the turning of the year.

The Tondo Pride had killed during the night, of that we were sure. We had heard the thunder that was not the thunder of the skies, but the rumble of stampeding buffalo. Later we heard the distress calls of a single animal. That meant they were close, very close, within a quarter-mile of camp. But we had not gone out to seek them. Bill and Dougie had left, and no journalists had arrived, which was just as well. We needed only to complete the dismantling of camp, preferably before the rains.

Most of our heavy equipment was now in store at Mukango. George and I had made a series of trips between the two camps the previous day, and I had made a solo run first thing that day. The two gas fridges, the dismantled beds, the tables and chairs, the washstands were all there – for a camp run on minimalist principles it was amazing how much junk we had.

We reckoned that another day and a half would see the job done. We would leave the day after that, though quite where we would put ourselves into store for the wet season, it was impossible to say.

We talked about our plans a lot, but never for the next dry or hot or tourist season. We discussed instead our plans for the jaunt or expedition to Njovu. You did not need to be a field naturalist in the George Sorensen class to diagnose displacement activity here. We also discussed endlessly the changing patterns of the bush as the year turned around us. I had many new bird calls to learn. The cuckoos delighted me. We said almost nothing of the past few days.

We called a halt for refreshments around eleven. The backroom team withdrew for mealie meal and relish; Sunday had made us sandwiches. He had insisted on baking fresh bread, despite the dismantling of his kitchen going on all around him. George had muttered about the inconvenience that Sunday's professional pride caused us, but the sandwiches were good. Sunday also made us a large pot of coffee. We had kept back two of the 'comfortable' chairs, as a touch of luxury, so we sat in the stripped sitenji, plates and cups on the floor.

'There! Didric cuckoo!' George's ability to retreat, or advance into the bush, its sounds and its stimuli, was a never-failing source of wonder to me. He seemed as immune to fretfulness as he was to the bothersomeness of tsetse flies and heat: a eurytopic man, George. While I had shifted about in my bed on the night that followed the shooting of the elephant and our almost equally horrific encounter with Mvuu, I had, within minutes of his retiring, heard the familiar sound of George's snoring through the walls of the huts. I could imagine George facing a firing squad with utter unconcern, his attention focused on a small brown bird singing behind the massed guns.

'Can't get it,' I said, meaning the didric cuckoo.

George whistled and then articulated the call for me, a soft announcement, a brief rattle of sweet notes. 'Di-di-diderc!' George insisted.

'Got it! Excellent.'

'Sunday!' George shouted. 'Can you do another couple of rounds of sandwiches?'

'I thought you did not want me to bake bread today,' Sunday answered, meaning, no doubt, that the sandwiches would be with us in just a moment. Despair seemed a long way from George's mind but perhaps he just wasn't concentrating.

We sat in silence, eating the sandwiches, drinking the coffee, both of them excellent. I heard the piping arrival of a greenshank on the exposed reaches of the river below us, and the quintessential Mchindeni sound, the fish eagle's triple scream. Thunder cracked again. I had an odd feeling of exclusion. Partly it was the end of the season, and I felt envious of the life that would continue here without me, the beasts that had no need to withdraw from the impassable, impossible conditions of South Mchindeni National Park after the rains had come. A thousand strange matters lumbered around my mind, a great flock of pterodactyls. Looking *up* at the elephant. The crumpling fall. The impossibly neat wound. A soft murmur of meditative thunder: a glimpse of forked lightning away towards the escarpment.

It was at this point that what we later called The Day of the Thousand Vehicles began. In fact, only five vehicles were involved, but since the normal daily arrival was nil, it seemed like a traumatic move to the South California freeway system.

'Vehicle,' I said, beating George to the sound of the engine. It is strange that when you are taking a game drive, you are seldom aware of the noise you make; you feel quite unobtrusive. But away from machinery, in the bush's normal noisy silence it is easy to hear a vehicle five minutes and more before it comes into sight. When George took a game drive and I remained in camp, I would hear his return from a couple of miles and more. Sometimes the sound was a prolonged early warning of visitors, a long moment of suspense until the guests, or invaders, swung into camp.

Eventually, the day's first vehicle arrived. It was a short-wheel-base Land-Rover with a closed cabin, not in its first youth. It was a Series Two, which meant it was old enough to bear the beer-bottle-opening shelf, but not the boss-eyed headlights of my own. For all its antiquity, it was a vehicle much tended, cleaned and polished, and it bore on its doors the insignia of the National Parks Commission. A small cloud of dust rose up beneath the ebony trees, and a young African in the lion-coloured uniform of a game scout leapt bouncily from the cab, walked around to the passenger door and opened it. Mvuu stepped awkwardly out, fat and ungainly.

Mvuu on his feet. Something was up, there could be no doubt about that. He was a pretty tall man, I saw for the first time, bigger than Leon but built on the same cubic principle. He turned and volleyed a series of instructions to his driver, who returned to his cab and drove a short way into the shade. He did not descend again.

We got up to greet Mvuu, and settled him into one of the two chairs. There was something not quite right about him, I thought. I walked up to the place where the oil drums that had fed the shower had stood, where I remembered there was a large mopane stump, irritatingly too large to fit beneath the hot-water drum. I carried this to the sitenji as a seat for myself, and offered our visitor a drink. 'Lion.'

'George?'

'Oh, why not, there's still a crate or so left isn't there? Shame to waste it, let's all have one.'

I walked across camp to the kitchen, the first of many such journeys I was to make that day. The beer was at least in the shade, and was apparently a little below blood temperature. Chambré. I decapitated the bottles and carried them to the sitenji. 'Sorry, it's a little warm, Mr Mvuu, but we put our fridge in store yesterday.'

'No matter. Do you have a glass?'

'Oh, sorry.'

I went back to the kitchen and collected one; Mvuu received it wordlessly and commenced his pedantic beer-pouring performance. It was then I realised what was wrong, or inappropriate about him: he was not wearing his usual khaki safari shirt. Instead he had on a white nylon shirt, clean, open-collared: unheard-of licence. It occurred to me then that I had never seen him smile.

Mvuu eventually completed his pouring, placed bottle and glass on the floor at his feet, paused, picked up his glass again, held it to the light, and finally placed it on the arm of his chair without letting go. He contemplated it for a long moment; I wondered whether or not to diagnose displacement behaviour, or merely an alcoholic's savouring of a brief but exquisite delay. Eventually he raised his glass and took one of his tiny sips; another; another. He returned the glass to the arm of his chair. 'I have some things to communicate,' he said at last. It was a shock to notice that I was trembling.

'The death of the elephant was regrettable. Very regrettable indeed.'

'I mean, I know –'

It seemed I had learned but little. I had the familiar, dizzyingly familiar, sight of Mvuu's raised hand, pale palm towards me. Since I was sitting some two feet below him, this was curiously alarming. I resolved to keep silent, knowing this was never one of my strong points.

'The death of the elephant was very regrettable,' he said, as if he could only continue with his recital by going back to the beginning. 'It is the first time that an elephant has been shot in this park in the presence of tourists. Very, very regrettable incident. The last time a shot was fired in the presence of tourists was in the previous season, when a warning shot was fired at a buffalo. The buffalo, an elderly male, withdrew, and the scout was praised for his prompt action. The season before that, no shots were fired. The season before that, that is to say, three seasons ago, two animals were shot and killed. One was an injured buffalo, an animal that had been damaged by a poacher's snare, and which approached too close to a party of tourists. A warning shot was fired, but the buffalo continued to menace the tourists. He was shot. No blame attaches. The second was a hippopotamus that was killed near Impala Lodge. The animal had taken to entering camp for grazing on a nightly basis, rendering it impossible for tourists to leave their huts without an armed escort. It had become a danger, and so a scout was given instructions by me to shoot the animal. No blame attaches. The licence-holder of Impala Lodge was recommended to take precautions against a repetition, and an electric fence was erected around the lodge the following season. So. You must see that the death of the elephant was very exceptional, and very regrettable. Am I making myself clear?'

'Yes,' I said. Mvuu chain-sipped his beer for a while.

'This week the South Mchindeni National Park executive committee held an extraordinary meeting in which the incident was discussed at full length. The committee is not satisfied on a number of counts. Number one: Scout Nyoka did not fire a warning shot. He was also in a bad position. He redeemed himself with very fine shooting under pressure, but we are not satisfied with his conduct prior to firing his rifle. He is not considered suitable for further touristic work. He has been seconded to a poaching patrol, with a recommendation that in future he is restricted to such work.

'Number two. Mr Lynch. We are satisfied with your knowledge of wildlife. The earlier decision to require you to re-take your safari guide examination is rescinded. But we are not altogether satisfied with your own conduct in the matter of the shooting. You were responsible for the wellbeing of the party. We are of the opinion that you could have prevented the regrettable incident from taking place.'

Fury overwhelmed me at this. The very injustice of it silenced me. The *Manual* spelt it out in its rules for walking: 'The safety of the clients and the wellbeing of all wildlife is the responsibility of the scout.' So I said nothing and Mvuu continued remorselessly: 'Also we understand that you rebuked Scout Nyoka before the clients. That is very unfortunate. We do not wish a repetition of such behaviours in South Mchindeni National Park. Now. Here are some of the findings of the committee. We do not propose to take away from you your qualifications as a safari guide. I say in addition that this was the decision of the committee, but it was by no means unanimous. It has gone into the minutes of the meeting that any request you might make for a permit to work as a safari guide in South Mchindeni National Park next season will not be looked on kindly. It is not considered that you are suitable calibre for working in a park that has been designated as a touristic destination for top-drawer international clients.'

I felt tears fighting for release behind my eyes, but I kept them in place with a fierce effort of will, and the help of three hard un-Mvuu-like swallows from my bottle of Lion. Rage, disappointment and distress fought for mastery.

'Number three. Mr Sorensen. You are the licence-holder for Lion Camp, South Mchindeni National Park, and therefore you are nominally responsible for the death of the elephant. Your licence to run a touristic operation in the aforesaid park is hereby revoked.'

George continued looking at Mvuu, in the manner of a trainer listening to an owner's bar bore.

'The committee wishes to emphasise that this is not a prohibition against your running touristic operations elsewhere in this country. The National Parks Commission, to which the executive committee reports, has added the rider to this finding, which is to say that the National Parks Commission is proud to be associated with George Sorensen. But it is felt that you are no longer suitable as a licence-holder in South Mchindeni National Park. It is felt that Mr Sorensen's style is not appropriate to a destination catering for top-drawer international clients.'

Silently, I got to my feet and went to the kitchen. I took three more bottles of beer, opened them, and carried them back across camp. The sight of beer seemed to unbend Mvuu a fraction. At least, he dropped some of his terrifying armour of committee-speak.

'Mr Sorensen, I am apologising for bearing this news to you. I am not wholly responsible for this.'

'Surely you have a casting vote,' I said, not without bitterness.

'No, Mr Lynch, no longer. I have taken the decision to take early retirement. I am standing down as warden at the end of the season, and I have already relinquished my chairmanship of the South Mchindeni National Park executive committee.'

'Who is taking over?' George asked, betraying, for the first time, mild interest in something Mvuu was saying.

'The minister, Mr Njiri, is taking over in both capacities. He is assuming temporary wardenship, and he also chaired the committee meeting.'

'As well as wardening the North Park? Busy man.'

'He is taking a personal interest in both parks, yes.' From the tone of Mvuu's voice, it did not seem that he was altogether delighted by this. The patronage of your wife's brother was clearly a more fickle thing than I, and no doubt Mvuu as well, had reckoned.

'Is this something to do with the road?' George asked.

'Naturally it is the matter of the road through the park that demands the personal involvement of a minister of state,' Mvuu said. 'Very important national concern.'

'I can see that.' I did see, too, or thought I did.

A pause grew up around us. Mvuu sipped his beer with concentration and method. At length, he was finished. He rose to his feet, not a straightforward manoeuvre. 'Well, I am sorry to bear bad tidings. But I am sure that you understand my position well enough. You will not shoot the messenger, no?' Mvuu gave a brief bark of laughter at his own joke.

'We never shoot messengers,' I said. 'Just be thankful you're not a focken elephant.'

But Mvuu had turned his back and was walking to his vehicle, and, anyway, my voice was discreetly low. The driver roused himself with a start, and leapt from the cabin to open Mvuu's door. Mvuu himself turned back and favoured us with a smile. 'I wish you good luck with your new venture.'

'What new venture?' I asked.

George, more intelligently, wished Mvuu well in his retirement. Mvuu nodded almost graciously, and climbed aboard his vehicle. In a roar he left us and we listened to the sound of the engine fading with extraordinary slowness across the vastness of the bush.

There was a long, long silence. I was unable even to summon up a petulant rage. After a while, George said: 'Dan, do you think it would be a sensible idea if you and I were to get pissed?'

'Why not?'

'Is that another vehicle?'

'No. Thunder.'

'No, it's not, it's Mvuu's vehicle, he's just taken the bend at the Tondo and turned south.'

'It's getting louder.'

I was right. Five minutes later, the second vehicle of the day swept into Lion Camp. Once again, the little fog of dust was summoned. The vehicle was quite something: a sparkling white Land-Rover Discovery, brand new, utterly covetable. Closed cabin, glass-windowed station-wagon back, the perfect expedition vehicle. The passenger door flew open, and out stepped a young African in city or business attire: grey pressed trousers, pale-blue shirt, white-striped navy tie. He looked about as appropriate here as a racehorse. He had about him an air of infinite capability. 'Mr Sorensen?'

George and I trailed sheepishly out of the sitenji like a pair of country bumpkins. George admitted his identity. 'Mr Sorensen, I am the personal aide of the Minister for Tourism and National Parks, Mr Jacob Njiri. May I present you to the minister?'

'Er, yes, all right,' said George.

The aide returned to the enviable vehicle, opened the driver's door, and the minister descended. He did so with a bouncing half-leap, a spry figure in a rather over-elegant cream safari suit. Gold-rimmed pilot-type spectacles framed his face. There was the slightest touch of grey at the temples, otherwise he looked alarmingly young. 'Mr Sorensen, yes, good morning, or good afternoon, if you prefer, it is a few minutes after twelve, is it not? I am delighted to meet you at last, truly delighted to meet you, for I have read your great book, and, truly, it was an inspiration to me as it has been to so many. And you are no doubt Mr Lynch; I believe you have done some important work on zebras. I would love to read your paper some time, if you could ever see fit to furnishing me with a copy. But may I ask you both a small favour? Could you be tremendously kind and put up with me butting in for a few minutes? I have a few things I would like to say to you both. I have heard so much about you, and what is more, I would love to be shown around Lion Camp, for I have also heard a great deal about your famous establishment.'

It is fair to say that Njiri's personality absolutely overwhelmed us both, it filled the camp. 'Jolly good,' said George.

Suddenly, I was the perfect safari guide. 'Of course, Minister, and welcome to Lion Camp. May we get you a drink? We are closing down, as you see, and we only have coffee and beer to offer you, both at roughly the same temperature since our fridges have already gone into store.'

'Thank you, Mr Lynch, a warm beer would be perfectly splendid.'

I went to the kitchen, and returned with beer. By this time, Njiri was standing on the edge of the bank, looking down at the still, but not for much longer, shrinking Mchindeni River. 'Thank you so much. Mr Lynch, this is sensational, the beer, of course, but also the prospect; every prospect pleases – Mr Sorensen, is that not so? – and only man is vile, present company, of course, excepted.'

There seemed no obvious reply to make to this. George and I showed Njiri around the camp; I continued to take the lead, since George appeared to have been struck partially dumb. The thatched framework of the huts Njiri greeted with a merry laugh. The site of the dismantled showers gave great pleasure. 'Truly, Mr Sorensen, you are a unique individual. Who else would have thought of such a thing as these showers? Not for you the mundanity of en suite facilities.'

Oddly enough he gave his greatest attention to the areas of the bank to the north and to the south of the camp. 'The glade is beautiful, beautiful, but the trees are too close together, are they not? How far to the end of the glade? Too far, I fear, too far. And behind it? No, the river is too far. N.G. as a position.'

But the north end found favour: 'Those two trees are really not bad, and the prospect here is still better. Yes, and you can also see the mouth of the Tondo from this point. Very good. Perhaps a little warm in the late season? But early season, this is tremendous. The combretum bushes are nothing, no matter. Oh yes, Mr Sorensen, this is a marvellous camp, it is full of potential.'

The task of throwing a minister of state into the pod of hippos below us in the Mchindeni seemed rather too much to take on just then.

'Now perhaps we could return to the sitenji and I could explain a few small matters to you both.'

'Another hot beer, Minister?'

'Excellent, how very kind.'

My head was just beginning to sing at this point: very very quietly and distantly, and not at all unpleasantly. I fetched beers. Any vestige of reality that had clung to the day seemed now to have dissipated.

'Thank you, Mr Lynch, thank you. Now, Mr Sorensen, you will be aware by now of the decision of the South Mchindeni National Park executive committee. I may say that I regret the decision very strongly, but such is the democracy of the committee system that my voice counted for nothing, alas.' He made an elegantly democratic gesture with both hands, gold-braceleted watch shining on his wrist.

'But, Mr Sorensen, I do have some small influence on North Mchindeni National Park executive committee. I feel very confident, in fact I think I could say without fear of contradiction, that we would welcome you in any form of touristic enterprise in the north. We are aware of the logistical difficulties attendant on all this. But I can say personally that I will afford you every possible facility. Anything at all that I can do to enable you to establish the first touristic operation in the North Park will be done. Everything, that is, short of financial assistance, which is beyond my brief, as I am sure you will understand.

'But when it comes to infrastructure, I intend to be of very great assistance. For example, I can organise the use of a grader for you at the start of the season to improve the access road to the North Park; we can make two, perhaps three cuts, for example. I can aid you by seconding to your operation two scouts, rather than the usual one. And I will, informally, be happy to accede as far as possible to any reasonable request you are pleased to make. If you were seeking to import a new vehicle, I would expedite the matter of an import licence, and negotiate on the matter of duty; such an import may well be permitted duty-free if it is considered beneficial to the well-being of the state. On all such matters, please be assured that you have my every good wish.'

'That is very kind,' George said, with an uncomprehending expression.

'Splendid! Then I can assume that you will be going ahead?'

George gathered himself together with an effort. 'Well, yes, it would be very nice, wouldn't it, but I am not sure that my company is capable of starting a new venture. It is no secret that we had a poor season. Our office in Chipembere had enough trouble finding clients to come to the South Park, which everybody in the business already knows about as a good tourist destination. I don't think that they would begin to be able to find clients to come to a place that is not on any of the tourist maps.'

'Mr Sorensen, you must sell them adventure! You must sell them the experience of travel beyond the maps!' Njiri was quite enraptured at the thought.

'My colleagues in Chipembere insist that there is no market for such things. They say that our clients want only comfort.'

'Then you must change your clients, Mr Sorensen, and perhaps you should also change your colleagues. Promise me this. You will think about it. Perhaps not next season. But I would like to take away with me your assurance that you will endeavour to find ways to refinance your company, to inspire your colleagues with new ambitions, and to pioneer tourism in the North Mchindeni National Park.'

'Well,' said George. 'If I find new partners, a new office,

new staff in Chipembere, a new vehicle, and a new set of contacts in the market countries, particularly in the UK, then I will be in a position to start thinking about it.'

'It is a problem. I can see that. But please give it your very best consideration. As I say, I will do everything I can to smooth your way, quite literally in the matter of the grader. Tell me you will think about it.'

'I will think about it, but to do anything more than think, I will need a miracle. Or failing that, a rather large sum of money – ah, hear that? Pretty Georgie.'

I don't suppose the minister had often been quite as dumbfounded. 'Emerald cuckoo,' I explained. 'It is supposed to say "Pretty Georgie".'

This didn't really help. The minister looked completely baffled, then a broad smile crossed his face. 'Ah, you are a man of the bush, Mr Sorensen, and you too, Mr Lynch. I must be away. It has been such a pleasure meeting you both. Now tell me, I believe it is possible to cross the river nearby and to reach Impala Lodge?'

'Certainly it is, Minister,' I said. 'Follow the road you came on, back past the ebony glade, until you see a truck spoor heading away on your left. Just follow it, and you're there. Or we could take you, if you like; the descent is a bit steep, and the vehicles get knocked about rather, and your new –'

'You are very kind, Mr Lynch, but I take a devilish pride in my bush-driving. I will endeavour to make the crossing unaided. If you hear the sound of crashing, you will no doubt come and rescue a much chastened minister. But for the moment, I have enough hubris to believe that I can manage.'

Njiri said his farewells, and climbed into the driver's seat, accelerating away, refloating the brief fog of dust. A thought struck me. 'Why the hell is he visiting Leon? I don't suppose he is sacking him from the park as well.'

'Some kind of tour of inspection?'

'George?'

'Yes?'

'What about this offer about the north?'

'Oh yes, it's a frightfully nice idea, isn't it? But I can't really see Joyce going along with it, can you?'

'Not exactly. The north isn't really bone-china cup country. But can't you talk Bruce round? Inspire him with the idea, get him to reinvest?'

'I suppose I'll have to try. But without any great hope of success – well, no hope at all really. Bruce has lost interest. He hasn't been out here all season, after all, has he? He used to be out here every few weeks, loved it, couldn't get enough.'

'Perhaps he needs to be inspired by the challenge of the north.'

'Perhaps he does. But he would still insist on employing Joyce, and that would bugger things up before we had even started.'

We kicked the idea around for a while, but it started to give us the glooms. So we had another Lion, and started to talk about Njovu instead, and its likely number of lion.

'I've just thought of something strange,' I said, during a pause.

'Really?'

'Did you notice that Njiri didn't once mention the road?'

'Perhaps he thinks it will make no difference to the park. Or perhaps he just doesn't care. Or perhaps he's got money in a road-building company.'

'Oh, highly cynical. If he's that devious, why is he making a tour of inspection of the South Park?'

'That's a jolly good question, actually. What the hell is he up to?'

'We really ought to get on with breaking camp, oughtn't we?'

'We're almost there. It's just a matter of making a few more trips to Mukango. Two. Maybe three.'

'Don't mind doing 'em,' I said. 'But I'm beginning to feel the slightest bit pissed. What if we load up, and I take the first lot out at first light tomorrow morning?'

'You can't possibly be pissed yet. Still, perhaps that should be remedied. Why not go and fetch another pair, perhaps I mean another pride of Lion?'

'Good thinking, George.'

'There's that emerald cuckoo again. Do you think we should take a look at him first?'

'Why not?'

8

'Of course, you know what we could do with two scouts,' George said.

We had found the emerald cuckoo, shouting out its absurdly inappropriate message of 'pretty Georgie'. The black cuckoo had then called close by, and we had spent a further thirty minutes looking for him. Eventually, we tracked him down, nice views, nice call, triply sibilant, the third note long and clear and rising. Then we returned to our 'comfortable' chairs and re-established the stated policy of the day by having another hot Lion.

'What could we do?' I asked obediently.

'We could do a walk with bearers. Split into two parties, us with the clients up front with one scout, party of bearers with all the gear following half a mile behind. Tents, cooking stuff, food, and everything. Go for days, and go where vehicles can't. Say two weeks. Seriously deep in the bush.'

'That's quite a thought. Have you got camping gear?'

'No. Well, only my own. Well, I think I've still got a tent. I used it last wet season, it's in Chipembere, at a friend's place, or at least, it was. I hope so, anyway; we'll need it in Njovu.'

'Not quite ready to lead a dozen tourists to adventure then.'

'Not quite, no. But you see the idea.'

'I think it's a cracker. Would we still need a new vehicle?'

'Well, we'd have to get the clients up to the North Park in the first place.'

'And back of course.'

'Those that remain.'

'That reminds me, will we be able to get off-road when we do the lion survey in Njovu, do you think?'

'Oh, I think so, don't you?'

'I was just remembering getting rather seriously stuck when I tried some wet-season bundu-bashing when I was working on my zebras. I wasn't too badly stuck to begin with, but it's amazing the way you can sort of dig yourself in.'

'Well, of course, once you start doing that you're in trouble, but mostly people make a lot of fuss about wet-season driving. It's just they're always in a hurry. It's amazing where you can get to, if you give yourself time. I mean, you get stuck a lot, you get stuck all the time, but you can usually drive out.'

'What, winch yourself out?'

'I'd love to have a vehicle with a winch, that would make it easy. No, the best technique is to use the high-lift jack, the Tanganyika jack.'

'How does it help, cranking the vehicle up in the air?'

'Oh, well, you see the trick is to drive off the jack. You sort of jump forward, and with luck you end up on firmer ground. Or a series of jumps. It's effective enough, even if it gets a bit messy. And time-consuming, of course. It works all right.'

'You must teach me the technique.'

'If we get off the road in Njovu, you'll have to learn it all right.' The thunder crumped again. 'Surely it must rain today,' George said, as if the weather was being irritatingly dilatory, much as he was wont to mutter to me about some inefficiency of Isaac the waiter.

'I thought we were trying to will it to hold off until tomorrow night, so we could keep the stuff dry before we got it all to Mukango,' I said. 'We really should be getting on with it right now.' I made absolutely no move to do so.

'I suppose so. Still, it's very pleasant here. Who knows when or for that matter if we shall ever spend the day sitting here again. Perhaps it'll hold off.'

A dry bark of a grey heron, flapping heavily upstream. A dry bark of thunder. 'I tell you, we're in deepish shit if it does rain,' I said. I took a studious pull on my Lion. There was only academic interest in my voice. I felt that I could take any amount of emergencies in my stride. 'Surely that's not another vehicle?'

'Can't be. No one left in the park but us, I think.' George cupped his hand around his ear and tilted back his head, towards the rear of the camp.

'It's coming from the other direction, isn't it?'

George leant forward, recupped. 'There's a vehicle crossing the river.'

'Bloody Leon taking a last bunch of clients down for a last look at our bloody lion.'

'They can't possibly have more clients. It's far too late.'

A few minutes later, we heard a roar, of engine, not lion or thunder, as the driver put his foot down hard to climb the steep bank. At this stage, the sound of any river-crossing vehicle normally grew fainter, as it passed behind Lion Camp to join the road that led to the airport in one direction, and to the Tondo Pride's core area in the other. But instead, the sound of the vehicle grew louder. The driver had taken the loop into Lion Camp.

'Your girlfriend come to rescue you,' said George, with mild malice.

'You bastard. No, I bet it's Lloyd with some ludicrous bird sighting, and he wants your support. Please George, I've just seen fourteen different Nearctic waders, and I want you to reassure me that I am not stringing common sandpipers and greenshanks.'

'Maybe it's Njiri to say he's changed his mind and he's going to become a partner in the company and invest a million kolwe in our future.'

'Or Joseph, wanting to lay flowers in the shower cubicle in blessed memory of the wet-bosomed Gianna.'

'Or maybe it's Leon coming to murder you, of course. That's a possibility to be born in mind.'

'Aubrey!' I called. Aubrey had long since departed; he had not been with us since the day of the elephant almost a week ago. 'Aubrey, if it's Leon, shoot the bastard! Don't waste time with bloody warning shots! Shoot him like a dog!'

We were still laughing at our jokes when the vehicle swung into camp. It was the Impala Lodge Land Cruiser, the new one, leaping impala logo on the door, paintwork still bright and green, as if even the copious dust of late season was reluctant to cling to it and mar its beauty. It was almost as covetable as Njiri's Discovery. Driving it, his face implacable, epigamic moustaches more bushy than ever, Leon.

He halted the vehicle and stepped out into the dust, cubic, uncompromising. He swung the door hard shut behind him. I was possessed by a fatal levity of spirit. 'Hullo Leon, we're trying to finish all our beer to save space on the journey to Mukango, besides, Njiri and Mvuu will confiscate it if we don't hurry. Care to help us?'

'Hullo George, Dan. Lion, yes please.'

I went to the kitchen, and did my stuff with three more bottles. I returned to find that Leon was in my chair, arms folded, giving a hard look at the dwindling Mchindeni river. Behind his habitual air of self-certainty, he looked uncharacteristically ill at ease. He didn't know how to begin whatever he had come to Lion Camp to say.

I handed out the beers and sat back on my mopane stump; sitting at Leon's feet had never been part of my game plan but there seemed no escape from it. 'Here's to a good close season for us all. And a successful new season for you, Leon,' I said unctuously. Leon grunted. 'Joseph well, I hope?' I added.

Leon took an un-Mvuu-like swallow from his bottle and fixed me with his eye. He said, fairly mildly but in a tone which made it clear that the mildness was costing him considerable effort, 'Don't get cute with me, son.'

'Leon, I hardly –'

'I said don't get cute. I am an upfront honest guy. I don't do things behind people's backs like some people in this park. When something happens, I confront it, I have it out face to face. Do you take my meaning?' Tyke my minning.

'I don't –'

'You know *exactly* what I'm bloody talking about, so don't get bloody cute. I have not come here to make a scene or to hit anybody. I have come here to have things out face to face.

But if anybody gets cute with me, then all bets are off. Take my meaning?'

I said nothing. I was beginning to get fractionally better at this. George too said nothing, but perhaps he was listening for cuckoos rather than showing colossal tact.

'George, I know this has been a rough season for you.'

'Well, it's been a little difficult in places, I suppose, yes.'

'I want you to know that there is no malice from me, and no malice from Impala Lodge. Not towards you. Do you understand that?'

'Of course not,' I interrupted. 'You just unmaliciously poach our brilliant safari guide, and our scout, and our clients, and our lion –'

'Shut the fuck up, you!' I had caused Leon to lose his temper: something of a triumph, but rather an alarming one. And I shut, for the time being, up. Leon held his muscled sausage of a forefinger under my nose, and his anger was an intimidating sight. It seemed unlikely then that I would survive the day unthumped.

Leon turned back to George. 'These things happened, yes. But it is not a matter of planning. Not a matter of a campaign against you. I know it must look bad in view of what has happened today. But I have come here to give you my solemn word that I had no idea what Njiri had in mind when he came into the park this morning. It is one of those things, George, just one of those extraordinary things that happen in this bloody country. But I want you to know that what Njiri did when he came to the bloody park today was just as much a surprise to me as it was to you.'

There was a pause, one that lasted for an uncomfortably long time. In the end, George realised that since I was forbidden speech, he had better say something himself. 'Are you talking about me having my licence to run Lion Camp taken away?'

'Partly.'

'I see,' George said, clearly not seeing. Leon took a hissing intake of breath, realising that he had to continue unaided.

'There's more to it,' he said.

George cocked his head to listen to the trill of a pied king-fisher, but made no remark.

'Look, George, it is hard for me to explain this. I thought you must know. The point is that Njiri has given me the licence.' Leon stopped, to let the announcement sink in.

'What licence?' George asked.

'What do you mean, what licence?'

'You've already got a licence to run a camp.'

'Of course, but there's something new happening out here.' Out year. 'No, George, Njiri has given me a second licence.'

'What on earth for? You're not setting up as a white hunter, are you?'

'Nott! George, will you please listen to me. This is *hard* for me. I thought you knew, I thought Njiri had told you, I didn't expect to have to explain myself. But listen, Njiri drove across the river just now, and completely out of the blue, I want you to know that, *completely* out of the blue, he told me, not asked me, he told me that I was to start operating Lion Camp from next season, and I am to have a five-year licence to run Lion Camp as an extension to Impala Lodge.'

There was a long pause, as George listened to the mutterings of the ebony glade. A mutter, too, of thunder, now very distant again. The sky seemed a little darker. At length, George said: 'Jolly good.'

'Look George, I had no idea –'

'I'm sure you'll do an awfully good job.'

'It's very exciting professionally.'

'Of course.'

'I thought I would groom Joseph up to be in charge of Lion Camp in the second season. He will get his safari guide's licence in a couple of days, he has his exam with Philip Pocock tomorrow, and he'll bloody cruise it, man. You know how bloody good he is. And then give him a season to learn the ropes. And if he trains on, he will be in charge of the whole camp. No matter how big it is by then.'

'Jolly good. Very pleased for him.'

'George, you don't make it easy for me. But I've got some more things I want to say.'

'What about the road?' I said intemperately. But I didn't think this counted as getting cute.

'I don't know anything about the road,' Leon said, a strange reply for one who always prided himself on being well informed. 'What can you do in this bloody country but go ahead and hope for the best? They might change their minds tomorrow about bloody anything.'

'But I thought it was all settled and fixed.'

'Of course it's all bloody fixed, man, except that nothing is ever fixed in this bloody country until it is finished. And not always then. That's how things work out here.'

At this point I returned to silence.

'Now look, George, Njiri says you are thinking about starting up an operation in the North Park.'

'Njiri is talking about it, not me. I can't afford it. The company was in danger of going broke in any case; this will most likely finish it off.'

'I would still like to make a suggestion. If you do get round to starting up in the north, you will need to overnight your clients somewhere on the way.'

'That's one of the logistical problems, of course.'

'Well, you can put them up at my place. I would like to offer that as an olive branch. Put them up, for free, grub at cost price, work something out later, for as long as we are both in business.'

'That's very handsome of you, Leon. But I don't think it's something we will take you up on.'

'You think about it, George.'

'Oh yes. Yes.'

Leon stood and drained his bottle with a flourish. 'I got to go.' He turned and looked George in the eye, man to man and face to face, seizing George's hand in his own steak-like one. The theatricality of this manoeuvre was rather spoiled by the fact that George did not get to his feet, nor offer any answering manly clasp. It looked like someone warmly wringing the hand of a maiden aunt. 'Good luck, George.'

'Thank you, Leon, and jolly good luck to you, too.'

Leon walked off to his vehicle without another word. I kept quiet. He slammed the door once again and drove off in a roar. I went to the kitchen to fetch more beers.

'I am getting used to Leon ripping us off,' I said, sitting back on my warm-seated 'comfortable' chair. 'But I don't think I will ever get used to his need to be congratulated every time he does so. I wanted to say, "Leon, it may feel like it to you, but from where we are sitting, it really doesn't feel as if you are doing us that great a favour."'

'Is that what you think?' asked George. 'I thought it was pretty good of him, really. The overnight is quite a good offer, worth a lot of money. I mean, potentially, if we set up, and all things were equal. Of course, they aren't and we won't, as I said, but Leon wasn't to know that.'

I sat in silence for a while. The pied kingfisher called again, and then the pretty chatter of pied wagtail. For a moment, I contemplated flinging myself in among the pod of hippo. For a long moment, it was all my fault. All my fault. I hadn't helped George at all. I had ruined him. 'George?'

'Yes?'

'You know I – I had a bit of a fling with Caroline?'

'Oh. Yes, well, I did notice, yes.'

'Well.'

'Well, I don't blame you, splendid idea, nice chick, you know, I'd have done the same thing myself.'

'Leon knows, doesn't he?'

'I suppose he was a bit short with you. Perhaps he does. Or perhaps he just sees you as a threat, or a danger of some kind. So he is stimulated into this defensive threat behaviour.'

'Do you think he's been having a go at Lion Camp all season as a matter of revenge?'

'Oh, what an interesting theory. I hadn't thought of that.'

George seemed to think that this required no further comment. 'It's been worrying me, you see,' I said, worriedly. 'And it's worrying me a lot more now.'

George returned his mind to the subject, which was something of a triumph. 'I think the point you miss is that Leon is a businessman,' he said eventually, as if that explained everything.

'So?'

'Well, he wouldn't take on new staff, let alone a new camp, if there weren't sound business reasons for doing it. I suppose if he could have influenced getting you chucked out of South Mchindeni Park, he might have enjoyed that on a personal level. But everything else is business.'

'God, all I did was take his girl away for a single night. He has taken the whole bloody bush away from me for bloody ever. The *bush*, George.'

'I do see that. From me too, when you think about it. But Leon'll make a grand success of it all; at least, he will if they don't build the road. Brave of him to continue really. He will have to invest a hell of a lot of money in Lion Camp if he wants it to be anything like Impala Lodge. That's quite frightening when you consider the threat to the park.'

'I can't stand it, George. And most of all, I can't stand the thought of flushing bloody lavs in our camp.'

'Me too. But Leon's still pretty brave, taking it all on right now. He's quite brave and effective really. I mean, for a complemental male.'

'George?'

'Yes?'

'What's a complemental male? I looked it up, but I couldn't find a reference in any of the books.'

'Oh. Well, it's – how does the definition go? – it's a thing you find with invertebrates, something like "a male that lives permanently attached to a female, often small and degenerate except for well-developed reproductive organs".'

9

By late afternoon, the day still thundery, still rainless, George and I had reached the subject of the bone-arse. This was a particularly delicate and sensitive business. 'I mean, Sunday deserves a double bone-arse at least,' I said. 'Considering he did most of the caterer's job as well as the cook's, we really owe him. We'd never have managed without him, and he knows it.'

Bone-arse was Sunday's pronunciation of this desirable addition to wages, paid at the end of every season. It was rather a subject of his: 'Isaac, you drunk again. You lose your bone-arse, Isaac,' he would shout, clearly and in English, in a voice that carried across the camp, so that George and I would hear and Isaac would be soundly teased. 'Great meal, Sunday.' 'Oh, very good, Dan, my bone-arse is assured.'

So that was inevitably how George and I pronounced it as well. It was no longer a joke in that it made us laugh, but it had become a ritual shared drollery: an aspect of bond reinforcement. The problem of the bone-arse was that the end-of-season thank-you was considered a half-promise and more of employment the following season. 'I want them to get the extra money all right,' George said. 'But I don't want them to receive a bone-arse under false pretences.'

'They must know the situation anyway,' I said. 'Gossip being gossip. Especially in the Valley.'

'But I'll still have to explain. I suppose I'd better talk to everybody tomorrow morning, or afternoon, more like, before we take them back to the villages. Oh dear. It won't be easy for them to find work next season.'

'Well, there'll be work here, won't there? I mean, at Lion Camp.'

'I hadn't thought of that. I'd thought that Lion Camp would

be no more, since we won't be here. Silly of me. I suppose most of them will get taken on then. Joseph knows who's good. And Caroline had one of Sunday's meals, didn't she, so I suppose she'd give him a job. I hope so. But I'm a bit worried about Isaac. Everybody knows he's a bit of a pisscart. Not everyone wants to put up with that.'

'Didn't you cancel his bone-arse already? I seem to remember some hard words along those lines, when we picked him up after two days off at his village and found him ripped to the tits. Needed twenty-four hours to sleep it off.'

'You're quite right, I did say that. Oh well, I expect I'll have forgotten about it again by tomorrow. In the circumstances.'

'I bet you do that every year. Regardless of circumstances.'

'Do you think Leon would take him on? He was reasonably presentable when Caroline was here, wasn't he?'

I didn't have an answer to that. This was perhaps, for all that the competition was stiff, the question that gave me the most heart-scalding. I couldn't bear the thought that Caro's visit to Lion Camp had been purely, or impurely, one of reconnaissance. Or was she relishing the taste of a double betrayal: betraying the friendship and the love so briefly shown to her at Lion Camp, where she had briefly betrayed her own greater loyalty to Impala Lodge?

'I don't think I am capable of giving you a sensible reply about Caro,' I said. Lion, I found, had unlocked my tongue. George and I were sitting not facing each other but side by side, eyes out over the Mchindeni River and the bank beyond. It was a reasonable alignment for self-examination and confession.

'I thought she was such a nice chick,' George said.

I sought firm eye contact with a yellow-billed stork, standing back agape in the stream. 'So did I. But things change, don't they? We don't know precisely what the Impala Lodge people have been up to, but it doesn't fill my heart with love.' I raised my gaze to a male puku, announcing his descent to the beach with a sharp whistle. 'But on the other hand, if she should turn up right now, and pray God she doesn't, and she asked me to, say, jump into the Mchindeni and swim with the crocs, or to pick a fight with the Tondo Pride, I rather think I'd do it. Jaysis, you couldn't stop me.'

'Is that another vehicle?'

'Focken Jaysis,' I said prayerfully, wondering what and who my words had called into being.

It is always the sound of a gear change that carries, breaking the unmechanical patterns of the bush. We heard such a sound then.

'Dan, I really think –'

'Jesus, no. Please God, no.'

'Dan, it didn't cross the river, did it? Came from this side.'

'Thank Christ for that. Who is it, then?'

The roar swelled, and at last the vehicle appeared. It was a Land Cruiser with game-viewing seats, but it bore no game-viewers, and no leaping impala logo on its door. Instead, it had a silhouetted, spread-eared elephant, and the words 'Philip Pocock Safaris'. Driving it, most unusually, was Philip Pocock himself. He stopped, opened his door and stepped down a little stiffly. He was wearing a bush jacket, and a cravat with his khaki shirt; the cool – it was barely 80 – clearly affected him, with his thinned old man's blood. We walked over to greet him.

'What the hell are you doing here, Philip?' George asked him.

'Is this the famous Lion Camp hospitality? Really, George, it's not often I drive across the park these days, and I expect something a little bit more cheering when I arrive. I think it will rain tonight, don't you?'

'I suppose it probably will, yes. I've been telling Dan all day that we need to get on with packing up, but he insists on sitting about drinking beer.'

'Me?' I asked, outraged. I offered Philip a beer, was accepted, and went to the kitchen to do my stuff. George and I seemed to have reached a pleasant plateau of semi-intoxication, on which we were perfectly capable of performing anything save precision tasks, but where nothing had very much reality. An enjoyable way to deal with the end of the season and its troubles, in fact.

I returned to the sitenji and distributed Lion; once again I took my seat on my mopane stump.

'Thank you, Dan, thank you very much. I suppose you have all heard the news?'

'News?' said George, looking hard at his bottle.

'We know the news about us,' I said. 'I'm sure you know that George and I have both been kicked out. Out of South Mchindeni National Park, anyway.'

'Well, that's not quite the news I meant, but that's why I came to visit you, of course. To say that I am very sorry to see it happen, George. I spoke in your favour, of course, yours too, incidentally, Dan, but as you know, I don't have a position of authority here any more. I'm not the person they turn to these days.'

'I wish I could have that walk again,' I said. 'Just to *try* something different. Just to see if doing anything different would have changed the way things turned out.'

'Oh, I read all the reports,' Philip said. 'Assuming your own report was one hundred per cent accurate, and I have no reason to believe otherwise, then I don't see anything else that you could have done. Something spooked the elephant. It might have been because someone in your party ran. If it wasn't that, then the running made everything a hundred times worse. The blame almost certainly lies with the person who first broke into a run, one of your two clients or your scout. The fact that the scout was not between the clients and the elephant was shocking, a sackable offence in my book. But *you* did get between the clients and the elephant, and you didn't run. You staked your life on Aubrey Nyoka's marksmanship, and that's not something I would do in cold blood. Especially as you didn't even know if Aubrey was still there. Incidentally, that was an extraordinary shot. Quite extraordinary. I've shot elephant myself from sideways on, but it's very difficult to make a clean kill that way, hardest shot in the book. And Aubrey fired no warning shot. I think myself that he *did* fire a warning shot – and that it killed the elephant. He didn't lay off enough.

'And as for the elephant, well, I have lived my life with elephants, as you know, spent more time with elephants than I did with any of my wives, to their everlasting irritation. And when I have been on foot, and an elephant has taken exception to me, I have scarcely ever seen anything other than a mock charge. That is how elephants work, isn't it? Look as big as possible, as fierce as possible and frighten the buggers away. But when you are caught in a real charge, there is no mistaking it. A real charge doesn't *normally* come straight out of the blue, but I have known it happen once or twice, and your description made it perfectly obvious that this was what happened.'

'I feel so bad about my elephant,' I said. 'Not just the elephant himself, though that's bad enough, but the fact that the bastards used the death of the elephant to get at George and to steal his camp.' My tongue, Lion-loosed, spoke what had haunted my mind for days.

'Dan, if it hadn't been the elephant, it would have been something else. They've been talking all season about Lion Camp's failure to bring foreign exchange into the country. That would have done just as well. If you'd had a rush of clients, they'd have done you for inadequate facilities; there was some talk of that, too. The elephant was just a heaven-sent excuse. It simply made it easy for them.'

'Will you still be here next year, Philip?' George asked.

'Oh, yes, if I'm saved, you know, if I'm saved. I don't plan to feed the lions just yet.'

'Still in business?'

'Oh, yes. The young people are doing a good job of running Mukango. They are very tolerant of the old bugger in the planter's chair, humouring him, making him feel wanted, pretending to involve him.'

'I just wondered if you might call it a day. With the road and everything.'

'Oh, my goodness me. Then you *haven't* heard the news, have you?'

'I thought we were the news.'

'And I thought Njiri had been out to see you.'

'Briefly, yes. He came here to throw us out, look at the view and then drove across to Impala Lodge.'

'He came to visit me first. Told me about you, of course, but also told me about the road.'

'Well, what *about* the road, Philip?'

'The fact is that they are not going to build it. Yesterday, the government decided on a southerly route, missing the bottom end of the park by a good twenty miles, so we even have a decent buffer zone. Of course, it puts an extra seventy miles onto the journey, but they agreed to it. It's a complete triumph for Njiri.'

'Was he against the road? I thought he was all for it.'

'He changed sides, you see, that's what swayed the balance. He changed sides about halfway through the season.' Philip began to laugh wheezily. There seemed to be a joke hidden in there somewhere, but I could not see it at all.

George was aware of this as well. 'Out with it, Philip. What's happening?'

'How rich that you didn't know. How very rich that you had no idea.'

'Know what?'

'Njiri joined Leon's firm as a partner halfway through the season. He now owns a chunk of Impala Lodge and, naturally, he wants to expand. That's why Leon got the Lion Camp licence. And that's why Njiri stood out against the road. He's got money in the park, now.'

'But that's pretty small beer, by ministerial standards,' I said. 'Leon's doing pretty well, but it's not exactly Swiss bank account stuff, is it?'

'Well, this country has two recognised destinations for international tourists, does it not? South Mchindeni National Park and Palmyra Resort. On a standard package you fly into Chipembere and overnight there. And there are two decent hotels, the Grand and the Victoria. Njiri owns the Grand and has a share in the Vic. He has a holding in Eagle Air, so he makes money from all the connecting flights. And barring a couple of lodges, there's only one place to stay in Palmyra Resort, and that's the Palmyra Hotel. Njiri owns that outright. And here's the punchline: he's on the verge of getting parliamentary permission to open a casino in the hotel, the first in the country. It's an empire. Leon's operation, and, for that matter, all of South Mchindeni National Park, is just a way of bringing the punters to the roulette tables.'

'The bastard!' I said. 'That bastard Leon. He has betrayed the lot of us, hasn't he? He has betrayed the entire park.'

Philip regarded me mildly but disconcertingly. 'Dan, I know you are very young, but I think it would be a good plan if every now and then you tried to conceal the fact. For you are completely wrong. Leon has not betrayed the park. Leon has saved the park. If it had not been for Leon, the road would certainly be built. It really is as simple as that. It was he, not you, not me, and not George, who persuaded the minister that it was possible to place a serious dollar value on wildlife, on the bush. What other arguments can you use to persuade governments, after all? True, Leon probably also stressed the negative publicity that would follow if they did go ahead and bugger up the park. But plenty of countries are prepared to live with that – look at all the places where there used to be rain forests. No, Dan. Leon is our saviour. I hate to say that, but it is true. The park had to be saved, and you are the price, you George and your young friend here.'

'I see,' I said slowly. 'You know, I have sometimes thought that I would gladly die to save the park. Or to save just the Tondo Pride, for that matter, or just the ebony glade. So I suppose the park comes cheap at the price really.' More Lion talk. 'I shouldn't grudge it, perhaps, though I do. Saving the park at the price of leaving it for ever. That's going to take a bit of adjusting to.' I also thought, but didn't add, that the idea of Leon as out-and-out bastard was one thing, and a matter I could handle with only intermittent flashes of paralysing rage, but Leon as hero – that was far too bewildering a concept for my poor brain to grasp.

'I have looked after the interests of the Valley as best I could for nearly fifty years,' Philip said. 'But I am out of step with modern life and, besides, I am tired. Leon seems to have taken on my role as defender of the bush. I opened the park for tourism. Leon has made it safe for the next generation.'

'Do I have to like him then, Philip?'

'No, Dan. But you have to admire him. There's no getting out of that.'

'Oh, I admire him all right,' said George. 'I rather like him, too. I envy him, in a way. I can't do the things he does. Committees. Money. Deals. I don't understand any of it. Even the bits I understand, I can't actually do. And the bush needs someone who can do all that. I do see that.'

'You can't change, George,' Philip said. 'But the point is that the park has changed. Not the bush, but the park, the people in the park, the way the park is used, the sort of people who come here, the numbers they come in. And you can't go back on all that.'

'Dollo's Law,' George said. 'Evolution is irreversible. Structures and functions once lost cannot be regained.'

'Very good. The park is a ghetto, a controlled ghetto, managed for wildlife and funded by tourism. We have to accept that. It's not the limitless bush any more.'

'I have spent a lot of my life thinking about the natural processes,' George said. 'I have often wondered what it would be like to go extinct.'

'Local extinction is not final extinction, George. You must migrate, found a small but viable population elsewhere. You are not extinct, just driven to the fringes of your range.'

'Philip, if anyone else tells me to go to the North Park, I will hit him on the head with a beer bottle. As I keep explaining, though not a single person has actually listened, as I have spent the entire day telling one deaf person after another, I have neither the money nor the organisation to set up a crazy venture like taking tourists to the North Park.'

'If I had any cash, George, I'd invest it all with you. But Mukango doesn't make vast profits, it just keeps going. But if you think of any way I can help, just ask. You know that.'

'Thanks, Philip. We could rob a bank, perhaps?'

'Good idea. I think I have it in me to become a senile delinquent.'

'We could rope in Aubrey as well,' I said. 'He's got what it takes all right.'

'Excellent, excellent. Look, I must be away, the sun will be down soon, and I ought to leave the park before it gets dark, you know how querulous the scouts on the gate are.'

'Why not stay for a sundowner anyway.'

'Thank you, no, I must be well behaved. The young people at Mukango will be sending out search parties for me if I'm late – the old fool's driven into a herd of buffalo, that sort of thing. I must be considerate.' He got to his feet, and we walked across camp to his vehicle.

'We'll be passing your way tomorrow to fill the storeroom.'

'I'll look forward to seeing you, George. And I'm going to get you north somehow. You just see if I don't.'

He drove away, leaving the small fog of dust. 'Any beers left, Dan?' George asked, his mind as ever on the essentials.

'Not many now. Some, anyway. I'll get a couple. After all, it's nearly time for a sundowner.' I went to the kitchen. Sunday was squatting comfortably at his cooking range, which was a metal grill over a mopane wood fire. Exuberant smells filled the air. 'You making us a curry?'

'Ethiopian curry.'

'Hot-hot?'

'So hot you will surely double my bone-arse.'

After Philip had left, I had a fancy for a fire, but George said he didn't dare ask Isaac. So I found Isaac and asked him myself, but I told him it was very important because George had asked for it specially.

'But we have no clients.'

'George thinks it is important.'

'George only has fire for clients.'

'Oh, Isaac, you make a fire, then George will pay you a bone-arse without fail.'

Sunday's argument tipped the scales in our favour, and Isaac built a nice fire for us. George and I sat, each with a beer, on either side of the small flames, facing the river and playing I Spy With My Little Ear. For some reason, one not unconnected with the amount of Lion I had drunk in the course of the day, I felt it was vastly important to write down the source of all the sounds we identified. I have the list still, because I wrote it on the endpapers of my copy of *Roberts' Birds of Southern Africa*.

'There's the Heuglin's.'

'And the – shut up George, I know it – black-headed oriole.'

'Mvuu will be impressed.'

I made a phallic gesture at him. Another call: a pretty, lisping cadence, a charming little journey down the scale. 'Oh, I know that one too.'

'Of course you do.'

I thought. I grimaced. I held my head in my hands. I ran through every African bird I had ever heard in my life. I was playing the game with Lion-inspired intensity. The sound was infinitely familiar, infinitely obscure. I closed my eyes and listened: another sweet, soft cadence: but no answer came. Eventually I had to give up.

'Willow warbler.'

'Oh no!' My cry was anguished. Obligingly, the bird did it again: a song I had heard every English spring of my life. The patch of hawthorns just beyond the stable block normally held two pairs, and in May and June, the two cock birds would sing to each other furiously from either end of the thicket. A tiny scrap of feathers; you could hold a dozen in your cupped hands; it had flown from northern Europe to the banks of the Mchindeni River. 'Amazing. And to think it will have to go back again in a few months. Unbelievable.'

'What's so unbelievable? You did it.'

'Ah yes, but with a crucial difference.'

'You can't fly.'

'Good spot, but not the difference I mean.'

'No?'

'I'm not going back.'

'That's what I thought, when I was your age.'

'But you never did go back.'

'Precisely.'

The last exchange, somewhat Lion-driven, left me a trifle dizzy. After a pause, I said, 'George?'

'Yes?'

'Were you ever as deep in the shit as we are now?'

'Oh yes. Quite often, actually.'

'Aren't you worried though? This all seems disastrous to me.'

'It's potentially disastrous, Aubrey.'

'George you are *unworried*. I don't see how that can be. Do you think things aren't especially serious? Or do you have faith that something will turn up?'

'Oh, well, I haven't thought about it really. But we're going to end up doing something, aren't we, even if it's not exactly what we wanted.'

'But the bush, George.'

'Well, I decided when I was about your age that I was never

going to leave the bush. And I never have. I haven't always done exactly what I wanted in it – I've never really worked out what I wanted to do, come to think of it. But I've always been in the bush.'

'I used to think something of the kind about racehorses. But it's the bush now.'

'Dangerous things, horses.'

'But it's nothing to do with danger, is it? It's bush. Or the horses.'

'Well, you'll stay in the bush, since you seriously want to, and that, in one sense, is an end to the matter. And so will I. It would be nice if we could work together again – I mean, after we have done the Njovu expedition. But, well, either we do something together or we don't. We'll both be in the bush somewhere or other. There's still quite a bit of it left, you know. Bearded woodpecker.'

'Got it.' I wrote the name down laboriously. A flight of hadeda ibis came tumbling down onto the beach, shouting their name in loud comic voices. A high-pitched chattering came from the glade. 'Ha! Lizard buzzard.'

'Oh, very close, it's –'

'It's that bloody little sparrowhawk, you can't fool me.'

'Precisely.'

The light was fading, but the sun did not sink, at any rate not visibly. 'A cloud-downer?' George asked, drinking thoughtfully.

'They're not exactly going down,' I objected. 'They are just changing colour. From grey to sort of blue-black.'

At this, the sky scrawled a rapid signature of light over the blue-black clouds then a crack of thunder, louder and more sudden than before. There was a new note in this thunderclap: a note of urgency.

'We're going to be washed out if it rains tonight,' George observed, untroubled. 'I am by no means sanguine of the thatching on our huts.'

'Do you think the sitenji will leak?'

'Perhaps.'

'Well, if it does, it does.'

'It'll last longer than our huts, at any rate.'

'Remember they did both our huts on a single morning, when we were collecting the first clients of the season? It always looked like a botch job. But it didn't matter, did it, until now?'

'How very true.' A pearl-spotted owlet began its extravagant sequence of calls; a few minutes later, a barred owlet, monotonous and breathless, welcomed the night. On the far side of the ebony glade, we heard a sudden row among a roost of guinea fowl, fat morsels of birds always keenly aware of their own edibility. Then, loud and very clear, the whoop of hyena. 'Ah. Hyena must be moving onto the buffalo kill,' George said. 'The buff that the Tondo Pride killed last night. The lion must have pulled out. Wonder where they have gone to lie up.'

'Odd not to have visited them, isn't it? Odd to be too busy to find a lion kill.'

'It's always odd at the end of a season. Charging in and out of Mukango, hoping you don't see any good game, because it will hold you up. Trying to beat the rain. And you always fail. At least, I always do. By about a day. Always.'

'Listen. Behind the glade.'

A sound halfway between a cough and a large saw cutting through a log. Unmistakably leopard. 'Nice spot, Dan, *excellent*.' The radiophonic sound of the epauletted fruit bat. Night: and despite the fact that the long sit beside the river had given us the best possible night vision, it seemed very dark indeed. The cloud cover was dense.

'I'd like to bring a hygrometer here. You can really feel the jump in the relative humidity.'

'And the temperature has dropped quite sharply,' I said. 'I'm going to my hut to get my jacket. I bet you're glad I got Isaac to make the fire.' As I stood up, there was a brief scribble of light, and for a moment the opposite bank of the Mchindeni was brightly visible. The world cracked and crumped.

I returned to my chair in my belt-flapping, over-pocketed

and epauletted jacket, and resumed my seat. Isaac brought us big platefuls of Ethiopian curry, which we ate on our knees. 'Any more beer, Isaac?'

'Not so many. Maybe some.'

He brought us two more. George ate furiously, with his usual total concentration. The curry was distinctly bone-arse-worthy. George spoke again when his feeding frenzy had died down and his plate was clean. 'I needed to perform alimentation. Soak up some of the Lion.'

'Not too much, though.'

'Certainly not.'

Above our heads, a wood owl called. The second bird joined in and the pair performed a duet.

'I hope my Land-Rover starts,' I said. 'And finishes, come to think of it. I am by no means sanguine of its ability to reach Chipembere.'

'We could do the journey in tandem, if you like.'

'That's a sporting offer. It won't be quick, though. It won't do more than about eighty Ks.'

'Never mind. We could make it a two-day trip, if you like. I know a nice stretch of woodland where we could camp out, do a spot of birding.'

'That's a thought.'

'Have you decided what to do when you get to Chip?'

'Well, I'll be able to sleep on somebody's floor for a week or so. I'll look around. Thought I'd pick Philip's brain tomorrow. Some of the operators from the other parks are likely to be in town. Some of them will be going to the World Travel Market, so if I can catch them before they leave, I can sound people out about work for next season, before we go to Njovu for the lion. Hadn't thought beyond that.'

I feared that another fit of the glooms could be descending. We sat in silence for a while. Then George said: 'Can I hear another vehicle?'

'Surely not. Must be thunder. No one will be driving out tonight.'

'Listen. Over that way, from the riverbed.'

226

'Simply not possible, nobody will be taking a night-drive tonight.'

George stood and walked to the edge of the bank. 'I can see lights.'

I went and joined him. On the far side of the Mchindeni River, twin headlights were moving steadily north towards us. They proceeded slowly, sensibly along the far beach: but there was no bright beam of a spotlight. Even without clients, you use a spot. The light is not just for finding game; it is also for finding your way. A spot is an important safety device. It helps you to follow a path over the deceptive rises and undulations of ground when you are bundu-bashing in the dark. This was unusual; this was also distinctly risky. More than a touch mad.

It seemed that the vehicle was following the truck spoor laid down by all those crossings of the Mchindeni River, seeking the Giraffe Crossing. Yes: it veered to the usual crossing point, the lights briefly flashing into our eyes. 'How more than odd,' George said. He sat down and rolled himself a cigarette. I took the completed work from him without asking or thanks; uncommenting, he rolled a second for himself. I lit mine from the fire, at arm's length. The engine proceeded, more smoothly now, towards the steep slope up the bank. And then a shrill gear change, and a sudden scream of engine. The driver of the vehicle had his foot flat to the boards.

'Someone's playing silly buggers out there.'

'I think he's reversing,' George said. He was on his feet again, cigarette glowing between his lips. 'He's crazy, he'll fall off the bank. Wild driving. Now he's back in forward gear.'

'Christ!' I said. For the headlights suddenly, almost absurdly, rose and probed skywards, twin columns clearly visible in the dusty air, sharply defined inverted pyramids of light against the backdrop of cloud.

'He's climbing. God, it's steep. Not far off vertical. He'll roll in a second. Someone has gone completely crazy out there.'

We heard the engine in a frenzy of effort, and then the lights swung sharply downwards. 'He's made it, whatever he was climbing.'

'Just. He was bloody lucky.'

The beams pushed forward, level now, and then startlingly, they disappeared altogether. All we could see was a spooky glow over the outline of the bank. And then the engine screamed again: louder and shriller than before.

'Stuck,' said George. 'Spinning all four. Has he engaged low ratio?'

'Couldn't have climbed the bank without.' The vehicle called out like a pained animal. 'He's digging himself in deeper, I reckon. We'll have to go and rescue.'

'Even if it's Leon?'

The engine sounded quieter as if the driver were trying a more rational approach: slowly feeding juice into the engine, hoping to gain a little traction by being careful and logical. For a second, the vehicle seemed to respond; then once again it screamed. 'Come on, Dan. We have to go. Whoever the idiot out there is, he's in trouble.'

'I'm a bit pissed for rescue work,' I said. 'Still, we have to go all right. Shall I drive?'

'I'm OK. You get the spot.'

And so George and I set out on the last night drive of the season, George in the driving seat, me standing high behind him, not looking for leopard but lighting the way ahead.

'We'll follow the truck spoor towards Giraffe Crossing,' George called back over his shoulder. 'Take it from there.'

'Why not?'

We veered off the road and bundu-bashed out along the river bank. Ahead of us we could see the lights of the other vehicle. I could hear no more screaming sounds; presumably the driver had seen us and was waiting for rescue.

'I wonder which bloody idiot we'll find,' I said.

George was driving with apparent sobriety, certainly without anxiety. We breasted a small rise, and the stranded vehicle was before us. And all at once, two simultaneous terrors struck me. 'Jaysis,' I said. 'Oh sweet focken Jaysis. Tell me this isn't happening.'

George looked over his shoulder again. 'All your favourite girls in all the world,' he said.

He was right. In the vehicle, Caro. All around the vehicle, the lionesses of the Tondo Pride. They were lying across the truck spoor, in unmoving splendour, replete, content, the nearest six feet from Caro. They were all lying on their fronts with their heads up, watching the two vehicles with increasing interest. They were animated and intrigued: not relaxed. Certainly not unworried. 'Ah,' said George. 'Of course. It all makes sense now.'

He raised his voice: 'Hold tight, er, Caroline. We'll be with you in a moment.'

He performed a ragged three-point turn, commenting as he did so: 'Well, they'll have come down to the river for a drink after they were finished with that buff. And they just couldn't be bothered to move any further. A lion never looks for a safe place, does he? A lion is a safe place. How many did you count?'

'No more than seven or eight.'

'Nor me. Tricky. The others will be around, surely.' He reversed carefully back along the truck spoor. I stood as high as I could, lighting the way and shouting directions. 'Stop. *Stop!* Or we'll kill a lion.' She was lying smack across the path, unmoving, unwinking. 'Jolly good,' I said, a trifle breathlessly.

'Can I get off the wheel tracks here?'

'I think so. It looks firm enough for the next ten yards or so.'

'Wouldn't do to get stuck.' George went backwards with unaccustomed care.

'Stop here. Good. This is where the loose sand starts. Better not risk any more.'

George switched the engine off. I shone the light at Caro, not the full beam, just the edge of it. She was wearing a big, loose shirt, unbuttoned, over her usual umbrella-thorn singlet. 'You all right, Caro?'

'They wouldn't move,' she said. 'I had to go round them. So I got stuck. They just wouldn't move.'

'No, they don't, do they?' George called cheerfully to her. 'It always surprises me, but once lion have been accustomed to vehicles –'

Caro gave a laugh, quite an impressive one in the circumstances. 'I mean, this is all very interesting, George.'

'Oh yes, well, I see what you mean. We'd better sort you out. I'll attach a tow rope, shall I?'

I said, quietly: 'George, it's a gallant idea, but have you noticed that there are an awful lot of lion about?'

'It's all right. Don't worry. Pass me the rope, will you?'

I scrabbled about, found it.

'Look, I'll do it, George, that way if I need to jump –'

'Dan, just work the spot.'

'Spot the lion for you, you mean?'

'No. Keep it on me. I want the lion to see me. It doesn't matter about me seeing them.'

'Shit,' I said.

'Ready?'

'Oh *shit*. Are you sure about this?'

But George stepped from the vehicle. Stepped towards a crowd of lion, seven or eight in view, all between ten and twenty yards away, plus four or five lurking God knows where. I stood in the back, shining the light on him, like a stagehand illuminating a prima ballerina. I distinctly heard him mutter, in rather amiable tones as he stepped down: 'Off you go, girls.'

The nearest female stood at the instant of his descent. Another stood, and then another. The rest of the lion, those that I could see, watched George, unbelieving. And then the middle one of the three abruptly turned on her haunches and trotted briskly away, twenty yards or so. And then the second and the third did the same. 'Spot 'em quickly, Dan.'

I did. They were sitting in a row like three domestic cats, watching, not terribly sleepily, with rather noticeable resentment.

'Back to me.'

I shone on George, as he walked on, round the back of our vehicle, to attach the rope to the tow bar. And then he walked across the ten yards of loose sand to Caro's vehicle. At the edge of the spot, I saw two more lion rise to their feet and trot away. I caught a glimpse of Caro: disbelief as much as terror in her eyes. George attached the rope to the bull-bars at the front of her vehicle. 'All right, er, Caroline? Let's get you out.'

He walked back to our own vehicle, still brilliantly lit by my spot. I was awestruck by what I had watched. 'All right?' George said. 'Let's go.' He turned the key contentedly.

Nothing. 'Oh dear,' he said. Turned again. 'Oh dear.'

'All right, George. My turn. I'll give you a push.'

'I hate to ask.'

'It's OK.'

'You'll have to untie the rope.'

'Sure.'

Heart thumping, I jumped to the ground, got behind the vehicle and lifted the slack loop of rope from the tow bar. I shoved mightily, then again: nothing. We seemed to be on a very slight incline, and I couldn't overcome the vehicle's inertia on my own. I pushed again, muttering and blaspheming. Then I heard footsteps behind me.

'Hello, Caro,' I said softly.

'Jesus,' she said. 'Who is rescuing whom?'

I wanted to embrace her, tell her she was beautiful, tell her she was wonderfully brave, wanted to ravish her then and there among all the lovely lionesses. But instead, she and I shoved, and George's vehicle rolled forward and then grunted softly into life. George moved forward a little under his own power, then backed up, and I replaced the tow rope. 'I must work the spot for George,' I said.

'Fine.' She turned, and walked back to her vehicle. The walking, that was impressive. And then we were all moving forward. George pulled her a hundred yards or so along the truck spoor, as far as the road, and then stopped. He backed up a yard or so, and I jumped down. I released the rope from our tow bar, and then, not without difficulty, undid George's strange and complicated knots on Caro's bull-bars. I wanted very badly to jump into the vehicle alongside her, but I did not. I blew her a cheerful kiss instead, and returned to my station with the spot. In stately procession, we drove into Lion Camp.

I leapt to the ground, but Caro was before me. And she was in my arms. It was then that I started to feel bewildered.

Her clasp was tense, tight and strong, possessing neither passion nor affection: only desperation. She said 'Oh Jesus' a few times. After a while, impressively, though disappointingly quickly, she had mastered herself, and amended this to 'Oh Jesus, get me a beer.' She released herself from my arms.

'Isaac! How many Lion left?'

A voice from the kitchen answered: 'Maybe three.'

'Please bring us three beers then. Caro, what's happening?'

'Jesus,' she said. 'There were a lot of lion out there.'

A thought struck me. 'Did you see the alpha male?' I asked.

Caro looked at me with appalled disbelief, for once lost for words. And then Isaac appeared, carrying three opened Lion in a single hand. 'Caro,' I said, 'come and sit by the fire and drink some beer.'

'Thank you, Dan. I believe I will.'

So far that day, I had sat at the feet of Mvuu, Njiri, Leon and Philip. Perhaps it was inevitable that I should now sit at Caro's. Once again, I took station on my mopane stump, as Caro took my chair. She looked beautiful to me in the firelight, just as she looked beautiful to me in full sunlight, or at sunset, or for that matter in pitch darkness. The fire illuminated the maculations of her limbs and the unbuttoned epauletted shirt, sleeves half rolled up, worn over shorts and umbrella-thorn singlet. Her hair was longer than before, and needed attention from the wire-cutters.

Taking rapid pulls from her beer, Caro told the story of a terrifying drive. Caro, I knew, was a good bush-driver, and certainly good enough to know that bundu-bashing on a black night without a spotlight and a good spotter is likely to be hair-raising. But she had found the truck spoor easily enough and had pulled off the road on the Impala Lodge side and followed it down to the river. She had made the crossing without incident: in the middle of the river, with the reasonable amount of ambient light available in the open, she had felt relief, and had believed her task more or less complete.

She was sadly deceived. She followed the wheel tracks onwards, and shortly before the steep ascent, she had found the entire Tondo Pride, lolling about in the middle of the truck spoor in their usual self-applauding way. 'Classic lion behaviour,' George said. 'Idle buggers, you see, don't give a bugger about anything, or anyone.'

'I'm glad to know why they were there, George,' Caro said. 'Thank you so much for explaining that to me. That makes the whole thing so much easier to deal with.'

'That's quite all right, Caroline.'

Caro had tried to drive around them, picking a place that was steep, but just about driveable. 'I was quite happy then; the vehicle was doing its stuff. Kept finding some grip from somewhere and got over.' But a few yards further on, there was a dip in the bank which she saw far too late, impossible to see without a spotter, a freakish hollow filled with loose dry sand, too far from the stream to be reached by subterranean damp. 'Worst possible place. Right by the lion, and spinning all four wheels. I made myself not panic, but it was impossible not to dig in. Jesus, I thought I was there for the night.'

'We heard you from camp. Guessed you were stuck.'

'I'm surprised you two buggers didn't stay to watch the lion.'

'Oh, Caro, you do us an injustice.'

'We'd only have done that if the alpha male had been there,' George said. 'Incidentally, did you notice that it was Auntie Joyce who gave the others the lead to pull out? I was rather counting on that.'

'You two,' Caro said. 'I'll never get over you two.'

'But, Caro, there's one thing you haven't explained,' I said. 'What the hell were you doing, driving about the bush in the middle of the night?'

'Have we got any more beer?' Caro asked.

I thought, we?

'I'm afraid not.'

'Oh God. Have you got any of that Malawian special occasion Scotch then?'

'Believe me, if I'd known this was going to be a special occasion I'd have ordered a couple of cases. But there's none.'

'Don't you have clients' drinks then? I don't mind being a client.'

'I'm ever so sorry, Caro, but I packed up the clients' bar and took the bottles to Mukango early this morning.'

George looked at me sternly. 'Did you do a proper stock-take on the bar?'

'Well, I sort of did a quick check, and I was going to –'

'You mean you did absolutely nothing of the kind.'

'That's it in a nutshell.'

'Had you looked at the book, you'd have noticed that the Old Boys between them consumed an entire bottle of Ballantines Scotch whisky.'

'But they only drank the odd beer – ah! I see. I believe you have stolen a bottle of whisky. I'm rather shocked.'

'No, no, I haven't stolen it, I've *embezzled* it. That's quite different.'

'That's all right then.'

'Caroline, could I invite you to become a – what is it – an accessory after the fact of peculation?'

'George, I think you've just saved my life.'

While George went to his hut for the whisky, I went to the kitchen and found three glasses and some warmish but drinkable water.

When I returned, I regarded the bottle with approval. '*Ballanites*. My favourite.'

George poured, we drank. 'Where were we?' I asked. My mind was swinging about the place very merrily, but I tended to lose the thread every now and then. I seemed to be alternating moments of brilliant, crystal-clear insight with bouts of amnesia. 'Oh yes, Caro, you were going to explain why you were driving round the bush in the dark.'

'You've not guessed, or worked it out, or anything mildly intelligent and obvious like that?'

'Caro, I can't really think straight. I can't think straight when I've spent most of the day drinking Lion, I can't think straight when the day has brought one weird shock after another, and most of all, I can't think straight when you are sitting beside me. In fact, I can't think straight even if I just think about you. You are simply not helpful to me when it comes to inductive logic.' Once again, the Lion was talking hard. 'Caro, please tell me why you spent the evening roaring round the bush flattening lion and writing off vehicles, instead of staying in your nice camp behind your nice electric fence.'

'Then stop talking for a moment and I might tell you. Listen, I have just had the most shattering row with Leon, as a moment's thought should have told you. I've just walked out on him, a hard thing to do in the middle of the bush. Hence the mad drive. All my gear is in the back of the vehicle, packed in a terrible temper, lots of shouting and screaming and all the staff agog. Took the second vehicle as you see, didn't dare take the new one, Leon would have stopped me somehow. Drove off, with Leon shouting, "You'll fucking kill yourself, you fucking bitch."'

Softly I repeated this remark in my well-practised Leon voice. Caro laughed suddenly: 'Oh, it was highly melodramatic stuff, staff'll be talking about it for months.'

'What does a lovers' tiff matter when the end of the season has come and you have your bone-arse in your pocket?'

'Not a lovers' tiff, actually. A permanent parting. That's for sure. I was planning to leave quietly, at the end of the season, go back to England for the World Travel Market, and I was thinking, maybe I won't return, get back into the travel business in England and set up life again there. That sort of thing, perhaps. Hadn't really planned anything, just possibilities. Certainly hadn't planned all this melodrama. But that's it, you know, all over with Leon and Impala Lodge.'

'Melodrama,' George said. 'Erroneously considered a hologynic phenomenon but which in fact occurs regularly in both sexes.' He sipped his whisky.

It was at about this moment that my mind caught up with

events and their implications. Unreasoning hope and anticipated disappointment commenced a mad game of chase about my already whirling head. I was eager for more details, but there seemed to be no polite formula for requesting them. However, as usually happens in moments of personal crisis, the victim assumes, and rightly, that there is no point in even pretending to discuss anything else, and that no introduction or apology is needed. And so we were plunged into a discussion at a level of intimacy quite unthinkable in normal and crisis-free times.

'It's not Leon's *fault*,' Caro said. 'It's not as if he has changed or anything. He has exactly the same qualities that he had in London. The thing is, I don't like those qualities as much as I used to.'

Was it possible, I wondered, for a person to share a life with someone like, say, Leon, and then to transfer all that affection and loyalty to some quite dissimilar person, like, say, to take a quite random example, me? Surely not, I thought. Leon and I were of different species: sympatric, dimorphic. A female could not swap from one to another, any more than a puku doe could leave her herd and mate with buffalo. And vice versa, of course.

'It was putting you out of business that was the last straw,' Caro said. 'All this evening he has been talking about his plans. Build six extra huts on the north side of Lion Camp. Put in a floating jetty and run wet-season trips by banana boat. I asked him what was to happen about you two; he said you weren't good enough for South Mchindeni National Park. He said he was doing the right thing for the park.'

'Well, he is,' George said. 'There's no arguing with that.'

'I quite agree with you,' I said. 'Leon is *right*. That's why I hate him. I really should have got Aubrey to shoot him.'

'I asked him if he had anything to do with getting you a bad scout,' Caro said. 'He just kept saying it was not his area of responsibility. But I'm half convinced he had something to do with it, you know. Of course he couldn't have guessed about the poor elephant getting killed. But I am sure he thought that something would happen. He might as well have shot the elephant himself; I am sure he was responsible. I feel responsible myself, in a way, I wish I had done something about it all. Just to stop him, you know. Jesus, I really am well out of all of this.'

'So what now, Caro? Back to England, as you said?'

'I suppose so. But I have had half an idea in my mind for a few weeks now. Sort of a pipe dream. And I thought I'd at least like to talk to you about it before I do anything drastic like get on the actual plane. Anything more drastic. But I'm rather afraid of talking about it, it all sounds a bit crazy. And anyway, I expect you've got lots of plans worked out already, you two.'

There was a pause. George seemed to have sunk into a coma after his comment about Leon. I would have answered, but it was to George the remark was addressed. Why was that? I could feel life beginning to go odd on me again. Caro was forced to repeat: 'I mean, George, I expect you've got lots of plans.'

'Oh yes, well, short-term plans, yes, certainly, Dan and I are going to Njovu National Park to count lion, you know. After that we'll have to see. Try and find a job, I suppose.'

'You mean that Lion Safaris will cease to trade?'

'You're very businesslike,' said George, amused and rather insufferably patronising. 'I suppose we must. We can't do much without a camp, can we?'

'Can I ask you some business questions, George? I mean, say if you'd rather not.'

'Try.'

So Caro started firing hard, tough questions at him. George, vastly taken aback, was for once jolted out of his cloud of vagueness. He certainly answered them all clearly enough. He explained that when he got to Chipembere, he would meet his partner, Bruce Wallace, and they would almost certainly agree to wind up the company, and divide up such assets as remained. 'Which is not much. The fridges and all the hardware in store at Mukango. Kitchen stuff, bedroom stuff. Nothing, really.

237

The vehicle was originally mine, and I don't suppose Bruce will want it. And that will be that, I suppose.'

'What would he say if I offered to buy him out?'

'Why would you do that?'

'Never mind bloody why. What if I tried to buy him out? Would he be reasonable?'

'Well, he's a businessman, but he's never really seen Lion Safaris as a profit-making concern. I'm sure he wouldn't object to rescuing something from a total loss. But what is there to take over? This is a company without assets.'

'Not quite. It has George Sorensen.'

'How very flattering. Who is banned from South Mchindeni National Park.'

'George, will you be very kind and listen to me for one moment? Concentrate, I mean?'

Her firmness compelled obedience, even in George. And Caro spelled out her idea, or vision. A safari operation in North Mchindeni National Park. To buy a second vehicle. To market George Sorensen Safaris as the Last Adventure: the last great trip into the great unknown: the last patch of darkness on the dark continent: the world's last area of true wilderness. Lion. Lion on foot with the world's greatest lion man.

'But I'm not –'

'Yes, you are.' Clients to be found by her connections with the travel business in England. Her former partners already specialised in adventure holidays, they had a long mailing list of people who had made such trips before, they could reach the people who would be ready and eager to take 'the ultimate wilderness trip'. 'The problem with Lion Safaris was that you had no infrastructure. No proper agency in the client countries. No decent financial organisation in this country. And not enough money. I can put all three things right.'

'Have you really got money?' George asked, amused and intrigued, as if this were an odd phenomenon, possibly not altogether unpleasant once you got used to it.

'I'm good at money, George. I told Dan that; didn't he tell you?'

'It wasn't the aspect of your personality that he tended to stress, no.'

'Well, you know I can organise, you've been to Impala Lodge. I can organise you, not into a second Impala Lodge, perish the thought, but so that you can run a real George Sorensen operation in your style, your way – but with financial backing and plenty of good clients.'

'I see,' said George, ruthlessly organised already.

'George Sorensen Safaris,' Caro said slowly.

There was a pause. I said softly: 'Let's do the show right here. Rogue Lion Safaris Rides Again.'

No one said anything. George took off his glasses and polished them, an operation I had seldom if ever seen him perform. Then he rolled a cigarette, and passed it to me. Then he rolled a second for himself, and lit it with his undisposed-of disposable lighter. He drew a lungful of smoke, and blew it out across the river. Then he turned to me. 'Rather overwhelming, this girlfriend of yours, Dan.'

'I don't know about girlfriend,' I said. 'But I know about overwhelming. In fact, I'm an expert on the subject.'

There was a further pause for what was perhaps thought, after which George suddenly made a prolonged performance of throat-clearing. 'It's all very interesting, what you say, of course,' he said. 'Do you have any other plans in this package? About staff, for example? About an assistant, for example?'

For most of this conversation or interview, Caro had been looking hard at George, seeking eye contact, most of which George effortlessly avoided. But after George's remark about 'girlfriend', the directness of her gaze had wavered. She darted several little glances at me. There was more to come, I could feel the punch of that realisation in the pit of my stomach. Sorry, Dan, but this is going to be a tight ship. That sort of thing. Her hand, holding her whisky glass on the arm of her chair, was quite steady. But then she raised the glass, took a sip from it, and lifted it a couple of inches higher, so that the knuckle of her thumb rested against her mouth. I had, like George, or not quite like George, been feeling rather overwhelmed. She seemed twice my age, infinitely my superior in wisdom, experience, knowledge of the real world. Yet with these little flicked glances, that odd movement of her hand, she seemed for a moment not frightening at all: almost frightened. And then confusion struck me again, and I could perceive nothing but contradiction.

'George, this is very impertinent of me, but could I ask you a favour?' Caro had resumed, with a slight effort, her controlling tone. 'Do you think you could leave me for a few minutes to talk to Dan?'

Another flashing signature of light crossed the sky, revealing for a fragment of a second ramparts and turrets of cloud. Then, almost at once, a sustained clatter of thunder. Highly melodramatic.

George filled each glass with whisky, picked up his own and announced: 'I shall go to my hut.' He walked stately and straight across the camp, taking the paraffin lamp from outside the door and vanishing from sight. Light shone through the interstices of the matting.

'Bugger,' I said. 'I forgot to ask him for another cigarette.' Thunder cracked and rolled.

11

The courtship of puku is an enchanting business. The females are so lithe, so feminine, and the males, despite their arguably epigamic antlers, are scarcely less fragile. Mostly, the process involves a delicate tiptoeing around each other: the utmost consideration, the utmost understanding. I know that the male's tasting of the female's urine does not *sound* enchanting, but the act is performed with supreme delicacy, with an oenophile's fastidiousness. The taste tells him of the female's degree of receptivity; there is no room for ambiguity in that. After a little more tiptoeing, the male then approaches diffidently from behind. With a single, exquisite, pointed ballet-dancer's foot, he taps, with great gentleness, between her rear legs, a delicate hint with a pleasing whiff of coarseness. This is repeated a few times, and if willing, the female responds each time with a more and more inviting presentation. It is a ritual of foreplay: pointed foot, tap-tap. It is all so well mannered, so refined, you can almost hear the rattle of bone-china teacups and see the extended little fingers. And then the male courteously mounts and completes the dance. It is a quiet, restrained performance in which both participants know exactly where they stand. There is never an instant of awkwardness.

There was no such ritual to fill the void between me and Caro. We sat side by side, for I had taken George's chair beside the fire. Ungallant hound that I was, I kept silent. Eventually, Caro said: 'Do you blame me for all this, Dan?'

'All what?'

'Leon. Joseph. Phineas. The elephant. Lion Camp.'

'Oh that.'

'Well, do you?'

I thought about it, as well as I could, for a while. Then to my considerable surprise, I heard myself replying not only honestly, but giving an answer I didn't know I knew. 'Every time I think about blaming, I can only think of the most wonderful twenty-four hours of my life.'

I was not looking directly at her as I said this, but I saw her beginning to smile. 'You really did feel that too?'

Too?

'It was perfect, Caro.'

'I know. It was a time set aside from the common run. I think maybe everyone has one such day.'

'Just one?'

'I don't know, Dan, I've only had the one myself. And that was the cause of all the trouble, I believe. It takes a while for the magic to wear off. So when I was back in Impala Lodge, well, I couldn't talk about anything else. And I could hardly say to Leon, I've just had the most marvellous fling with that nice young man from across the river. So I kept talking instead about the marvellous game-viewing on the other side, the brilliant location of Lion Camp, how absolutely brilliant Joseph was, how absolutely brilliant Phineas was, and how all it needed was a little bit of business sense – Leon and I were always talking about business, you see, it was rather our thing – to turn Lion Camp into the best operation in the Mchindeni Valley.'

'Distraction behaviour.'

'I suppose it was. But it must have planted all kinds of seeds in Leon's mind.'

'Did he know about us then? Did you tell him? Did he guess?'

'I think he knew without being aware that he knew. I think all the joy I had at Lion Camp rather got to him. He got very intolerant about George, and especially about you. He felt some of the magic of the day, you see, but it all came out the wrong way in him.'

'Oh, magic. That sort of stuff is always about round here. You just hadn't been close to it before.'

'You're partly right, Dan. And also you're partly completely wrong.'

'Yes, I know. I'm glad of that.'

'I'm glad of that, too. But tell me, Dan, you haven't said, are you happy about George Sorensen Safaris? If it all happens and so forth?'

'Well, I'm pleased for George, obviously.'

'Not for yourself?'

'Me?'

'Yes, bloody you.'

'Well, from the way you were talking, I thought you didn't want me involved.'

She said quite sharply: 'Well, obviously I do.'

I said, rather inadequately: 'Oh.'

'Just for a start, I know that you and George are the best bush team in the Valley. For purely business reasons, let alone everything else, it would be insane to separate you.'

Everything else? I tried saying 'Oh' again. And then after a while I added: 'The best team in the bush is George and anybody. But thanks for saying it.'

'But tell me, Dan, don't you want to be a part of it? I mean, if it works, if we decide to go for it, if everything really starts to happen – I mean, are you in? I don't know if I'd want to do it if you weren't in.'

For a moment, I knew what it felt like to be struck by a thunderbolt. I thought about this for a while. 'You mean, do I want to work in the most wonderful place in the world, with the most wonderful colleague in the world, and with the most beautiful woman in the world? Is that all you are offering?'

She smiled at this, and pondered a while. 'Yes. Though perhaps not all.'

This statement hung in the air, fizzing and crackling. Not being a puku, there was nothing I could think of doing. Gently tapping her crotch with my foot was not quite the answer. My mind, filled with desire and fear, simply stuck, all four wheels spinning, silently screaming.

Caro said: 'You're very unforgiving.'

The remark jolted me, and all at once my mind found grip again and was going hard. 'What? Me? Caro, there's nothing to forgive, not a thing. I tell you, I'd swap everything that has happened over the past four weeks for a single hug from you and count it a good bargain.' Suddenly, the Lion inside me was up and roaring: where had such eloquence, such honesty come from? I was half-turned towards her, sitting on the edge of my seat, and my hands flew up towards her: at the same moment, her own came to meet mine. In a series of slow, elegant moves of almost puku-like grace, we proceeded from double hand-clasp to kneeling hug to prone embrace beside the flickering fire of mopane wood. Inside me, the Lion silently sang a full pride chorus.

'Do I get to sleep with the boss?'

'I didn't know you felt that way about George.'

'You horrible tease.'

'Oh, I'm not, Dan, I'm really not. I really am awfully serious. And when I get serious, all sorts of things tend to happen, you know.'

'Oh, I know all right.'

The sky crumped again, but now the Lion was silent, over-whelmed. For I had now caught up with the fact that Caro had given me the greatest gift it was possible to give.

The bush. The north. Already, I could see Rogue Lion Safaris marching across the roadless wilderness of the north, George and I leading a group of avid, adventure-crazed clients, walking towards a new and unknown pride of lion. And everything working: Caro back in Chipembere fixing and turning the wheels and then driving north, again and again, to join us. Already, I could taste the early moments of delight and of doubt, the shadow of Leon slowly growing less substantial until it vanished altogether. I could see her force and her efficiency converting Rogue Lion Safaris into a roaring success, opening up North Mchindeni National Park for the world, George and I at the cutting edge of her ambition. And already I could experience the joy of her visits to the north, the delight of evenings under the fig tree in the Nice Place that Phineas had found for us. And the visits growing less frequent as the business grew and prospered and took more and more of her time. Other operations would move into the north, but we would remain the brand-leader, the operation by whose standards all others were measured. Caro's boundless will would keep us there. And already, far, far into the future, I could hear her saying to me: 'It's up to you, Dan. It's me or the bush.' And already, I knew the only answer I could give.

But that lay far in the future, and the road that led there was paved with joys. And I was back in the bush. Nothing else mattered. Passion seized me: in truth, it had never for an instant relinquished its hold.

The bush. And then another crack of thunder, and then, without any more ado, any more teasing, any more foreplay, the rains arrived. It was not much like rain, but rather as if someone had slashed open a vast sack of water. It all seemed to come down at once, but it kept on and on coming. One minute dry, the next, deluged. And we were both now African enough only to rejoice: I turned to lie on my back, she half turned with her head on my shoulder, both of us shouting and laughing at the tumultuous rain which was soaking into the ground, filling the empty reaches of the Mchindeni, and bringing with it life.

Now the lagoons would fill, the plants would grow, a soft green flush of grass would cover the concrete-hard flats we had driven and walked over. And all the herbivores, the buffalo and the antelope and my lovely zebra, would leave the riverine strip and would wander deep into the park, hidden by the rising growth all around them, seeking the largesse of the rains. Only the Tondo Pride would find life hard now, their prey scattered and spread and infinitely harder to discover and to catch, but their time would come again when the year turned once more. Life soaked all around us.

I could hear George's voice behind me, through the clatter and chatter of the rain. 'Oh, I see, that's all right then. But all the same, I think you'd better fetch your sleeping bag from your hut, Dan, before it's completely soaked, the thatch on those huts might as well not be there.'

'Caro, we must get your gear out of the vehicle and under the thatch of the sitenji.'

It did not take long to complete these emergency measures. Before long, we were sitting in the sitenji speculating on how long the thatch would keep out the rains. Towels and warmish, dryish garments had been seized. Three dryish sleeping bags had been collected, but there was no hurry to get into them. A sleepless night doesn't officially start until you try to sleep, after all.

It is one of those odd but ineluctable facts of life that there comes a stage of drunkenness in which the only possible course of action is to sing hymns. And so we did, loudly and lustily. George and Caro had the chairs again, I was sitting on my stump, elbow now on Caro's knees, her hand on my shoulder. George sang out well, his voice strong and unexpectedly tuneful. Caro, of course, knew every word of every hymn in the Anglican hymnal. Among many, I remember her leading us through 'Hills of the North Rejoice', which was splendidly appropriate. We had 'Jerusalem', of course, and the arrows of desire sped along the banks of the Mchindeni while the rain drowned out every sound of the bush but itself. Then we sang 'I Vow to Thee My Country'; Caro knew the second verse as well, an unusual accomplishment, and she sang it as a solo.

'And soul by soul and silently, her shining bounds increase,
And her ways are ways of gentleness and all her paths are
    peace.'

And the level of the Mchindeni rose and the level of the whisky sank, and the rolling words, the rolling melody seemed to bring out in George something of a whisky *tristesse*.

'I suppose the north will last me out,' he said.

'And me,' I said.

'Perhaps. Perhaps. But think of it. Farming, poaching, roads, minerals, gas, oil, people, people, people. The best that can happen is tourists. But I expect when the park becomes civilised like the south, we shall have to move on again. And the trouble is that this time there won't be anywhere. Still, as long as the park itself is all right, that's the thing, isn't it? I've just thought of a new theory about the history of the earth. People used to live in a state of siege, with the threatening wilderness all around them. Now it is the wilderness that is besieged, with the threatening civilisation all around on every side. Even the north is surrounded. It might last me out, but I doubt if the same is true for you two. Oh dear, I'm terribly sorry, I'm getting dreadfully morbid, aren't I? Sing another hymn, Caroline, and I'll shut up.'

Caro obliged.

> 'All creatures of our God and King,
> Lift up your voice and with us sing
> Alleluia, Alleluia.'

When the hymn was finished, George asked: 'Any whisky left?'

'Plenty, George. Plenty of lion left in the north, too.'

'Two very good points. Thank you for both of them.'

'When do we go?' Caro asked. 'Remember I've never seen the place.'

'Not till May, now,' George said. 'It will be impassable already. The roads will be all right, if you don't mind getting stuck every now and then, but the rivers won't be crossable. Be in spate tomorrow. But in May we'll be there.'

'God, how wonderful,' Caro said. 'How absolutely bloody wonderful.'

'Why are you doing this, Caro?' I asked suddenly. 'What gave you the idea?'

Caro considered the question for a while. Then she said: 'There are a lot of short answers. The challenge of running a business, breaking new ground. It would be a wonderful thing to have on your CV, you know, opened up an entire national park for tourism. And to get back at Leon, a bit, show him how things should be done properly. And because I feel guilty about the way you two have been treated. But mainly, because

– because of the magic time I spent with you. It was perfect. Everything, every single thing about that day was just so – well, right. And I felt that what you were doing was right, and that it was right to be in the same place as you two, doing the same things. That's what it comes down to. It's that what you do, and the way you do it, is *right*.'

'Shall I tell you something else?' I said. 'We'd still do it if it was focken wrong.'